Our Fair Eden

It's 2087, and the Earth's climate is in wild fluctuation. The Amazon Basin is a sun-baked graveyard, the Gobi is blossoming into tropical beauty, Europe is buried beneath icy tundra, and Manhattan is a swamp of the risen Atlantic. Old paradises are becoming new wasteland, old wasteland a new breed of paradise. Nowhere is safe. Millions flee the world's cities. But where do they run to?

The UN has an answer: the Eden Projects, colonies drawn from all nations, leading the charge in beginning anew, and developing new technologies to help start over.

Desh can't believe his luck when he wins the lottery to Eden Prime, most famous of all the Projects, hidden in the heart of Mongolia. But when he arrives in Eden, he finds himself caught in a struggle against a cruel autocracy, divided into gentry and peasants, all under the watchful eye of mysterious Texan matriarch, Mother Eden.

Subscribe to my newsletter to hear about discounts and new releases: http://eepurl.com/V4niL

For Emma

Our Fair Eden

Harry Manners

We crossed the Mongolian border sometime during the night. Morning brought word: we were getting close.

The light reaching over the cragged Altai Mountains cut into the carriage's dank interior, illuminating dozens of intertwined, unwashed bodies lying on soiled sheets. Each pair of eyes was ringed with purple, gazes deadened by fatigue and the impossibility of sleep.

Nobody had spoken since we left Saint Petersburg, but I suspected everyone was thinking about what awaited us, mourning the homes and lives we'd left behind forever.

Ma nudged me. I looked up into her ruined face—sunken, wilted, and chapped. "Drink." She pressed our water bottle close to my chest.

I shook my head. "I drank last hour. You take some."

"Drink." Even withered, her countenance set my heart aflutter with a twinge of fear. I remembered her temper when she'd been strong. She'd always gotten her own way.

I gripped the shuddering bench beneath me and kept my gaze level. "It's your turn."

"You need your strength."

"I can be strong." I bit my lip and then added, "For you." Those last words emerged as a melodramatic whisper. But if a little melodrama got her drinking, so be it.

A few moments of tense silence passed, and then the thinnest of smiles appeared on her lips. She drank.

She'd never been beautiful, but she had been pretty, with a heart-shaped face and skin pebbled with Irish freckles. Vitamin deficiency had put an end to that. I knew she'd been slipping me her ration of multivitamin supplements crushed in my juice for months, but I'd never dared challenge her.

Now, I wished I had. Maybe she'd still be strong enough to stand without shaking like an autumn leaf.

"I wish your father could be here," she whispered. Leaving father in Fremont had sapped the last of her strength. The Oasis Lottery in California didn't permit public-sector employees to be entered into the draw. Father had been senior manager of the Water Treatment Sector—too valuable an asset to let go.

"The lottery doesn't pick families, Ma, just people. It's a wonder we both won," I said.

The vital quota of scientists, artists, farmers, and other skilled workers had been selected for the Eden Program years ago; today, the lottery picked out handfuls of civilians, building islands of civilization in no-man's-land.

I reached for the bottle and tipped it back to her lips. "Keep drinking."

She relented, her eyes glistening. "I know, dear. I just wish…"

"I know." I lowered my voice. "But look around. We're not exactly among peers."

Only a handful of the faces in the carriage were Caucasian. So far as I knew, we were the only people from the States in the entire shipment.

I saw her throat working. "You're right. We're the lucky ones."

I nodded, closing the bottle tight.

We're the lucky ones.

So why did I feel like I'd been sentenced to a long, slow death? To exile in an alien land?

Ma had been brave in front of me when we had heard the news, but I'd still heard her and father through the paper-thin walls of our tenement flat on the outskirts of Fremont. Heard her hacking cries.

That had scared me more than anything, hearing my mother weep; at first I had thought they were of fear for leaving father behind, but now a part of me thought maybe they had been of blind, mindless joy.

"You always talked about winning a place in Eden. I know it's what you always wanted." I sighed. "But leaving him behind…"

She blinked, stared like a wounded animal.

"Did he make you take me?"

I couldn't bring myself to say what I really wanted:

Would you have come if he hadn't?

Her cracked lips parted. "He wants a life for you, Desh. We both do. I'd give my heart to have him here, but… but the ticket was mine. And that's that."

I nodded.

At Eden I would have opportunities I hadn't had in a long time. I had more qualifications than the other arrivals put together, and I had been on the road to being a prodigy before the recession hit.

Maybe here I could finally make a difference.

"He knew you were meant for greatness, Desh," Ma said, watching from deep behind her dark hooded eyes. "And now you can have it."

Father had come to sit quietly on my bed the night before we'd left and made me promise to use my gifts, to look after Ma and live a good life.

"I know, Ma," I muttered, fighting the tightness in my throat.

Whether we'd wanted to come or not, we'd beaten the odds by a country mile to be selected. Flung out to the far reaches of the world, we would have to go on, once a world primed to consume itself had broken its tenuous armistice. Peace had lasted this long, but the superpowers would soon annihilate anything still green and good in the civilized world.

It had taken every drop of diplomacy to keep red buttons from being pushed. That's why the Eden Projects had been founded, microcosms of great leagues and nations sent to the far corners of the earth, where it was hoped the climate would change for the better, and a precious few would be safe.

Mankind in a bottle.

The Skyrail we were riding in was an old model, one from the days when pre-laid tracks had only recently become obsolete. I had seen luxury models owned by mega-corp directors that could hover over a hundred feet in the air and push Mach 2.5, but this tin-can barely scraped ten feet of clearance from the dunes. The supersonic hover-train was over a hundred feet long, yet the vibration from the far end still had us pitching and yawing every other moment. But it was still a Skyrail. Even the oldest models barreled over land or sea at more than three hundred miles an hour, and we'd been traveling for a few hours now. Now we were slowing down. That could only mean one thing: we had arrived.

Emerging from their blank stupors, people clamored around me, buffeting my ears and shoulders as they tried to wrestle some window space. They gasped at the view and gabbled in myriad tongues.

"Tell me what you see out the window, Desh," Ma said. Early cataracts clouded her formerly electric-blue eyes, and she relied on me to do her seeing for her.

I turned to join the others, staring out at the waste beyond the dust cloud kicked up by the Skyrail's advance. We had left the desert behind and hovered to a standstill, surrounded by fields of gnarled tufts of grass. I called it grass, but it had no doubt been cooked up in a lab somewhere, some engineered weed that could grow almost any place on Earth. It spread for several miles around the settlement before petering out to bare earth, as though the nearby mountains graced the area with rainclouds every so often, and the valley acted as a natural bowl.

In the heart of that small valley—surrounded by a thin halo of thicker, greener foliage—sat a twinkling sprawl of simple geometric shapes. An island of shimmering greenery. An oasis. Eden Prime, the first and most famous of the Eden Program sites.

Despite having dreaded coming here, my heart skipped a beat. I leaned close to Ma and whispered, "We're here."

Her milky eyes danced. I could almost see her mind's cogs working. "W-what does it look like?"

I turned back to the horizon and squinted. "It . . . it looks small."

Those were the only words that came to me, but at least they were honest. Our destination looked very lonely indeed, the merest pinprick of human habitation amid an endless ocean of scorched sands and sun-bleached sandstone bluffs.

I clambered away from the bumbling masses still hollering around me and hauled our luggage from the alcove where I'd stashed it before departure. I felt Ma's hand on my sleeve, gripping hard, more a sightless groping than anything else.

"What are you doing?" Ma asked.

"Getting our things ready. We're getting off first. There might be a rush. I don't want you to get hurt."

Ma smiled benignly, an almost childlike grin. "Desh, they're civilized here. All of them. That's the whole point of the Eden Projects. To carry on in peace." She straightened her back. "Once we arrive, we'll be just like them. Just as civilized."

I didn't say anything, just pressed her bag firmly into her grasp and guided her away from the bench. I kept a wary eye on the others until I could feel us pulling a few Gs as the Skyrail decelerated in earnest. Then I shunted us toward the door and waited.

***

Extract #1
USGS Geological Survey

Climatological global assessment of potential candidate sites for colonization, commissioned by the United Nations Environmental Committee.
    Objective variables:
    - Elevation above sea level
    - Average rainfall
    - Bedrock composition
    - Native flora and fauna
    - Current state of development
    All candidates were considered on the merit of projected changes to local climate relative to global climate shift as predicted by current simulations.

Results — Primary candidates:
- Tibesti Mountains, Chad
- Atacama Region, Chile
- Northern Territory, Australia
- Ömnögovi Province, Mongolia
- Papua New Guinea
- Qaasuitsup, Greenland
- Denali Region, Alaska, United States of America
- Antarctic Peninsula, Antarctica
- Dead Sea, Israel

The chief members of the board confirm their recommendations for the candidates listed in this report as suitable potentials for the program code named **Eden**.

Extract #2
Saint Petersburg Gateway Memo

Memo to all staff:

After the recent discovery of contagious pathogens—notably, a known strain of the superbug Orvin Constanta (ZN17)—in the subcutaneous technological implants of several draftees en route to the Dead Sea Project, all technological augments and unauthorized personal devices will henceforth be confiscated from draftees before departing the gateway, without exception.

Dr. Gordon Bilton, Senior Physiologist
Saint Petersburg Gateway, Eden Program

"Hey, y'all," the loudspeaker sang. "This is Mother Eden speaking. I just wanna welcome every one of you to our little slice of heaven. Those disembarking, please make your way to the processing tent." The accent was one I'd never expected to hear out here: I guessed Texan. A lilting, motherly voice that reminded me of honey and bed warmth.

There was no one to greet us, only blinding gusts of ash-dry wind. The voice emanated from a bank of speakers thronging a dented line in the ground that hinted at previous Skyrail pit stops.

A few hundred yards away armed guards patrolled a chain link fence, but none of them were looking in our direction. The Skyrail had swooped in over the fence and I had the sense that they had been watching closely.

Behind us other carriages were popping open, their passengers dog-piling into the dirt. The engines were already spooling up again; the Skyrail would depart back to Saint Petersburg as soon as possible. Every minute cost the Project sponsors more than a common man's life was worth.

So here we were, slap in the middle of nowhere. Just a line in the dirt and a row of blinking dullards, uprooted from their homes and cast into the unknown. Even though the Skyrail's whine was building to close to a hundred decibels, it was eerily quiet.

Then the loudspeakers donged, and the same sweet voice came again. "Those disembarking, make your way to the processing tent. Come on now, don't keep Mother

Eden waiting."

A squeal of static was accompanied by a low thrumming as the Skyrail departed behind us. Then, bar the whistling wind, true silence.

I started walking. I might have been the first to move. It didn't matter. I only cared about getting Ma away from the others. I had been right about them. Ma and I had made it onto the blazing sand just moments before they had tried to squeeze themselves through our carriage door all at the same time. I'd managed to get us clear just as they came careening to the ground as a single mass of limbs and tattered cases.

No trace of the civility Ma had talked about. Quite the opposite. Almost feral.

I wasn't surprised.

Some countries were better off than others, but I suspected any of these people would drive a steak knife through my neck if it meant another blanket, another meal. Who could blame them?

Certainly not me. It was a survivor's world. Those who shoved, bit, and scratched got what they needed. I had done what I did on the Skyrail to keep Ma safe, but at heart I was a farmer, not a hunter.

My family had barely survived the Second Great Depression, when half of North America had starved. Many were still dying. And it was only going to get worse as the Earth's climate took its final plunge.

"Desh?" Those milky eyes, full of trepidation and excitement.

I took Ma's arm. "Come on, let's go."

"What about the others? It's only good manners to wait for our future neighbors."

"They'll find their way."

I steered her in the right direction and we started walking. All the while I eyed the ground underfoot, which still bore signs of recent cultivation from savage parched rock.

The climate was changing, fast. But it was such a complex system that, even now, the most sophisticated computer models failed to make accurate predictions. There was no knowing which places would grow hotter, which cooler, which continents would grow luscious, and which would shrivel and bake. Rainforests were becoming dust bowls, prairies graveyards, and land that hadn't seen rainfall for centuries was blossoming into fresh paradise. The rising oceans had swamped over fifty cities and displaced their populaces, while the farm belts of the world had wilted and blackened. They were even setting up a Project in Antarctica. The ice sheets would all melt away in time. The colony founded on the bare rock underneath would be humanity's last stand, if it came to that.

Here at Eden Prime, Ma and I made our way toward the billowing white tent before us, ahead of the rest, luggage to our chests, her hand clutching my sleeve.

"What do you *see*?" she hissed.

I was obliged to take a quick panoramic glance of our surroundings. Close up Eden Prime was a sprawling spatter almost a mile across, interspersed with screenings of date palms. Nearby was a central mass of low-lying buildings carefully regimented into neat rows, alleys, and thoroughfares.

The thicker greenery I'd seen turned out to be crops. Live crops. Whole fields of them. I hadn't seen such things except in history documentaries and news feeds of far-flung places like the great Amazonian Farming Plains or parts of China, where the ground hadn't grown too dry. All our food had been grown in supplement labs since Ma and Father had been young. Seeing those twinkling faraway crops made my mouth water.

Ma's vicelike grip tightened on my wrist. It was starting to cut off the circulation to my hand. I glanced at her and looked into those milky orbs darting to and fro, looking but not seeing. I saw raw fear from a woman I'd always thought of as too strong to be scared of anything. My heart leaped. "Lots," I croaked. "I see lots."

Her fingernails dug further into the flesh of my arm.

"Trees," I said. "Buildings."

There were faces too, hovering in shadowed doorways, peering through lace curtains. I hadn't noticed them at first, but once I'd seen one, I saw them everywhere. "There's lots of people watching." Soon I heard a trickling from nearby irrigation channels and then, despite myself, I was smiling. "Water. I hear water."

There were as many rivers running over the earth as ever, but their courses had shifted by hundreds of miles. There would soon be bountiful paradise where before there had been only wasteland, and wasteland would replace former paradise. The world's gardens would fall and be reborn elsewhere—as the Gulf Stream stalled in a torrent of polar meltwater and the great ocean gyres whorled into a mess of worldwide El Niño insanity.

For most it would be too late. The new gardens would sprout many centuries after our great cities had crumbled to dust.

Only the Eden sites had some assured measure of preservation.

I'd pored over the endless news of the planet as it changed before our very eyes, consumed by the terrible truth. Before I had been forced to work two eight-hour shifts a day, there had been hope for me. My test scores put me in the ninety-ninth percentile for IQ, and a John T. Everett Scholarship had gotten me a degree in Mechanical Engineering from Princeton.

But then things had got really bad, and taking care of Ma had become my only purpose in life.

Here and now, maybe I would finally get my chance.

We kept walking until we came to the tent's entrance. It was a simple thing, a far cry from what I'd imagined when watching the ads. I'd pictured a utopian jewel, alight with meta-materials and marvels of technology.

This was a tepee, woven of sturdy but cheap material. Inside were stainless steel fold-out tables set into the bare earth. Most were surrounded by cardboard boxes stuffed with dog-eared files, manned by secretarial folk with half-moon spectacles and conservative uniforms.

I hesitated at the door and blinked.

"What is it?" Ma said.

"We're here."

She smiled. For a moment, her old self shone through. "Then let's introduce ourselves." She squeezed my wrist once more, gently this time. For a brilliant moment my apprehension melted, and I ducked us both inside.

***

Extract #3
CDC Spokesperson

Considering the destruction wrought by the infamous LX27 outbreak of 2052, it remains imperative to this day that all citizens maintain sufficient concentrations of TOPO-2 isomerase enzymes and macrophagous nanocytes in their bloodstreams, along with standard practice of conventional hygiene, to counteract the proliferation of superbugs. While the success of the modern world in combating the surge in antibacterial superagents has reversed the fall of western medicine endemic to the end of classical antibiotics, such agents continue to exist and are as much a danger today as ever. Any isolated communities lacking in such modern countermeasures will most likely lead to isolated pockets in which new agents can evolve and proliferate, and as such pose grave threats to the rest of the world's population. Lack of resources, not technological prowess, has become the world's greatest threat. Government organizations crumble, and funds run dry daily in dozens of nations per year, and it falls to the strained reach of organizations such as the UN, UNESCO, WHO, etc. to compensate.

Food and water are prioritized by default, naturally. Yet I maintain that additional funds must be allocated to ensure that all populations are kept supplied with biotic countermeasures, lest more outbreaks occur in the near future.

The danger posed by these agents remains one of the primary grave threats to the population of the globe. An outbreak among the millions of displaced refugees in Asia Minor, Western Europe, or the Eastern seaboard of North America could result in a runaway effect not seen since the Black Death in the Middle Ages.

✐

We were received without address or even direct eye contact. The Eden folk scribbled signatures, stamped papers, and cast stacks of medical files into ring binders. I guided Ma forward after they waved us on. Ma spoke the whole time of how much she looked forward to joining the good folk and how she promised to be an upstanding addition to their flock.

They didn't look so civilized to me, but perhaps I was

expecting too much. The ads, the way people spoke of these places—it gave the impression that everyone swept around in monk's robes, their minds buzzing with the wisdom of the ages.

At least the others' quarreling had been quelled. They'd rolled up to the tent entrance as a single mumbling mass, shoving as though room was at a premium, cursing and spitting, set to bite chunks from one another. As soon as they entered, however, blinking and glancing about, they readily fell into line and were silent.

Culture, social standing, upbringing—I saw all of it dissolve in that moment. We'd been drawn from the four corners of the earth, but we'd all seen the same ads. The same Elysium Fields caricature, the same picture of serenity that we expected to slot into like a glove.

Here, people didn't bite. Didn't scratch. They held their heads aloft, thought thoughts of immaterial things. They said good morning, leaning over their white picket fences to chat with neighbors who had emerged for a bit of gardening.

In our desperation, I bet most of us had believed it. Still believed it. I was sure Ma did.

The prospect of three hot meals and a place to sleep was enough to keep us in check. Maybe that was the whole point of the ads: to turn us into lambs before we arrived, and make sure we crawled up to the front door on our knees with our hands held out for scraps. If that was true, it was working like a charm.

Ma and I were waved through the tent and out the

other side. The weight of our things was beginning to wear on me, and with Ma clutching my arm, I staggered every other step, sweat beading on my brow. As we made our way along the winding path outside, I began to puff like a racehorse.

Then suddenly the weight was gone, and two grinning nymphs had appeared on either side of us. A pair of young women, identical in dress and amiable smiles—aloof but nonthreatening—had wrested our cases from my shaking hands, handling them with ease.

"Just this way, stranger," the one closest to me said. Her accent seemed affected and was eerily similar to that of the sweet old lady we'd heard over the loudspeaker.

Ma's grip had tightened on my arm as she'd sensed the proximity of newcomers, but at the sound of the woman's voice, she relaxed. "Hello, there," she said, enunciating with a clarity that I'd never heard before. "It's very nice to meet you indeed."

The other woman replied, "A pleasure." She had a clear-cut, melodious tone that somehow didn't carry a trace of emotion. Was that how things were here? Maybe they had their own language. I could imagine the dictionary entry:

Pleasure [Eden-Speak]: That which is banal, mind-numbing, and utterly devoid of enjoyment.

"Please, this way," she continued. "Orientation will begin shortly." She didn't sound enthused in the slightest.

"Oh, of course, much to do, of course!" Ma gabbled for a while as we walked closer to the settlement.

We were now close enough to see the buildings without a blinding halo of reflected sunlight. I could make out municipal-looking structures, the lower-lying rectangular behemoths I'd seen from the Skyrail. Interspersed between them were trees and lawns, perhaps even parks.

Everywhere between were streets lined by quaint identical bungalows. Painted an inoffensive pale yellow with fake mahogany trim, they were large enough for comfortable living space and three good-sized bedrooms. Their lines seemed odd, the style impossible to place. They reminded me of no particular architectural norm, of no one culture. Perhaps an amalgamation of all, perhaps something decidedly neutral.

I blinked in surprise when I saw that each sported its own little patch of grass, space for a flower bed, and a four-foot-high white picket fence. Just like the ads.

Farther away, however, I could just make out the edges of other buildings markedly different, but they were hidden behind thick screenings of palms.

"We are honored to be a part of the Eden Program," Ma was saying. Slow, clear, with a ring that bordered on reined-in hysteria.

That same flat tone in reply: "On the contrary, it is we who are honored to be receiving you. I'm sure you'll all make excellent additions to our community."

Collection, a tiny voice said somewhere deep down in my mind. *We'll make excellent additions to their collection.*

I blinked. Why had I thought such a thing?

The women were smiling, Ma was at ease. The Eden settlement looked to be nothing but what we'd been told to expect. So why did I feel more unsettled by the moment?

Behind us, the others were emerging one by one from the white tent. Still blinking, still shuffling in an orderly fashion, almost like newborns emerging from the womb. Each of them was flanked by escorts who looked very much like our own—the same simple white robes, the same blank, detached smiles. From afar their voices carried on the wind like a lullaby. All with that same blank tone, that same affected Texan drawl, despite their countless nationalities.

We were now nearing the first buildings, and already it was difficult to believe we were in the middle of the Gobi Desert or that this place, in part, comprised the lingering hopes of all the civilized world. It almost looked like a holiday camp; a diffuse sense of lazy contentment seemed basted over every roof tile, every blade of grass. I could see people walking between buildings, sedate silhouettes under the shade of lampposts and waving fronds, some arm in arm, all talking with sweeping gesticulations, robed in things eerily reminiscent of togas, like the scholars of old.

"When did you arrive at . . . what is it that you call this place?" Ma was saying.

A brief silence followed, and then the young woman beside me spoke up. "Eden," she said. "Just Eden. Formerly Eden Prime." Another pause. "We used to prefer that. But then Mother Eden convinced us to change it.

Now we all like Eden better."

"Yessir, better," the other said. "And the both of us arrived a little over nineteen years ago."

I squinted at them both. "You couldn't have been here that long. You'd have been babies."

The young women stopped and turned to me, standing side by side. I hesitated under their identical, flat stares. Their lips were upturned just slightly, not quite smiles. Plastic, emotionless. It almost looked as though they were presenting a studied display—as though they'd practiced smiling in front of mirrors but had never done so spontaneously.

They weren't twins, or sisters, or even related. One was a redhead, short and sturdy, and the other peroxide blonde, slender and tall. Yet I was finding it hard to tell one from the other. The slight angle of their upturned lips, the delicate lines of their eyebrows. The touch of rouge upon the ridges of each cheek.

Like dolls. China dolls.

"Longer than that. We're natives of Eden."

They turned and resumed walking. We were drawing close to a hall marked with a banner reading, *ORIENTATION.*

"You were born here?" My voice was had taken on a queer high-pitch. I looked at them afresh.

Their skin appeared tanned, though not naturally white. Not quite. There was a note of something more than just a good bronzing, but whether it was from Mediterranean, Hispanic, Asian, or even African heritage, there was no telling. Perhaps all of them—mongrel, like the architecture. It wasn't just in the skin but the eyes as well. Slanted, though only just. And the noses, robust, yet long. The hallmarks of a great many races, all present upon single faces.

"I didn't know the Eden Program permitted breeding that long ago," I said. I blinked and trained my gaze on the floor.

Don't stare. Mustn't stare.

But their faces.

"Wasn't in the initial UN plans, but Mother Eden saw we needed fresh pups to build a real community. It takes wisdom like that to see the truth the heathens out there in the world tried to hide from our eyes."

Good God, they've deviated from the plans. The plans that took the world's best sociologists and psychologists ten years to develop.

"How many others were born here?" I said.

"Still a minority. But the number's growing!"

"Why haven't we heard of this before?" It hadn't been on the ads.

The young women said nothing, just kept on walking, hips rolling voluptuously, the same slight upturn to their lips—the same reticent reptilian stare.

"This is supposed to be a humanitarian mission to save our species," I said. "Not a staging area for a cult. People all over the world pay taxes they can't afford to scrabble enough resources together to keep the Eden sites in operation."

Ma's hand on my arm. Fingernails pinching my flesh again. "Desh, mind your manners," she hissed.

I shook free. "What's going on here?"

Her fingernails dug in deeper. "This isn't civilized." Ma's voice at once became laced with humility as she turned to the nearest of the women. "I'm so sorry about this."

The young women shared a look. "It's quite all right," one said.

"The journey through the desert can wear out even the strongest," the other finished.

An awkward moment passed between the four of us, and then they continued walking ahead. My arm was certainly bleeding by now. Ma leaned close. "What's come over you?"

"I don't like this," I whispered. "They're not telling us something. Don't you feel it?"

For a moment I thought I saw her eyes flicker. Then all at once her fingers slackened, and she set us on a rolling gait in the same vein as the young women's. "No," she said sweetly. "I don't. You're just tired. Come now, Desh. Smile. It's all downhill from here."

I said nothing, trying to ignore the lump in my throat.

She was afraid. Years of hardship had made her a master at showing strength, but she had never been able to hide anything from me. Her eyes never lied.

I wasn't surprised. She'd put all her hopes in coming here. She didn't have anything left, and we both knew it.

In time we came to the hall, where the young women

paused once again and turned to us. "This way, please," they said in unison.

"Oh, you are too kind," Ma said. And just like that, for the first time since her sight had faded, she released my arm and marched toward the doors. "You are *too* kind. What civility. What angels." Effusive, unending babble.

The young women were staring at me again. I thought they were staring directly into me.

"We'd sure be honored . . ." said the redhead.

" . . . if you'd step inside," the blonde finished.

Then, in unison: "Mother Eden is waiting."

I mouthed soundlessly for a few moments. My surroundings were more beautiful and tranquil than I could have hoped. It was all so perfect. More than I could have asked for. Yet, for some reason that I couldn't formulate, I wanted to run—turn tail and run straight back to the desert.

I hesitated a final time. Then Ma vanished inside those big double doors and I sighed with defeat. I joined her in a few bounding strides, gladly leaving the china dolls behind. I swore I could feel their stares, the heat of twin laser beams on the back of my head. I didn't look back.

The hall was long, low, and immaculate. A congregation of rickety folding chairs had been arranged in a wide parabola around a stage occupied by a single imposing figure.

A skeletal woman of some six feet, with features taut as tension cables and eyes swimming with watchful intelligence, the woman moved not an inch for the full first five minutes we were in her presence. Composed in an erect posture, a studied picture of serenity, she moved only her eyes—round, saucer-like orbs that seemed to focus on nothing in particular yet absorb every detail.

Ma shuffled along the aisle leading to the front row, beckoning me forward. The first to enter the hall by some margin, we sat in absolute silence. The creaking of our chairs under our weight clawed at my ear like two pieces of polystyrene rubbed together.

I wanted to tell Ma everything would be fine, but my tongue seemed cemented to the back of my throat. The space around the woman standing over us seemed charged with static, one that pushed my buttocks against the chipped plastic of my seat and made the blood in my ears sing.

I was willing to bet this was Mother Eden.

She was so striking, it took me almost a full minute to notice there were others in the room. Like planets orbiting too close to a parent star, the others had been entirely lost in the glare of her radiance. Once I'd noticed them, however, it was plain there was something different about them. There were at least a dozen, dressed in the same simple robes as the twins and Mother Eden herself, save for one detail: theirs were a faded brown, the color of the desert. And the people themselves were identical in their thousand-yard stares, impassive expressions and perfect postures. Every one of them stared fixedly at the floor some ten feet ahead of them, unblinking. One could have been forgiven for thinking them a troop of powered-down cyborgs, were it not for the steady rise and fall of their breathing.

Mother Eden gave the impression of having registered our presence, just like the crowds outside had seemed so intent to go about their lives and ignore the Skyrail-load of bedraggled immigrants stumbling forth from the horizon. Yet these floor-starers seemed utterly ignorant of everything around them, ensconced in catatonia.

For the briefest moment I thought I saw one of them looking at me, but when I turned to her, I found her eyes lost in the same dead gaze as the others. A glimmer there, perhaps, but nothing more. Maybe it was only because she was young, a dainty pre-teen with unmistakably British complexion—no other skin could have been so pasty, nor hair so fire red.

I couldn't help watching her for some time after, still trying to get a hold of myself, but whatever twinkle had been about the girl was gone.

The others arrived after what seemed an eternity but couldn't have been more than a couple of minutes. Under the hall's strip lights, their motley, dirt-streaked faces looked like those of bewildered newborn lambs. They were followed by their escorts, and the twins who had guided Ma and me, and still more from the settlement. More Eden-folk swept in until the rear of the room was packed, while the newcomers took their seats in awkward silence, wide-eyed and hunchbacked.

After even the doorway was crammed with empty maddening half smiles, more began to appear at the windows, from behind the stage, and even upon a balcony above our heads. Soon, the hall had become an amphitheatre. I had the feeling that Mother Eden's American nationality had something to do with us gathering here, of all places. I couldn't help imagining those on the balconies as wealthy spectators and us as the enslaved gladiators ripe for the slaughter. Or, perhaps, the whole place was an enormous microscope, bringing into focus a group of intriguing amoebas.

Among the spectators' many colors, features, and races, not one china-doll visage bore any trace of ill intent. Yet they were all different, somehow, a little touched, and empty. Vessels stark as the Gobi.

Ma was gripping my arm again. Pain radiated from the punctures made by her fingernails, but it quickly faded to a dim scream at the back of my mind.

What's going on? I thought. *Why are they all staring? Why is everything so quiet?*

They had all been so keen to ignore our very existence at first, yet now they were clamoring for a view of us. What had changed?

My back was slick with sticky sweat, and a pungent animal pong of fear wafted up from under my collar.

An electronic squeal of feedback heralded Mother Eden's first true movement. The stoic, ancient figure's composure fractured in a moment, and an easy southern drawl, entirely at odds with her stately persona, flooded the hall. "Welcome, y'all! I'm Mother Eden, and I run this joint. I gotta say how fine it is to see so many fresh faces among us. I can't rightly remember the last time we had so many turn up like this all at once."

No applause. Just silence.

Unperturbed, she continued. "Now I know y'all must be mighty tired. Even wonders like a Skyrail-ride can take it outta you, let alone after all those nasty examinations the good doctors on the other side must have put you through.

"But if you'll bear with me, I'll say my piece, and then we'll find you somewhere to sleep for the night."

I peeked over my shoulder, saw a sea of blank stares, and felt stark alienation pervade the room. Most of the settlers were of Eastern descent, and I was willing to bet my left arm that only a few spoke any English, let alone understood Mother Eden's soup-thick twang.

Utter silence. Not even a shuffle. The only perceptible noise was the soft hiss of an industrial air conditioning vent.

Mother Eden didn't look fazed. A warm smile heralded the remainder of her speech: "We all want to give sincere congratulations on winning those lotteries back home. All of you are most welcome here. You probably seen our little outfit out back—lots of men in uniform and ugly-looking military gear—but it's all there to keep us safe, so don't you worry none."

She leaned over on her podium. "We got a book

around here, you could say it's our bible. Chock full of all the cleverness that's come outta this place over the years. You might hear folks quote a line or two here and there. My favorite goes something like this." She cleared her throat. "'And the lost, wearied by strife, came from penury to the bosom of Eden and vowed to begin anew.'"

Her smile widened, an ugly expression that brought her lips back over her gums. "We're all family here. One big happy family."

"Family," chorused the surrounding robe-clad onlookers, all in perfect unison. I didn't fail to notice that the many onlookers all emulated her accent exactly. All the same. All perfect.

The room smiled down at us.

⌒�〜◯

Mother Eden took us to our new home herself, leading us just as a shepherd leads a flock of bleating sheep. The crowd of onlookers had dispersed, returning to their business as though nothing had happened: some in white robes were conversing, arm in arm, dignified and regal; others in blue were playing with their children in the park or buying groceries; a few in brown were pumping water, weeding gardens, tending the fields. It was almost as though we hadn't arrived at all. Yet anyone we passed gave a cheery smile and cried, "How you doing, neighbor!"

Ma blushed the first couple of times and said, "Fine." She still had a firm grip on my arm, but now it was less a pinch, more an embrace. "Desh, they're so polite!" she twittered. "What lovely people."

I didn't say anything. The hard lump in my throat persisted.

I caught sight of two men down a narrow alley between the main thoroughfare of stores and public buildings. One was carrying a box of dates and humming an old ditty, the other was wheeling a barrel of water and whistling. It was strange to see the two of them so readily engaged in idle amusements so typical of Western workaday folk, for both seemed of indigenous Oceanic origins. When the man with the dates noticed the other, he cried, "How you doing, neighbor!" The man with the water responded, "Fine, and you?" Then both men went back to their tasks.

Mother Eden took us beyond the center of the settlement, past a motor pool of Humvees and heavy-duty trucks, and onto a sleepy little neighborhood lined with young apple trees. Two streets of the same cookie-cutter houses lay before us, each gleaming with fresh paint, most with tarps still hanging from the doorways, fluttering in the wind. In the distance I could see a general store, another small park, a laundromat, a mess hall, public bathrooms, and even a rec room.

"Brand new, spick-and-span!" Mother Eden cried, gesturing to it all.

I couldn't contain myself. Before I knew it, I'd exclaimed, "We get our own house? All to ourselves?"

It was unbelievable. Anger was rising in my bowels, catching me by surprise. While Ma gasped and rushed forward, hand on heart, and the others around us marched forward to claim their prizes amid ecstatic gabbling, I suddenly found myself alone with Mother Eden. Moments before I was sure I would have fallen mum in her presence, but now I found myself too aghast to stop. My hands, curled into fists, were shaking. "We can't . . . we can't accept this," I said.

Mother Eden's eyebrows disappeared into her iron-colored bangs. "Nonsense, darlin'! Don't be standing on ceremony, now. This here's a present from everyone. We all pitch in for the new folks."

I choked as Ma vanished into a house that our twin guides were gesturing toward.

Mother Eden's voice rang out again, this time from just above my shoulder. I jumped; she was mere inches from my face, and her eyes bored into mine. "Don't be worrying about owing anyone nothing. Here everyone gets a turn at everything. It'll all come back around."

"It's not that." I took a step back. "You could fit a dozen people in any one of those houses, with room to spare." I spun around to take in the surrounding streets and cul-de-sacs that surrounded our own. "They can't all be like that. Tell me you're doubling up, this is some kind of welcoming gift, some settling-in time before we bunk with other families."

Mother Eden's face remained impassive the whole time I was speaking, her smile utterly identical to those of her disciples. "Some folks are fine enough to make the sacrifice for the rest of us by sharing, sure," she said. "But you don't have to worry none about that. There's plenty of room."

She was walking me toward the house that Ma had ventured into, hand planted on my shoulder. "I can see you're a special one," she muttered. "You see things other people oftentimes don't wanna see. A strong head on those shoulders. Bet your mama raised you up to question things proper, huh?"

I said nothing, my eyes caught between hers and the house. We came to stand beside the twins, those eerie white-robed clones, listening to Ma's distant gasps and giggles of delight.

How many people back home would give all they owned, all they hoped and dreamed for, to get a shot at coming out here to one of the Eden Project sites? How many people would give their lives, even, if it meant their families could escape the destitution and uncertainty that blanketed all the free world?

Before Ma and I had left, there had been reports of mass exodus from over a dozen countries—vast herds of homeless refugees, wandering from their homelands into the great unknown. Mega-slums pockmarked the globe like acne. Without leadership, ungoverned by any state, these wandering masses would surely perish.

The voice of one newsreader's reports echoed in my head: "Some of these rootless tribes number in the millions."

Presently I grunted. "How many applications are you turning down every day so you can have a lovely palace all to yourselves?"

The twins blinked in unison. Smiled, in unison. "We don't have anything like that," said the taller.

"They're all bungalows," said the shorter. "No palaces around here."

"All the same model."

"Every one."

Mother Eden raised a hand, and their smiles vanished. Almost as though struck, they cowered and looked at their toes. The hand that had been held on my shoulder found its way to my chest. "We could use strength like yours. Can't teach what you got: vision, and the guts to call things like you see 'em. But we all got to work together here. What we're doing out here, all we've accomplished, the wheels only keep turning if everyone does their bit. And sometimes that means taking a few unpleasant truths on the chin and just getting on with it."

I said nothing, couldn't. My mouth was cemented shut with oatmeal.

"I gotta be honest, you remind me of myself when I first got to these parts," she said quietly, turning to sweep an arm around at it all. "Confused, scared, angry as hell at how the Lord had seen fit to make things just so." Her hand squeezed my chest. "Worried sick about the people I'd had to leave behind. Guilty to the gills that it'd been me to win the Golden Ticket."

My throat had constricted to a pinhole, my inner monologue at war with itself. Her voice carried such sincerity. But something made my guts twist up in a bunch.

She was walking again. "We need people like you 'round these parts. Always have, always will. But we gotta work as a team here . . ."

"Desh," I said.

Another flowery, maddening smile. "Desh, we have to put our heads together, for the greater good."

"Desh, get in here!" Ma cried. "Oh, my word, this living room—our own *air conditioner!*" Girlish giggles continued to issue from within the house—my new prison. Her gushing was interrupted by a choked sob. "Oh, Desh . . . Desh, glasses. They've given me a pair of glasses. They're even my prescription. My, how did they *know?* I haven't had glasses since I was twenty-two. They must have cost a fortune!"

Along the street, similar squeals and cries filtered out through each gleaming doorway.

"You get your first duty cards next week," Mother Eden murmured. "Don't be too put out if yours ain't the most glamorous. Some people have bad luck. It's all random." A knowing look had invaded her eyes. "But don't worry, now, you'll get your turn at something a little nicer. Just remember what I said."

Extract #4
Eden Project Welcome Pack

Welcome, citizen! You've taken your first

step to making history. Eden welcomes you to your new home. You'll find you have all the necessaries prepared for you, plus a few comforts (see attached itinerary for full details).

All new arrivals are allocated to the same neighborhood for the duration of their first week and are exempt from project duties for this time to help everyone settle in and make nice. Be sure to take advantage of this time and get to know your neighbors; you'll be seeing the same folks for many years to come, and sometimes all you'll have is each other. Everyone has to pull together in Eden.

Once your welcome week has elapsed, you will receive weekly duty cards detailing a 'job' that is randomly assigned to each individual by our central computers. Paradise this might be, but make no mistake—life depends on elbow grease and sweaty brows! Everyone has to do their part.

And so we have a fine little system worked up. Hard work is rewarded. We're big believers in Karma here. What goes around comes around, and the random selection applies to your housing, too. Every week you'll get a duty card and your fresh robes; every month you'll get your housing allocation.

It's a little like musical chairs sometimes, what with everyone moving here, there, and everywhere, but fair's fair! You might notice that things might not seem all the same around the Project, but rest assured everyone gets their turn in the finer places, and everyone spends a spell roughing it.

Remember, we're all the same here. Everyone benefits off each other's backs. All we are is what we choose to be. Choose to make the lives of Eden's folks better, and apply yourself to the fullest, citizen. The fate of the world depends on you!

- Mother Eden

"Ma," I muttered into the gloom, peering around her bedroom door. I expected a sleepy grunt to answer from the darkness, but instead her reply was alert and immediate.

"Can't sleep?"

I crept over the threshold, feeling like an eight-year-old who'd come running after a nightmare. We had turned in early, but still it was pitch black out here in the desert, and Eden had precious few streetlamps. The house creaked with the wind and the settling of its wooden supports, and my bed smelled clean—not fresh, but sanitized and unwelcoming. "No."

"Me neither." She patted the sheets, and I crept forward to perch on the side of the bed. With the world quiet bar the creaking wind and only a few scant moonbeams to light the room, it was almost possible to believe I really was a little kid. We could have been back home in Fremont, with Father silently asleep beside us in our one-bedroom tenement.

"What are you doing up?" I said.

"I heard about a broadcast that goes out every night."

"From who?"

"Her. Mother Eden." She sighed. "What a wonderful job that woman has done out here. I'd like to hear more from her before tomorrow. We need to make a good impression, Desh. The more information we can get, the easier it'll be. It should start any moment."

A heavy silence fell over us, and I turned my head to listen. Somewhere outside crickets were chirruping, and some pipes gurgled underneath us.

Then with a static squeal, the street thrummed with the sound of a familiar honey-sweet voice. "Evening, newcomers! This is Mother Eden, just checking in to make sure you're all settled and set to rest."

The broadcast was coming from the streetlamps, I was sure. It was loud, almost intrusive. I felt it would still be audible even if the windows were all shut tight.

I tried to ignore it. "You miss him, too?" I said.

"Your father?" Her voice wobbled.

"Yes."

"Of course I do." Another pause. "I wish he was here. But we both have to be strong and make good of what he's provided for us."

"I should have stayed with him," I mumbled.

"No, darling." Her bony fingers clasped mine somewhere in the shadows. "No, he's where he needs to be. He worked the graveyard shift at the plant every day since you were born, just hoping he might get us out."

"But *he's* still back there, Ma."

She was silent. In the dark I thought I might be able to pick out the reflection of her spectacles and the whites of her eyes, fixed on the moonbeams spilling in through the window.

Mother Eden was talking. "We've got an early start if we're gonna get all of you up to speed. We need good hands and strong backs to succeed out here. Every link in the chain has to . . ."

I was sure I could see Ma's eyes now, and they were definitely fixed on the window, unfocused.

"Ma," I said.

She jerked and turned to me. "I'm sorry, dear." She smiled, and it was the same weak smile she'd worn for over a year. But she was wearing those spectacles, horn-rimmed frames that gave her an unfamiliar dignity. They gave a hawkish sharpness to her gaze. It was a wonder how much stronger they made her look.

"Maybe if I make some headway with my research, they might make an allowance and let Father in," I said. There was no chance of him ever making it here, but I still said it.

"Maybe," she said.

I frowned in the dark. The tremor in her voice had waned to almost nothing since we had come to the house.

Such a transformation in only a few short hours. It was as though the mother I had once known was shining out through the cracks in her decrepit exterior. Although, she didn't seem as broken up about Father as I was.

"It's not fair," I said. "I know it's a godsend, Ma, but I don't know if I can do this without him."

"I know, dear." She was looking at the window again, squeezing my wrist tight. "I know." She settled against her pillow and muttered, "But maybe we should listen to this, eh?"

I nodded, swallowing in vain to clear the lump in my throat.

Do you even care? I thought. *It doesn't sound like it.*

What did I want? For her to break down in front of me? Would I prefer that?

No. But this . . . this isn't right. She must *be missing him, too.*

It might have been the excitement of arriving. She had been overjoyed at the state of the house, and had gabbled about it all evening. In time, I was sure, the reality of having lost Father would sink in.

I made a mental note to keep an eye on her. It could crash down on her all at once.

"I wonder if we can get our hands on a copy of that book Mother Eden was talking about," Ma muttered. "It would be good to get ahead, read up on the proper way to live out here."

I nodded again, but now it was my turn to say nothing. I listened to the broadcast with her a while longer, then said, "I'm tired, Ma."

Without a word I slunk back to bed.

"Goodnight, dear," Ma said.

A trickle of warmth dripped down into my chest. Though, if I was honest, she seemed more focused on Mother Eden's voice than mine.

The next morning was eaten up by the tasks of unpacking, tearing away the plastic wrapping on every surface, and opening up the house. The air outside was alive with tiny cracklings as our neighbors did the same.

Besides that, however, there was a surprising silence, so deep that I could hear the faraway whistling of the desert wind. Vehicles seldom drove by, and the long intervals between lacked the rattle of radio or television. When I thought about it, I hadn't seen either one among the vacuum-sealed essentials we'd been given—there wasn't even an allocated space for a TV or wall-screen in the living room.

Before I'd had a chance to stop and eat breakfast, Mother Eden's voice— emanating from speakers atop the street's lampposts—called us away to another orientation. I planned to take a minute to fix some food for the walk over to the hall, but Ma appeared the moment the announcement had ended and took my arm. Her spectacles stood proud upon the ridge of her nose. She was moving decisively now, with purpose. The sharpness to her gaze was uncanny. "How can you think about food when we're so *late*?" she said, bustling me out the door.

"They only just called it," I said.

"And look how far behind we've fallen already!"

She was right. People were spilling through their front doors with plastic still trailing from their hands, hurrying up the street, dragging struggling children, straightening the clothes they'd slept in with desperate swipes.

I mouthed wordlessly, searching for a reply, but then Ma was shoving me in the small of the back. The power of each push caught me off guard, a wiry strength I'd thought lost to her for years. Against my will, we gave chase. We arrived not last, but certainly among the stragglers. Ma whined the whole way about how embarrassed she'd be if we had to walk in with everyone staring at us, and I did my best to comfort her, but my attention was absorbed by looking around at the Project.

Things were the same as they'd been the day before. I'd imagined that what we'd seen at first had been a tidied-up cheeseball show, the kind you always saw when being shown around a new place. But things hadn't changed a bit.

Everything was perfect, neat, and clean.

We took seats at the back of the hall. I suspected Ma would give me hell when we got back to the house—somehow it would be my fault—but I put the thought to the back of my mind when Mother Eden took to the podium.

"I hope y'all are having a good morning. Word around

town is that the lot of you are settling in just fine. Always good to hear we got no problems with anyone." A palm-sized projector at her feet lit up a wall-screen behind her. It looked strange here in Eden, by far the most advanced piece of technology I'd seen since the Skyrail had departed. Upon the screen were pictures from around camp.

"This morning's just to fill in the blanks and help get your heads in the right place for how we all live here. First, y'all probably noticed how we got no locks on the doors. That's 'cause the first rule 'round here is trust. We all believe in one another, and the Project trusts every one of you to be good citizens and behave in a way that's proper.

"Second, you'll notice we've got none of those heathen squawk-boxes and tele-screens and computers you all got back there in the wide open. We've had a philosophy build up here over the years, and right at the bottom of it is the idea that all those gizmos and distractions are what got the world in such a mess in the first place. So you won't be finding any of that here. Nothing but honest entertainment—good old-fashioned books from the local library and our very own evening broadcast."

Ma's hand touched my leg, sensing my agitation. A knowing look was in her eye. "Books, Desh," she whispered. "They work just as good."

I wasn't so sure.

How can anyone survive without the net? I thought.

The rest of the talk stretched out for almost an hour, detailing the duties that everyone was obliged to carry out, tasks to keep the community in working order, which would start the coming Monday. Then there was a briefing explaining that only a few of us would remain in our homes for very long. The lottery was prone to shuffle around the housing arrangements by a large margin.

"Stops people from make cliques and little societies," Mother Eden quipped brightly. "Keeps grudges on the slide. We get along when everyone knows everyone." She didn't mention anything further about the housing arrangements, even though I felt there was more to it. But I put it to the back of my mind, because after that came the subject of the drills. The wall-screen changed to an image of the perimeter fences.

Mother Eden's face had grown serious. Suddenly her cartoon drawl seemed suppressed. "Y'all know what it takes to keep places like this on their feet," she said. "I'm sure y'all have seen the news reports again and again on Projects ransacked by desperate folks displaced from their homes. Refugees come knocking, looking for help, and they get desperate when there ain't enough to go around. That's what all this is for." She stepped around her podium. "We make a point to take all the ugly fences and big, strapping army men in our stride and just get on with things, but it's important to remember they're there. Just keep them in the back of your mind because—while I promise every single one of you that this here Project is as safe as they come—every second there's someone out there fixing to take it all away from us. Don't let all that empty sand fool you, because there's millions of homeless people all over the world, and they show up in the unlikeliest of places."

A few faces were starting to twitch into uncomfortable frowns. But everyone held composure, wielded by Mother Eden's splayed arms.

"That's why, every now and then, we might have a little drill. Just for safety, just to let y'all know that danger's on the horizon. Nobody's gonna be expected to do anything so nasty as fighting, mind you, but things might just get a little . . . loud." She clicked something in her hand, and suddenly the hall was filled with a deafening siren. I ducked instinctively, dragging Ma down with me. Over the racket I could hear dozens of muffled screams.

Then silence.

My ears ringing, I dusted Ma's disheveled form. "Are you all right?" I said, yelling over the ringing in my ears.

Wide-eyed, she nodded.

I turned back to Mother Eden who, though still grave, looked distantly pleased with herself. And I could see why: every one of us had ducked down, like the terrified children from the 1950s I'd seen in history class, cowering under their desks in terror of nuclear warheads. She had total control over us.

"That's our raid siren," she said sweetly. "Y'all listen out for it. But remember," her smile widened, "we're all safe here. Snug as bugs."

Snug [Eden-Speak]: In mortal peril.

Extract #5
Archived Interview
 The following is an excerpt of a televised interview between Hubert Abernathy, spokesman for the United Nations Climate Change Council, and Pulitzer Prize winning reporter, Jennifer Tinson.

Q: So, once again, Mr. Abernathy, I'd like to draw attention to a sensitive issue: Eden Prime, the former flagship settlement in the Eden Program, which seems to have been swept under the carpet in recent years.

A: As we've already established, Ms. Tinson, Eden Prime is still very much our flagship program. Satellite images confirm that the site has expanded in size steadily for the past twenty years, in line with even our most optimistic projections. The intensive innovation of new GM crops seems to have brought the entire region into a flourishing state of plenty.

Q: All highly commendable, of course. But how can you attest to the success of the program when we haven't heard a single word from anyone on the site for several decades—since only a few years after the program's inception, in fact?

A: As we have already established, a policy of total communicative blackout is enforced with the Eden Projects to ensure their complete autonomy. Only through these means can we be certain of fostering true independent communities capable of preserving our civilization.

Q: Sounds like the UN is conducting something closer to a sociological experiment.

A: It's nothing of the sort. This policy was crafted by all the founding nations many years ago.

Q: If such blackouts are in place, why are the programs equipped with dedicated 500-kilowatt radio transmitters?

A: Such things are to be used in emergencies to signal for aid. Their secondary use is for communicating and coordinating with other surviving communities in the event of a catastrophic worldwide climate shift.

Q: Or a world war. Isn't that right?

A: We don't anticipate warlike scenarios, Ms. Tinson. The Climate Change Council concerns itself with, unsurprisingly, climate change.

Q: I see. There's been some concern around the control center constantly manned at the United Nations Headquarters. If the blackouts have been in place for so many years, how can you justify the expense?

A: As I have said, the transmitters are

in place in case of emergency, and as such we must be ready to receive such a distress call and coordinate rescue operations. Each Eden site represents an investment in the billions of dollars. We can't afford to lose any of them.

Q: And if you were to receive a message that wasn't a distress call? People on-site, or their descendants, might decide that they've had enough. Being isolated out in the desert for the rest of your life would surely erode even the hardiest resolve.

A: That is very unlikely. The specialists in command of each site were selected from pools of many thousands of candidates and given the most rigorous training.

Q: But just for sake of argument. Say we received a message. What do you think they would say?

A: Well, I should think that one day it'll be us calling them, asking to join them!

I woke to the sound of muffled cries. I groaned, bleary-eyed, and blinked in the harsh blue light of morning. Staggering out onto the front lawn, I saw one of our neighboring couples across the street gathered on their doorstep, struggling with a thrashing figure at their feet.

Without thinking, I hurried over. Halfway across the road I caught a good look at what was going on. The parents looked grim and moved with the slow determination in the face of trouble that people develop by late middle age. I guessed they were from somewhere in Indonesia.

Thudding on the concrete doorstep was a young girl, limbs a twitching blur, her mouth touched at the edges by creamy foam. While she whimpered and whined like a wounded dog, her father grabbed at her bucking neck, and her mother turned her onto her side.

Their stiff aged bodies were awkward in the narrow doorway. The girl beat herself bloody on the sharp edge of the step, and her legs made sickening cracks against the doorframe.

I reached them moments later and reached down to hold her shoulders. Her father's eyes met mine, and I saw behind his steely gaze—one that looked used to dealing with attacks like these—a frank, human fear.

Between us we held her torso, but her legs still kicked and thrashed.

I'd seen epileptic fits before, but this one was far more violent, and it didn't seem to be stopping. And, looking around, there didn't seem to be any sign of an ambulance.

Where is everyone? I thought, scrabbling for calm and failing. *Surely the whole street can hear!*

But the street was empty.

"Ma!" I bawled. "Ma, help!"

She came running out moments later. Ma, running. I

couldn't remember the last time I'd seen such a thing. "My goodness!" she cried.

"Call somebody, we need a doctor—"

"No!" The girl's mother had surged forward, dropping her daughter's shoulder, and took hold of mine instead. Her eyes were inky pits surrounded by milky oceans. "No doctor!"

"What?" I screeched. "She's in trouble, lady. She needs help!"

"No!" Now it was the father. He didn't lay a hand on me, but he didn't need to. I had the feeling he'd skin me alive if I suggested it again.

"What, then?"

Neither of them spoke. Instead they looked at one another, then dropped their eyes to the floor and took to holding on grimly.

I blinked, stuck for words.

The girl went on whining and thrashing. Her legs would be bruised badly by now. "Ma, get over here, hold her legs!"

I reached down beside the Indonesian family and held tight. We'd get answers after the worst had passed.

Please let this be something that'll pass, I thought.

But the girl's legs continued to fly about. When I looked up again, Ma hadn't moved from the grassy verge, frozen midstep. Her eyes danced in their sockets, moving up and down the street, from house to house.

Now I could see that we weren't alone after all. The street might have been empty, but we had quite the audience: from the windows of every house peered the other new arrivals, all stock-still and stoic.

"Ma!" I cried.

Ma took another half step forward and then danced back again as though burned, looking around like a cornered animal. "What's wrong with her?"

"I don't know. Get over here and help me!"

But instead she just stood there, still frozen, cracking her bony fingers in distress and hopping from foot to foot. "I don't know how to help. Let the doctors take care of it."

"The doctors aren't coming, Ma!"

"Oh, I'm sure they'll be along any moment." A pause, then she cleared her throat. "Why . . . why don't you come on inside? It looks like her mommy and daddy have it all covered. We're just getting in the way."

I gaped at her, then glanced back to the girl. Her burnished skin was draining of its vital sheen, taking on an ugly drained tone. Her eyes had rolled up into her head and the foam at her mouth was dripping down to her chin. "Ma, she's going to break her legs if you don't get over here."

"Don't be silly, Desh, she'll be fine. Your Aunt Hillie used to get the epilepsy. It all blows over. I'm sure they have these problems all the time." She gave an exaggerated smile and nodded jerkily to both the parents. "All fine, yes?"

Neither of them even looked up. The mother was weeping quietly as she held on.

Why aren't the others coming out? They're just going to

watch this?

"Ma," I barked. "Now!"

"Deshun, I'm not going to say it again. You're just getting in the way, now." Ma had her arms akimbo, but her voice still sounded off, as though she was trying to convince herself as well as me. "She shouldn't have come to Eden if she had a condition."

"*Ma!*" I was almost screeching now. But then the man's hand fell on mine, heavy as a hunk of ham.

"Go," he said. "Go away. We will help. You go." He eyed Ma and then all those faces staring at him from behind net curtains and pane glass, and his lip curled. "You both go away."

Before I could muster a reply he had thrown me back onto the grass. "Go!" His eyes were suddenly red with fury and pain, and he returned to his flailing child. The mother continued weeping.

I stumbled back onto the grass and Ma was beside me a moment later, pulling me up and dusting me off. "Good, good, that's right. Come along, dear," she said briskly and began shepherding me back across the street.

I balked and protested the whole way, delirious with the surreal absurdity of it all. Everyone was staring. I could feel it now. As one, just as the china dolls had stared at us all during the welcome speech. Judging, disapproving, cold.

Ma got us both inside and slammed the door, leaning up against it and breathing a deep sigh.

Even through the door, I could hear the little girl

choking on her own vomit.

⟡

"Desh, come on now, eat your soup. It'll get cold." Ma was eyeing me from the kitchen doorway, her voice an odd blend of timidity and firmness.

I looked at the bowl before me, blinked, then sighed and sat back. "I can't believe you." I sounded cold and blank, unlike myself.

Ma flinched.

"People had been talking about them, Desh. A few people came knocking to warn us about that family." She sniffed.

"Warn us?" I looked at her, but I wasn't sure who I was seeing. "About a little girl?"

The Indonesian parents had taken their girl inside, and I hadn't seen her again. But word had traveled fast along the street. The girl had wound down, got quiet, and just stopped.

Her mother's wailing had echoed in every crawlspace in the new arrivals' area until it had cut off sharply. A twist in my gut told me her husband might have had something to do with it.

At last an ambulance had pulled up outside and two women in green had hopped out. But there hadn't been any great urgency about them, and when they had emerged they hadn't wheeled a stretcher, but instead a long covered black box.

"They knew, Desh," Ma said. "They knew she was sick, and they lied. Even though they couldn't bring in the medicine, they brought her here anyway." She took a decisive step into the room and stretched a dishtowel taut between her hands. "Took up a spot at an Eden site that could have gone to somebody healthy, who could have made a difference."

I shook my head. "They must have thought she might have had a chance here."

"All the medical screenings the rest of us had to go through to get here to make sure we were worthy!" Ma's brow was so furrowed her face seemed carved in two. "They cheated and lied. That's not the right way to be, not around here."

"So we all just line up and watch her die? A goddamn little girl, Ma?"

She said nothing, just bunched the dishtowel up in her hands, wringing and twisting. Her eyes, however, betrayed a wounded regret, shining with unshed tears.

"I don't care what the others are like, Ma. I don't care if *they're* animals. I'm not going to be that way."

She stood with her hands clasped, shoulders hunched. "Desh, we have to make a good impression. We have to make sure we're neighborly and proper. If we want to make a good life here—"

"We have to dance to their tune?"

"Yes, Desh!"

"They stood and watched their own kid beat herself to death on the floor. You want us to be like that?"

"No, I . . . of course not," she flustered. "I just . . ."

"What, Ma?"

"I . . ." She fumed. "They shouldn't have come! It's their own fault, not mine. It's not my business, Desh, nor yours. And now we're involved and people might talk. This is our one chance, young man, and I won't have you ruin it for the both of us." She stormed across the room, took up my soup, and carried it away, her eyes glistening, guilt-ridden and angry in equal measure. "You let it get cold," she snapped and left me sitting at the table.

While she banged around in the kitchen, I looked out the window and saw the little girl's mother totter out onto the sidewalk, taking out the trash. She kept her head low, but the burgeoning black eye was still obvious. After a while she went inside and neither of the parents emerged again for a long time.

A few days later, the muttering still crept up and down the street. When the parents reappeared, they walked arm in arm, stony faced, and never said a word about their little girl. And everyone else seemed content to forget she had ever existed.

But I remembered. And even though she pretended not to, Ma remembered, too.

⁂

Another day went by, cooler than the last. Little stirred, and around us Eden ticked over its daily passings like fine clockwork, seamless and efficient.

I now missed Father so much that my chest ached. I had lived away from home before during my scholarships in Europe and my time at Princeton, but to know that I could never see him, hurt more than I would have imagined.

The little "welcome week" refused to be over and done with. We were supposed to be mingling with the other new arrivals, forming relationships that would make us effective additions to Eden Prime. But the others were insular, incommunicative; they didn't seem much interested in anyone but themselves, and a sneering competitiveness was rife.

I was keen to keep Ma out of it, but short of locking her up, I couldn't do a thing to stop it. And, though I didn't like to admit it, she had already established herself high on the pecking order.

To busy myself I made dinner—a finicky French recipe I had seen during my Fullbright year—that forced me to focus and took my attention away from Father. Ma clapped her hands in delight when I called her to eat, fussing over how well the dish had turned out. I let her, buoyed up for a while by the attention.

But when things got quiet and we turned to conversation to fill the silence, I found myself immediately talking about Father. As soon as I mentioned him, Ma stopped eating. An internal struggle showed in her fluttering eyelids and twitching lips. She cried out, spitting onion and potato across the tablecloth.

With a shuddering sigh she dabbed her eyes and excused herself. She went to her room, and for a while I heard her shuddering cries through the walls.

My chest ached all the more. But when I turned in to bed, I was smiling. After a while, I realized it was because now I knew: somewhere, deep down, she missed him.

"This is ridiculous, Ma."

"Just remember your manners and smile." Ma fidgeted beside me, pressing non-existent creases from her dress, and made a fuss of my evening tie. We were standing before the door where the welcome speech had been held. Dusk was afoot and the streetlamps were coming on. It was still hot, and I was sweating already, but there had been no fighting Ma.

The evening broadcasts had been talking about night classes held by the "fine ladies of Eden". They were mainly to help international newcomers with learning English, but I hadn't failed to notice the undercurrent hinting that it was a master class on how to play ball.

How to Climb the Ladder 101, I thought.

Ma had been talking about it all day. Her fixation with making good impressions and affecting all the wants and niceties of Mother Eden's inner circle was already becoming an obsession.

I didn't like it, but it made her happy. I would have done anything to keep her that way, if only to see her smile. That was what I had promised Father.

She took a deep breath, and we passed inside. A row of

seated middle-aged women lined the stage from which Mother Eden had spoken, all dressed in fine white robes or frilly dresses, cups of tea and saucers clasped in their hands. They chattered to one another, straight-backed and dainty, looming over a small audience. Most members of the small crowd were dark-skinned women, but some were men and others were the whitest of white. The former looked unsettled and nervous; the latter shifty eyed and coy.

"Ah, the Goldings!" One of the twins who had introduced us when we had arrived was standing, waving us forward. "Do come, sit! We'll have you both singing Eden's tune in no time." She covered her mouth with the back of her hand. "Give you a leg up on the rest, put in a good word and all that. You'll see the finer side of things here, trust me."

The women on stage and the shiftier members of the audience all giggled as one.

Ma giggled and waved. "Thank you, indeed."

She moved forward, and instinctively I started to follow. But my feet felt like they were made of lead, and my throat felt as though it had been slicked with battery acid. All of a sudden everything seemed wrong. I didn't want to be here. I was uncomfortable in my own skin, just being in the same room as the snooty women up on stage. They were creatures of comfort, at a glance.

The Eden Program was supposed to be all about fairness, sacrifice, and teamwork. But this . . . this was the polar opposite.

"I don't like this, Ma," I whispered.

"Oh, hush. Give it a chance."

I've given this place plenty of chances, I thought.

All this had the stink of a private club. It was a farce.

I held back, frozen in place. Ma was already some distance ahead of me, stumbling to a stop only when she turned and found that I wasn't at her side. The women up on stage watched closely, perched raptors eyeing up their prey.

"Desh?" Ma was beckoning me imperiously with her eyes. "Take a seat with me, why don't you, dear?"

I blinked and glanced between her and the circle of grinning faces. "Maybe we should go."

"Don't be silly. We're here, now."

"I really think we ought to go."

"Just sit down and listen. Don't be shy. I'm nervous, too."

I shook my head. I had to get out. "If you won't come, I'm going home alone," I muttered.

"Desh!" she hissed.

"Sorry, Ma, I can't. I . . . I don't feel so well."

She smiled, but there was no warmth to it. It was more of a glare. Her voice was loud enough for those on stage to hear. "Come on, now, don't be rude. Our hosts have put all this together for our sakes."

"I know." I swallowed, and forced myself to turn to the twins. "I appreciate it. But I need to lie down."

I backed away and Ma took a step after me, her lips parting. When I took yet another step she stayed where she was, her cheeks flushed. "I really think you should take a seat, Desh." There was a note of begging in her voice, mixed with a sweetness that I hated.

I shook my head. "Sorry, Ma. Not tonight. I'll see you at home."

I turned and left her there by the circle of chattering ladies in their dresses and teacups, and I walked home through pools of light thrown down by the lampposts. I thought she might chase after me, give me a hiding, and drag me back by the ear.

But she didn't even follow so far as the door.

I held out as long as I could., but eventually culture deprivation got the better of me, and I skulked into the library. It was a long, low building clear across the Project, set on its own some distance from any other area of activity. Though it sparkled with a pristine finish just like every other structure in sight, it had an unfortunate proximity to the garbage disposal area. A part of me wanted to turn tail and leave before I'd even made it to the door, but I'd only end up climbing the walls for something to do if I returned home. Ma now talked almost constantly about "the girls", Mother Eden, and the miracle of the evening broadcast.

So I walked inside the library, met by a blanket of silence inside. It was as though I'd passed through an invisible barrier; the sounds of the new arrivals' neighborhood—what I had started calling the White-Picket District—died in the single step I took over the threshold. Before I got adult privileges on my HUD—the heads-up display implanted on the optic nerve in infancy— in Fremont I'd been in a library to use the ancient flat-screen computers (awful, primitive things that used boards of letters for input), but I'd never seen a library like this outside history class.

There were thousands of books in here. Real, physical books, lined in shelves that took up almost all the floor space. I'd always known the dust-jacketed volumes we had in our apartment as little more than novelties Ma and Father liked to sit down to on occasion; it was their version of the echoes of the good old days that every generation clung to as they aged. After all, the bookshop in town rubbed shoulders with the vinyl record store.

The door squealed closed behind me, and I was left standing under the high roof, with the strange smell of musty paper blending with a faint note of garbage. The lights were turned down low. It wasn't mood lighting but instead was dim and uninviting.

The central space was occupied by only a handful of people, all of whom moved with the dull drudgery of the infirmed or senile. A single librarian sat at a nearby desk. Her smile was only slight and very plastic—what I guessed was Eden's equivalent of a sourpuss.

"Is this your first time?" she said. For a resident, she had a testy tone.

"Yes," I said, walking toward the shelves with uncertain

steps.

"Take your time. We get a lot of new arrivals in their first week." She paused. "Don't hold your breath. You probably won't find anything worth staying for."

Not the best promoter of the written word, I thought.

I reached the first of the shelves and looked toward the door. She was probably right. I wasn't one for sitting down to read just one thing at a time, especially for more than a minute or two. Nobody I knew could hold attention that long. We were used to our HUD feeds preparing the highlights of everything we needed to know for us.

But this was all I had. And I wasn't going back to sit silent in the kitchen. Not again.

I sighed, tilted my head sideways, and started reading titles.

⌒◎

I dropped a four-foot-high pile of dusty volumes onto the front desk. "What the hell's going on here?"

The librarian barely looked up. She was flicking through an old housekeeping magazine—"How to Throw a Garden Party That Puts Your Friends' to Shame!" was the title on the open spread—something I vaguely remembered Mother Eden's broadcasts encouraging.

She raised her eyebrows. After a strained moment, a thin smile touched her lips. "Can I help you?"

I gestured to the books, drawn from disparate corners of the library and covering myriad subjects. "Where are all the missing pages?"

She blinked sweetly. "Excuse me?"

"The missing pages! Every one of those books has pieces torn away. They've been cut out; I can see the stubs still bound to the spine! You've got a vandal making a mess of this place. You'll have to put an order in for replacements."

"Sir, I think you'll find they're intact."

I reeled. "Intact? They're the very definition of un-intact!"

My one remaining resource that might have kept me sane, ruined by some bored delinquent. I had yet to find another person my own age, but I'd been hoping against hope that when one showed up, we'd be kindred spirits. Now, I was betting he had a name like Todd, wore black mascara, and carried around a pocketful of razor blades.

I hadn't even wanted to read the books I'd selected, not really. But now they'd been taken away from me, my fists were shaking. I must have looked absurd, shaking like I had palsy there in front of her, but I couldn't stop myself.

"Intact, yes," the librarian was saying. "Just as they should be, after the necessary amendments have been made, of course."

Despite myself, I took a step back. "Amendments?" I looked at the books on the desk and then marched over to the nearest shelf and pulled off a book at random. I flipped through and, lo and behold, there was a wad of stubs halfway through. A whole chapter had been cleanly excised.

Speechless, I slid the volume back into place and returned to the desk. The librarian had watched me coolly, her finger holding the page of her magazine. I leaned over the desk now and found myself panting. "Censored?" I breathed.

"Edited." She smiled. Her eyes returned to the spread on garden parties. "Checked over for our benefit."

I shook my head. A strangled sound escaped my throat.

It was unbelievable. Almost one hundred and fifty years after the Third Reich's book burning, seventy since the Arab Spring and the blanketing of social networks, and at least fifty since the last Communist states publically condemned those who spoke against them. After all the UN had done to curtail such primitive breaches of human rights, here it was, right under their noses—funded, no less, by the very people who had fought against it!

"Am I to take it that if I were to take *any* one of the books in this library, I'd find missing pages? Or goddamn worse, *edited* pages?"

"Not all." She turned the page of her magazine and crooned at the sight of a plate of hors d'oeuvres. "We have *The Foundings*."

I shrugged, searching her for any sign of sarcasm. But when she turned her gaze on me once more, I saw only dry exasperation. "You really haven't been listening to those broadcasts, have you?"

"Please!"

She smiled, a wide, frog-like, indulgent thing. She was relishing this. "Our own beginnings. A full comprehensive history of the Eden Project, written by Mother Eden herself," she said. "It's been heralded as the foremost piece of sanctioned literature."

"You mean the only piece of sanctioned literature."

"Don't be obtuse, young man. The books under this roof have been checked over by trained analysts to remove any *trace* of harmful material. There are a lot of damaging thoughts out there in the world, all clamoring to get past our walls. It's for our protection. You should be glad we have such measures in place."

"To block all that pesky lingering free speech?" I said. I looked around at the other decrepit library dwellers, trying to make eye contact, hoping for some support. But the dozen or so hunch-backed cripples didn't so much as twitch at the sound of my raised voice.

"I think you'll find there's no drama around these parts, my dear," the librarian said. "It's one of the hallmarks of the way we live. In fact, if you'd been listening to the evening broadcasts, you'd know that.

"Now, shall I book you a copy of *The Foundings*? You'll need to sign up for a library card."

I sighed, defeated. That was it. No TV, no radio, no Internet. Not even an uncensored book. Not a single cozy mystery that hadn't had some oblique reference to a raunchy affair snipped out with a pair of scissors.

Anything that went against Mother Eden's divine words, torn from sight.

I was in more than one kind of desert here. A desert of scorching sand, to be sure, but one all the bleaker for want of a single errant idea.

"Young man?"

"Don't bother," I said and turned for the door. "I won't be coming here again."

I wandered across the Project to blow off some steam. I hoped to run into somebody who wasn't either a toddler or in the grips of middle age. Even those ghastly twins.

But I didn't see anyone. In fact, the entire Project seemed deserted beyond the White-Picket District. Probably locked up tight wherever their duties had taken them for the day. The only people in sight were the armed guards along the distant fences.

I recalled what Mother Eden had said the night before during her evening broadcast: "Now don't let the big guns and chicken wire get you worried. It's all for show, mostly; keeps some nasty people out there from getting any bright ideas."

Looking at the fences and those men now, I felt a sense of unease slither and grow. Chicken wire? I was looking at inch-thick curls of razor wire capping a few miles of chain link fences and concrete walls, lined by watchtowers covered in spotlights, manned by enormous guardsmen bearing equally enormous weapons. Sprawled between them were motor pools populated by armor-plated vehicles painted in camouflage colors and capped by fifty-caliber gun turrets. Entire regiments were on patrol along the fences, interspersed here and there—not in plain sight, but there, in the background.

They were all around us, encircling the entire settlement, protecting us from desert thieves and encroaching swarms of refugees—or stopping us from leaving.

After almost fifteen minutes of aimless wandering, I grew bored and decided to pay them a visit. Maybe some of them had a stroke of personality. I changed course and made for the nearest gathering of camo-clad silhouettes. It took far longer to get to them than I had imagined. At first it had looked as though the fences lay just beyond the main parade of homes and communal buildings, but the main road ended prematurely. I was forced through low hedges and across barren expanses of scorched dunes.

In fact, I was soon certain that it would have been all too easy to hide the fences, the armaments, and the guards themselves. The half-successful attempts at screening them from view that I'd taken to be in earnest were now clearly a double bluff. The powers at hand wanted these fences visible, wanted the heavy machine guns in the grips of so many he-men on display. And, I suspected, they wanted to remind us of what lay set against any dissenters. Or any deserters.

I pressed on despite growing hesitation, and soon the silhouettes had morphed into definite human forms. Tanned ruddy faces, necks thick with bulging tendons, and behemoth hands wrapped around anodized matte-black gun barrels. Truly impressive specimens. The rest of us were underfed androgynous wisps compared to such towers of ham.

The group I was headed for numbered around two dozen, and all of them bore the same impressive physique. Such physical prowess could only have come from the strictest exercise regime and enough high-grade protein to fill a medium-sized aircraft hangar.

How could the Project support a diet like that? The macroprotein supplements infused in our daily rations were no match for that kind of volume. Eden residents' diets consisted mainly of GM fruits, grains, and bread—hardy stuff that had been engineered to weather the sun and drought. It was never engineered to foster body builders. The few animals Eden Programs kept were for zoological and educational purposes only; the kind of inefficiency in sacrificing arable land for grazing pasture was strictly forbidden.

Then there was the question of the guards themselves. Who were they? Where did they live? I'd spotted no barracks anywhere, nor had I seen any of the men in the restrooms. Not even the convenience store. They instead seemed to eternally patrol the Project's borders, indefatigable sentinels. To my knowledge, there had never been a recruitment drive for military personnel at any Project.

But all that could wait. What I wanted most of all, after all, was somebody to talk to. I began to rehearse my introductions, practicing what I hoped was a warm smile. I'd had precious few excuses to smile of late.

I was so caught up in the act that when the guards dropped formation and charged toward me over the sand, waving their arms and bellowing, I continued approaching for a good few seconds, that same goofy smile still stretching my cheeks.

Then the closest of them cupped his hands over his mouth and his words leaped forth from unintelligibility. "STOP, KID! THE MINES!"

Mines. The word triggered something deep in my head, something that snapped with a metallic twang. Terror erupted up from my groin, bubbling somewhere behind my tonsils. I dug in my heels, great plumes of sand kicking up around me as I skidded to a halt. By then I could see the signposts.

It seemed impossible I hadn't seen them before—bright red, ten feet wide, spaced every few dozen yards across the dunes. Each one was emblazoned with luminous white letters and a skull and crossbones. CAUTION: MINEFIELD, they read.

In my desperation, I'd been blinded.

The guards had sagged in unison along a ridge some one hundred feet away. Between us lay a featureless band of sand, an unnaturally perfect level surface, a no-man's-land.

"Turn back now, sir," the nearest guard cried. His powerful voice had a bass that thrummed in my chest even at this distance.

I turned left then right, hoping to see a path leading to the fences; the guards must have some means of getting back to the Project, after all. But the no-man's-land stretched to the horizon on both sides.

"Sir!" Another of the guards had joined the first. He seemed much the same, complete with macho-man baritone and rigid stance. "Sir, return to Eden immediately!"

I hesitated, but they weren't going to allow it.

"This is not a request," the first bellowed. "This is a restricted area."

"What the hell is going on here?" I wanted to cry back, but my tongue was stopped in my throat. There was something about these men that invited frankness. Here were the first human beings I'd seen since arriving, far removed from the painted ceramic vessels walking the Project's streets. Grumbling, sweating, panting men.

I realized I wanted to be on the other side of the minefield more than anything.

But they were growing more irate by the moment. A lump leaped into my throat when the sun glinted off gun barrels being trained in my direction. I raised my hands, stunned, and stammered, "What? Shit, you gonna goddamn shoot me? Wrong side of the fence!"

"A flesh wound is better than tripping one of these mines, sir. Better for all of us," the second guard yelled. "They're liable to chain."

"You mean they could all go off?"

The rifle in his hand jerked. "We are *not* having a conversation, here. Turn around and return to your home, *now!*"

A dozen questions danced in my gullet, questions I suspected they could answer. Despite the coarseness of their voices, I didn't sense half the malevolence from them that I did from the robed denizens behind me.

I started, stuttered, and my arms fluttered in a single hopeless gesticulation. So close to precious truth. But there was no way I was getting at it now, not with guns trained at my chest and primed explosives buried under my feet.

"*Now!*" the first guard roared.

I sighed and turned away. I felt their gazes on me until I was climbing back through the hedges, by which time the strangest thing about the minefield hit home: all that firepower, all that razor wire, all on the outside. And then the truly formidable barrier of the mines on the inside.

Perhaps a last resort, in case all else failed. Or, perhaps, like so much else, another measure to make sure that nobody thought of leaving.

Then there was the guards themselves. They were different from the Eden folks—set apart from the rest— but they seemed very similar to one another. Almost too similar.

That night was dead quiet. We'd now unpacked the last box, but still the house was sparse, unfurnished, and beige. Only a smattering of the few possessions we had been allowed to bring marked it as our own.

Ma made a light meal of bread and bean chowder. We

ate to the sound of singing crickets, watching the sun set.

I'd never seen her look so happy. Radiant, even. I thought the novelty of being here might have started to wear off, that she must by then have been grieving the loss of Father, but there was no doubting the upturned edge to her lips. "It's so peaceful here," she said. "I thought it was too good to be true." She watched me eat, and her smile widened. "You can make something of yourself here. Actually make something of your life."

I grunted. I wasn't so sure. I had no idea how I was supposed to learn anything with only a few books—books gutted of anything worth reading, at that.

Being so cut off was suffocating. I hadn't anticipated that I would feel so alone. Computers were a thing of the past in the external sense, but I had been raised with my HUD, constantly connected to every person on the planet through the net. I had lived and breathed to the beat of network feeds, breaking news, and the comforting hum of billions of voices. I missed the scrolling text of my filtered personal feed, the popping images in my peripheral vision, the knowledge that I wasn't alone—that through cyberspace I could touch anyone, anywhere.

Its absence throbbed like a recently lost tooth. I must have been in some queer digital withdrawal, but I couldn't help myself.

After they'd given me every embarrassing battery of medical examinations under the sun, bombarded my skin with UV radiation, checked my family tree going back over two centuries for hereditary illness, and kept me in isolation for a full week for any sign of superbug contamination, they had declared I was in perfect health. And then they had lopped off my electronic link to the world—struck me deaf, blind, and dumb. It was a bad joke: make sure you're all spick-and-span, then cripple you utterly in one fell swoop. Without my HUD—hell, a computer screen, even—the horizon literally limited my range of sight. I had never felt so naked.

"How did you cope before HUDs?" I said.

"Hmm?" Ma said distantly, staring out the window. She shook herself, clearing her throat. "Well, I suppose we had computers then. Manually typing it all in. No AI to tailor your info-feed. Can you imagine the chaos?"

"I guess. But aren't you going to miss the net? Your radio shows?"

"I suppose. We'll get used to it. All of that's just a distraction, you know, to keep you from thinking about everything wrong with your life, about what matters. It'll do us good to get back to our roots and talk to people, really talk to them."

I frowned and stopped eating. The silence around us seemed thicker. "You've never said anything like that before."

It took her a long time to reply. Meantime, she just looked out of the window at the lamppost along the street. "Oh, I've always thought that. Anybody with a lick of sense does. But there was so much to deal with back home, what else was I going to do? I could never talk to our neighbors; they'd have tried to sell me something illegal or put the dogs on me."

I forced myself to take a bite of chowder, watching her dreamy eyes carefully. "You *never* said that before we got here. You didn't think it, either."

She let out a tired sigh. "Desh, don't be silly."

I tried another bite, but the food now seemed tasteless. "Every night for as long as I can remember, you've waited in the kitchen for *Ricky Gayle's NumberBall* to come on Radio Jive. I could sing every word of that jingle to you right now. You love that show." My heart leaped as I said that. Ma was all I had left of my old life. If she was prepared to let go of something like that . . . Was I already losing her to this place?

"I wonder when the evening broadcast is going to start," she muttered. "It must be late by now. Maybe something's wrong . . ."

I looked out the window and then back to her. "I'm sure everything's fine." I made to scoop up another spoonful of beans, but only streaks of tomato slurry remained on my plate. I must have eaten, but I had no recollection of taste. I was full but not satisfied.

I looked at Ma for a long time, wondering whether this was how things were going to be from now on.

Then the lampposts squealed outside. "Evening, y'all," Mother Eden's voice drawled.

"Oh, good!" Ma squealed, clapping her hands and sitting up straighter. Her gaze became hazy as she listened to the inane dribble, most of which was on how good and neighborly the newcomers were being.

I listened in for a while, too, eyeing her, trying to keep my dinner down. God knew I wanted to throw it all back up, because the only thing I'd been certain of for a long time was that, come morning, I'd hear Ma humming her show tunes.

And now she said it was just a distraction.

I knew where those words had come from. They were Mother Eden's.

⁓

Extract #6
Project Lottery – An Introduction

Eden Prime, as part of the Eden Program as a whole, has a directive to act as a foothold in regions of prospective future habitability and to develop solutions to environmental hardships the world over. As such, it is essential that mission-vital personnel are given every facility to ensure maximum productivity in research and development efforts.

However, the Project is founded on fairness and, as such, all citizens are entered into two lotteries to determine their weekly work duties and monthly accommodation.

In this manner, support personnel occasionally share in the higher level of health treatments, diet, and luxury reserved for researchers and administrative positions.

Accommodation is split into three classes, which vary in utility, size, and location. As duties require varying resources and commitment, accommodation allocations are usually in line with the demands on each citizen's current duty. However, it must be stressed that each selection is *completely* random, facilitated by dedicated on-site computers.

Those with skills in science, technology, and mathematics will automatically be entered into the duty-pool for R&D work duties. Those lacking in such skills will not; however, all citizens will participate in all duties at some time.

Duties are typified by a color-coded system, which corresponds to the robes distributed with each duty card:

Manual Labor/Support – Brown
Administration/Maintenance – Blue
R&D/Mission Critical – White

Naturally, white duties are afforded maximum resources, blue slightly less, and brown slightly less still. In exceptional circumstances, brown and blue duties will involve attending to the requirements of mission critical roles.

Thank you for your understanding,
The Eden Prime Management Team

I got my first duty card the next morning.

Anything but a researcher position in the Energy Research department would have been ludicrous; surely the lottery algorithm would take my abilities into account. I had things to do, projects unfinished, half a dozen simulations I could have been running. The labs on Eden sites were powerful enough to handle particle simulations of entire galactic superclusters—mouth-watering stuff, the kind of power I'd been slavering for since I'd been forced out of Princeton to take up the factory jobs.

I had my suspicions, after all, that that was why I was here in the first place. The lottery was supposed to be random, but perhaps they made certain exceptions for people like me? Perhaps they had wanted my brain, and our winning a place at Eden Prime had been to save public face.

I snatched the card from the girl on mail duty and opened it right there at the fence. There it was in neat printed type: CLEANING DUTIES.

I was a cleaner.

Liquid fire squirmed in my gut. I was going to be spending my time in the toilets.

"You . . . okay?" said a nearby voice.

I turned to see my neighbor smiling uncertainly as she stood at her own white picket fence, brandishing her own card. I'd gathered over the week that she was the mother of a family of two children—long considered the ideal family size by the Projects. They were a poor lot; Peruvian, or Bolivian—some damn place in the jungle.

When we'd arrived she hadn't spoken a word of English, just like most. But she had been attending the night classes with Ma, and already she had been transformed. They all had. Her ragged clothes had given way to a simple gown that could have come off the rack at Kmart, strangely similar to the white robes that the established residents wore. Her hair, before a tangled shock, was now tied up in a neat bun. Even the way she stood had changed—hands clasped, straight back, polite, blank expression. She'd already begun the journey toward being just another faceless resident.

I suppressed a shudder. I tried to smile, but she cringed. "Fine. Just fine." An awkward pause. I tried adding a strained, "Thanks."

But that didn't seem to help.

A smile eerily similar to the residents' was plastered over her lips, and she backed toward her doorway, vanishing as soon as she'd reached the awning.

Moments later the tinkle of cutlery and the hubbub of a bubbling pot emanated through the kitchen window.

Sweet, smothering, middle-class, All-American bliss.

Along the street it was just the same, coming from every window and beneath every door.

I hurried back to the house.

It was a hundred degrees in the men's public restroom, and perspiration soaked my clothes. Bleach, day-old piss, and the stench of shit clogged my nostrils.

"Cleaning duties," I grumbled. I'd been doing that sporadically all day. Most of the time I wasn't aware of it, but every now and then I'd catch myself.

Chances were I'd get an easy shift manning the emergency broadcast line next week—a duty purported to mean a week at the Ping-Pong table in the coms office—but I was the only member of the new arrivals to land janitorial duty. Every night when I dragged myself home, dog tired, Mother Eden's soothing voice rattled out through lamppost speakers. "Nice work, folks! That's pulling together. Go on home and get yourself some supper. Remember, now: we're all in this together."

All in it together. Because everyone was equal. Everyone shared in the good times and the hard, switched out between the plush houses and the bunkhouses, swapped the easy shifts and the hard.

Somehow, though, I couldn't imagine Mother Eden cleaning many toilets. In fact, I hadn't seen her since arrivals day. I'd only heard her voice over the speakers hidden in every nook and cranny.

Ma and I had settled just fine, with our rooms facing each other across the hall, and we sported an entire spare room. The guilt threatened to crush me most days. I could only console myself with the knowledge that we'd be swapping out for more cramped quarters soon enough.

For now, Ma had a double bed all to herself. I felt a

sinking sensation in my gut every time I saw her brave smile. She had come halfway around the world to end up staring at a man-sized space under the sheets.

After her evening sessions with "the girls", she had volunteered for executive-assistant duties, which saw her and a few others tiptoeing around the handful of larger houses, dusting and making beds.

Locked away inside the stark, dead-quiet mansions belonging to the researchers and other white robes, in the dreamlike heart of the Project's artificial greenery—it was the perfect opportunity to get closer to the dignified circle of ladies that seemed to hold sway over the Project's comings and goings.

I'd been called out there to unblock a cistern a few days ago. There had been an eerie, forced calm blanketing it all. Just like Mother Eden, those in the mansions never seemed to be around during the day. I guessed their duties must have taken them off somewhere, maybe the tunnels underneath the Project.

It was all a far cry from the bunkhouses, the other outliers from the cookie-cutter houses of the White-Picket District. I hadn't laid eyes on the bunkhouses yet, but the others on my duty all seemed to have drawn the short straw and ended up there this month.

I flushed the toilet I'd been scrubbing and wiped a slick of sweat off my forehead. Fresh moisture beaded immediately at my hairline. I stepped out toward the sinks and looked down at the row of cubicles that Peters and I, my cleaning buddy, had cleared.

Peters was resting against the hand dryer, a content smile on his face. He was an older guy somewhere in his mid-thirties, dark-skinned and foreign, hands toughened to the texture of sandpaper by a lifetime of manual labor. But there was something youthful about him, a roundness to his face and a lightness to his presence, touched by a glint to his eye that interested me.

"What the hell are you smiling about?" I said.

He shrugged. "Why wouldn't I be smiling?" he chirped. "Sun's shining."

I staggered to the door and propped it open. A gust of fresh air, a momentary relief, brought a swathe of desert sand with it, coating the floor. The floor I'd just mopped. "Sun's always shining around here," I said.

"Exactly! Never any excuse to go moping when you've got sun on your face. And here at Eden, you've always got that as a given. So you can always count on being happy."

I shook my head but said nothing, sinking to the floor with my back to the wall and my eyes closed. I drank slowly and steadily for a few minutes.

I liked Peters, and his rippling muscles weren't unpleasant to look at, but he'd been here too long. Like so many others, his Latino accent had blended awkwardly into a twisted bastardization of Mother Eden's Texan drawl.

"Don't be such a sourpuss." Peters looked out through the open door, staring fondly at the semi-arid wastes beyond the bioengineered grasses that lay around the White-Picket District.

I scowled. "How long *have* you been here?"

Peters smiled—a different kind of smile from the others'. Most of the people in the bunkhouses had a similar capacity for expression, one that made me think they hadn't been under Mother Eden's finger all that long. But Peters's answer put an end to that: "Don't remember. Doesn't matter, does it? Life's all good here." He swept a slick of sweat off his forehead. "Sure, the work gets tough and all, but at least we don't have to deal with the commotion always going on elsewhere."

I blinked. "Hard work? What do you know about it? Do you know how many shifts I had to work at the textile mill to help out at home? I bet I sewed the eyes on half the toy pandas sold in all of China last year."

God knew my fingertips had the scars to show it, and my lungs the fume damage to have shortened my life at least a year or two.

Peters's smile faltered—just for a moment, but I saw it. "Some of us work real hard."

I snorted. "You get to kick back on a non-duty before long, and you get a turn in the goddamn mansions eventually. You call that hard work?" My voice was raised and rough edged. The heat was wearing on me.

How could they all stand the endless heat?

When I opened my eyes, however, water bottle still pressed to my forehead, I saw that Peters's smile was well and truly gone. He shifted uncomfortably, his eyes still on the sand devils swirling in the doorway. "It don't always work out that way for everyone," he said. "Some people get a bad run of duties and accommodation sometimes. Some get stuck in some bad places for a while . . . sometimes a long while." He paused and shrugged. "Just luck. It's all chosen random-like. That's how it stays fair." Peters's voice cracked at the last moment, enough to bring the water bottle down from my forehead.

That last word—fair—rang hollow in the restroom's dank, dripping interior.

Fair [Eden-Speak]: The decree of certain *fine* ladies.

"How long since you had an easy shift?" I paused and then said, "How long have you been in the bunkhouses?"

Peters looked as though on the verge of answering but then shook his head and his eyes fell from the doorway. He took up his broom and began sweeping sand back outside with frenzied swipes. "I don't wanna talk about it no more," he mumbled.

I could only watch him. Questions paraded before my mind's eye: how had Mother Eden gotten such a choke hold on the whole place? How many people had found that things didn't always work out quite as fair as promised?

But I'd already learned that it was dangerous to speak against our fair Mother Eden.

"I can make a difference," I said. "I've been in research before. No offense to you, man, but I can't scrub toilets all day without trying to do all I can. They might have forgotten about it, for all their tea parties and get-togethers, but the world is counting on us."

He grunted. I sensed I'd crossed a line. I cursed myself

silently, aware I might have scuttled the only friendship I was bound to make here.

On top of that, I was blushing. I realized he might have made an impression on me. It had been a long time since I had been with somebody, after all. Two shifts at the factory hadn't left any room for romance.

Soon enough, I was sweeping alongside him again.

⌾

```
Extract #7
John T. Everett Scholarship Committee
```

Dear Mr. Golding,

Thank you for your recent correspondence. Words cannot express our regret on hearing of your change in circumstance. Once again, we apologize for being unable to allocate more funds to support your family, as tutorship fees for all candidates must take precedent in our budget.

But we must reiterate how vehemently we protest your refusal of next quarter's funds, along with the termination of your enrollment at Princeton University. Your original research as an undergraduate, and that during your Fulbright Scholarship at the Max Planck Institute, showed much promise, as do you as an individual. We beg you to reconsider.

King regards,

Abigail Hubb,
John T. Everett Scholarship Committee

Mother Eden talked about "citizens' advice" during the evening broadcasts, which I guessed was her way of talking about complaints. Of course it was dressed up so that it sounded like something else entirely, another way people could pitch in and help save the world. She often finished her broadcasts with, "Just go right on over to the office opposite the town hall and have your say. We always need more input from folks!" By now it was ingrained in my memory like a catchy jingle, but somehow it seemed almost like a taunt.

It didn't convince me much, but I decided to give it a try. I'd tried talking with anyone and everyone and had been met with nothing but silence. I might as well exhaust all my options.

I snuck out before sun-up while it was still fairly cool, holding my hands out to catch the breeze as I walked the empty streets. I got turned around a few times, still spotty on the Project's layout, but eventually I found my way to the town hall where Mother Eden had given her welcome speech, and from there it was a short walk to the office.

It was a shack, a mere ten feet across with a flimsy wooden door, squeezed in between a food-storage warehouse and a huge concrete complex I'd seen blue-robed people disappearing into all week—I had no idea what they did in there.

Well, you can't say it ain't here, I thought. I knew there wouldn't be anybody manning it at this hour, so I pushed my way in through the unlocked door. I found a mock-up of a waiting area, made hilarious because it was less than seven feet square yet somehow had a set of chairs and coffee table crammed into it, along with a decorative fern on a trestle. Beside this area was a receptionist's desk, backed by a set of cabinets overflowing with sheaves of paper. I took a chair, crushing my knees against the coffee table, and wondered how much of that paper was blank.

I drifted, retreating into memories of all those long hours spent on textile factory floors, sewing buttons on toys instead of working on my research. I could have had my doctorate by now, if things had been just a little easier. I could have had a fellowship somewhere out in Asia, maybe, and taken Ma and Father with me. We might have been all right.

For all my trepidation, coming here had seemed a blessing. Now here I was with Ma, half a world away from Father, and already I felt she was slipping away from me. She would give anything for a break, even if it meant compromising her moral core.

Daybreak sent sunbeams skittering across my legs, slowly sweeping across my shins as I continued to sit and stew. My stomach gurgled, but after a while it passed and I grew thirsty instead. As a warm amber glow crawled under the doorframe and the temperature began to rise in the tiny space, thirst too passed. I sweated alone in silence until, around ten minutes before duties were due to start, a *click* sounded overhead and an unseen air conditioner blew a blissful chill down over my shoulders.

I had just found a sort of peace when a great lump of a woman came crashing in, hauling her bulk through the narrow doorway and pushing her way behind the desk with some difficulty. She settled behind the desk and busied herself with sorting a few stray sheets of paper, studiously ignoring me.

I knew why. It wasn't 9:00 a.m. yet. Her duty wasn't set to begin for another two minutes. I bit my tongue, lest a complaint hurt my chances of being heard. I fidgeted every second of those two minutes, and when they were up, just as I suspected, the woman snapped her head around in mock surprise and that sickly false Texan accent spilled from her lips. Her voice was too high pitched for someone her size and too honey sweet for a face that looked so like thunder. "Oh, hello, darlin'! What can I do for you?"

I stood stiffly and ambled to the desk. I looked into her tight pudgy face, controlled to a tee, and sighed. "I want to lodge a formal complaint."

Her expression didn't change a mote. After a moment of staring me straight in the eye she reached under the desk, placed a clipboard in front of me, and handed me a pen. "Well, that's swell," she said, her voice still sweet. "Why don't you fill this in and hand it over when you're done? We appreciate every word from folks around the Project!"

She started to turn away, but I leaned forward toward

her emotionless face, which was slightly flushed and damp even with the air conditioning blasting over our heads; she was a big girl, indeed. "I don't want to fill out a form that you can file away and forget," I said. "I want to talk to someone, and I want to do it now."

Saying that felt sickly, forced, unreal. I had never lodged a complaint in my life. But I had to push them and test the waters. If I didn't, it could be a very long time before I lucked out in getting a white-robe duty.

Her eyebrows climbed her forehead, but otherwise her face remained blank as fresh snow. "Whatever about, darlin'?" she cooed.

"About my assignment to janitorial duties. I was an Everett Scholar in Engineering. I have skills to offer the program, as I'm sure others must who shipped in with me. I demand to speak to the head of research!" That felt strange, demanding anything, like I was owed something instead of having lucked out and won a ticket here from the San Andreas slums; people from the US hadn't been in a position to demand much of anything for a long time.

"'Those who demand of Eden often fail to reap its true bounty!'" she said. I'd heard that from a few others before. It was from *The Foundings*. People were always quoting its pages.

I said nothing, just stared.

Her smile was thick as molasses. "I'm afraid all the research teams are very busy."

"I don't care. I want to speak to *someone* who *does* something around here, because so far all I've seen is a lot of niceties and a few very clean toilet bowls."

She tapped her finger against the clipboard in my hand. "If you fill out the form, we'll get around to you as soon as possible."

"Don't give me that bull! I know I'm young, but I can help. There must be something I can do to pitch in."

Her smile only widened. "I'm sorry, young man, but as I said, all the researchers are very busy. And it doesn't look like they'll be any slowing up in pace any time soon. They're all running around like chickens with their heads cut off down there in the labs!" She spoke of them fondly, her eyes glazed. Then she shook her head primly. "I'm sorry, if you'll fill out the form—"

I scowled and dropped the clipboard onto the desk. The form wouldn't be read. There would be no testing the waters here. "Forget it."

❧

Later that day, Mother Eden visited. Ma melted into gabbling and hand-wringing at the door, sweeping in the old crone and seating her on the sofa in a whirling tirade of offers for tea, coffee, soup, cigarettes, magazines, Ma's very soul, etc.

"I'm sorry to intrude, Mrs. Golding, but I'm here to see your son."

Ma's eyes widened as though she had been slapped across the face. "Desh?" Then she smiled a smile that fell a long way short from her eyes. "Of course!" She ushered me forward with a stormy look that said, "What have you done?" and bowed out of the room, spewing yet more pleasantries until the door snapped shut.

Mother Eden turned to me. "I hope you're settling in, young man. I hear you're a swell addition to the Project. But I hear you wanted to make a complaint. Now, I know our system can be a little lax, but truth be told, it's a damn sight harder to get folks around here to speak up than you'd guess. Lot of yes-men around."

I thought of all those sheaves of paper sticking out of the cabinet in the office. That didn't add up. Either they were filed away and ignored by their thousands—and Mother Eden was lying to my face—or they were blank, a front to make it appear as though the system worked fluidly. But if that were so, why bother to go through the trouble if nobody ever complained?

I sat opposite her and cleared my throat. "I, uh—"

"Go on, now, young man! I'm always keen to hear anything that can help us make this place better!"

"I . . . erm." I swallowed and took a breath, then nodded. "Your complaint forms suck."

I half expected a stormy scowl like the one Ma had given me, but instead Mother Eden broke into a good-natured giggle. "Oh, damn, you caught us! We need to update the system, there's no denying it, but so few speak up that it's always at the bottom of my to-do list. But, noted, noted! Anything else?"

I shifted uncomfortably. This wasn't how it was supposed to work. I wanted somebody to rage against.

That was what I had prepared for. "Err," I heard my voice drone out for a full three seconds before I could rein it in. "What I originally went to the office to say was—"

"Yes?" She leaned forward, eyes twinkling. "What's that?"

"I think I can help . . . with the research. I'm smart, real smart, and I used to go to college before things got bad at home." I cringed inwardly. I sounded like a child, unconvincing even to my own ears. What had happened to the cudgel who had stormed into the office earlier? "I want to be on the research team."

Mother Eden sat back, her face still fixed in a half smile, and rocked back and forth on her behind for a moment. Her lipstick-clad upturned lips puckered into a mountain range of wrinkles. She mused a few moments longer, then snapped her lips and said, "I'm sure the nice lady at the desk told you how busy those folks are."

"I heard. But I know I can help."

She nodded, eyebrows furrowed, and reached forward to pat my hand. "And I hear you, believe me. But we got a certain way of doing things around here, one that's been in place a long time. I bet you got plenty to add, but you gotta play the game like everyone else. People who fight the system around here often find they run into . . . difficulty."

I swallowed hard. I hadn't meant to, but my throat convulsed of its own accord, loud enough for the dry squelch to fill the room. Her eyes twinkled at the sound of it.

"So what do I do in the meantime?" I asked.

She stood and laid a hand on my shoulder. "You just get along. It'll all be fine, I promise. We all look after one another in Eden."

Then she bustled out into the corridor, and Ma's platitudes began in earnest once more. Mother Eden started up a fine conversation with her as they headed for the door. I didn't fail to catch an invitation to one of Mother Eden's little soirees. Ma keened like a schoolgirl until Mother Eden had departed and then burst into the living room.

She was flushed, excited, and glowing. Yet still she advanced on me with her hands on her hips. "What did you do?" she hissed.

"I was just trying to help."

"Well, you settle in! Things are different here, and we gotta play by their rules. It's the only way we'll find a place around the Project."

"Yeah," I muttered, heading for bed. "I got that."

$\sim$

Extract #8
Duty Card

DUTY CARD 02 | DATE: 06/05/87 | NAME: MR. DESHUN GOLDING

Citizen,

Please find enclosed your duty card and robes. You will receive your next allocation seven days hence. As usual, all citizens are expected to present themselves to begin work promptly at 09:00. The duration and structure of workdays are individual to each duty. Directions, a Project map, and any further relevant details are attached to this letter.

DUTY: WASTE COLLECTION
CODE: BROWN

Have a nice day!

Ma had her duty card already: archivist. One of the plushest duties, I'd heard. A week of puttering in cool, softly-lit underground offices, recording the daily comings and goings of the Eden Project for future historians. Ideal for Ma, a born gossip.

She patted my hand over the breakfast table and poured me coffee. "Luck of the draw, dear," she said. "You'll get a better duty next week."

I gaped open-mouthed. "Luck of the draw?"

She blinked and froze, her steaming mug halfway to her lips.

"You're still going to the night classes."

Still, she didn't move.

She had been talking about the classes for days. The evening broadcasts made them seem like charming getting-to-know-you meet and greets, but by now I was convinced they were little more than indoctrination centers; sermons on how to act proper, diction classes that—as far as I could tell—were responsible for the ubiquitous Texan drawl of Project residents. I sensed my neighbors' derision whenever I admitted that I didn't attend.

Ma's gaze was furtive, restless. After a few seconds, she nodded.

I had to laugh. I was willing to accept the madness lurking beyond our four walls and live with it, for her sake. But now that same madness had wound its serpentine influence under our door and wormed its fingers into her mind.

They're getting to her.

"Why?" I whispered.

She placed her coffee down on the table and reached for my hand.

I pulled back before she could make contact.

Flinching, she said, "All the girls down the street go. It's only proper. It don't mean anything"—her accent was one step away from a bona fide, "*It don't mean nothing*"— "I don't need English schooling, after all. It was just to get to know folks 'round here a little better." She spoke vehemently, defensively, yet her eyes still twitched around the room, unable to meet mine.

"Folks?" I cried. "You've never said 'folks' in my life. You're starting to talk like *them*! Like the others. You can't go along to these things, Ma. They're trying to change you, they're trying to . . . brainwash you!"

Her face fell, but not in the manner I'd expected.

Instead of angry or appalled, she looked disappointed. Suddenly I could have been eight-years-old again, caught with my hand in the cookie jar.

"Desh," she said in a voice of calm reasoning. "That's ridiculous. You can't go 'round talking like that. You sound like some crazy conspiracy loon." Fear invaded her eyes. "You haven't been talking like this around the Project, have you? You can't, Desh, you can't."

"Ma!"

"No, Desh, you listen to your mama!"

Now it's "Mama". Good Christ, they've got their claws dug deep, I thought.

"We've got something here," she continued, her voice rising to a shrieking crescendo. "We've been offered a place among these good folks, and after all we did to get here—what your father sacrificed to give us a chance—by God and all that's holy I swear I won't let you throw it all away for the both of us!" In the aftermath, a ringing silence followed.

I sighed. "Ma, can't you see what they're doing? Mother Eden's got everyone wrapped around her little finger. She's taken control. This isn't what it's supposed to be. It's a dictatorship. If the UN knew about this—"

"Of course they know. You never stop harping on about how much places like this cost, Desh. If some shady cabal had seized control of a place most of the world spends their days dreaming of, do you really think nobody would have noticed?"

I was silent. I had no answer to that. I swallowed hard.

My dry throat rasped. "I don't know, Ma. But I know what I've seen. And it scares me."

She barked. "Scared? What's there to be scared of? Everyone's friendly here. We're *safe* here. Don't ruin this for us."

I halted and nodded to the duty card in her hand. "Where did you get that?"

Her eyes darted down to her hands, and a glimmer of guilt stirred behind them.

"They gave it to you early, didn't they? At the night classes."

Her voice had fallen to a whisper. "Don't you dare interrogate me, young man. I am your mother. If your father were here—"

"If my father were here, he'd have taken us far away from here by now. Or died trying."

"How could you say something like that?"

"Because that's what I'd have done, if I wasn't such a—
"

Coward. That word died in my throat, left me mouthing wordlessly until Ma stood from the table and shook her head.

"I don't know what's gotten into you," she said. "These are good people here. Righteous people. They don't mean anyone any harm."

"That the mantra they have you all chant?" I murmured.

She didn't answer.

"We're all supposed to get our duty sheets in the mail.

Sealed."

"Oh, Desh, really? What difference does it make?"

"It makes all the difference! These sheets are printed and sealed electronically every week. The first people to see them are those they refer to. At least, that's the way it's supposed to work. If you were given yours, it means it didn't come from the sorting computer."

"I don't know what you're trying to imply."

I stood from the table slowly, feeling her eyes burn into mine. My voice seemed to reverberate throughout the house, in every homogenous line, every plasterboard cranny. "What did you have to do before they put you on archive duty? How many times did you have to recite her dogmas, how long did you have to work on your southern accent?"

"It's not like that, Desh. God, what's happening to you?" The hysterical, worried edge to her voice cut at me like glass. She was fretting—it was as though she was afraid my words would pull a carefully constructed veil from over her eyes. Yet she was managing to keep her voice perfectly level; I was the insane party. "They hand out the cards to everyone who attends. Saves the folks on mail duty making so many rounds, is all."

"Ma, that doesn't make any sense." I swallowed. "They gave it to you once you agreed to keep attending, didn't they? And I bet they promised to make the duties a bit easier, huh? No more whittling away under the boots of the nice folks in the mansions."

Silence.

"Ma?"

Her lip trembled. "I can't keep cleaning those houses!" she sobbed. "They're so empty. All those abandoned neighborhoods." She shivered. "I . . . I can't—"

"You volunteered!"

"Yes, but—"

"But that was just to get closer to them, right?"

She swallowed hard. "I can't keep wallowing at the bottom of the pile, Desh. I've slaved far too long."

I stepped around the table and laid a hand on her arm. "Ma, I get it. I do. But this isn't right. The duties are supposed to be random, not divvied up according to who plays ball with Mother Eden. The houses, they're supposed to be the same. Having the mansions and the bunkhouses, it doesn't make any sense. Researchers and mission critical personnel need priority, but not marble floors—not maids and gardeners! And what's with the bunkhouses for brown duties? Where's the justification there?"

Ma drew back. "I won't believe that. I can't." She shook herself free from my grip. "You're a good boy, Desh, but you have to get help. You can't go around treating our saviors like this." She took my cup and set about clearing breakfast, running the dishwater unnecessarily, muttering and clattering.

I sank back into my chair, defeated, and watched her flit back and forth, scrabbling for the invisible veil still planted firmly over her eyes.

I thought of Peters and the others in the bunkhouses. I

was willing to bet my dinner that I'd be seeing more than one of them on waste collection duty with me today. I wondered how long I'd be staying here in the house with Ma before she ascended to the mansions and I was consigned to a bunk alongside them.

Ma left for her office without another word to me.

I reached the garbage float, the picture of a giant ironclad elephant beetle, before most people had set out for duties. The disposal dump was deserted, and a depressed pall of silence lay heavy over the area.

I wasn't surprised to see Peters.

I smiled and he smiled back. I hoped he'd forgiven me for the slight in the bathrooms. And I was glad for the sheer size of him. I didn't relish the thought of hauling large loads with my skinny frame.

He didn't say anything when I stepped up to him and pulled on my work gloves, both of us standing there in identical brown robes—more like jumpsuits than the sweeping toga-like white robes.

The others arrived in due course, and though I tried to keep my mind blank and just get on, I couldn't help but notice faces I'd seen the week before, bent over the toilet seats adjacent to mine.

Some were different, but that didn't bring any comfort; I knew the rest of the people who'd been on cleaning detail were probably elsewhere, manning other brown-robed drudge duties.

Worse, my thoughts kept turning to Ma. She was under my feet somewhere, amid underground tunnels—pleasant environs, surrounded by pleasant people, probably under the watchful eye of Mother Eden and her clique of blank-faced china dolls.

I realized then that I'd really lost her. It hit me with physical force. Eventually, Peters nudged me; I'd been standing dead still, staring into space. For how long, I had no clue.

I sighed and climbed aboard the garbage float. Like urchins clinging to the lumbering Beetle's carapace, invisible to anyone who looked our way, we made our way toward the gilded neighborhood of the merry mansions.

I sank to a new low when I saw Ma in the streets. She was out on her break, leaning against one of the low-lying blocks I guessed were the research labs, laughing with a few of the other new arrivals in the shade.

I caught her eye and waved, sitting up on the Beetle with Peters, swinging my legs and chewing on the remnants of a sun-baked sandwich. People were passing by on either side of the street, but we had had the good sense to park in the lee of an alley, out of the way. Not that anyone would have noticed us in any case.

I knew Ma saw me, but it took all of a minute for her to return a crooked smile and a hesitant wave. That was all

I received. Then she gave an odd twitch and turned slowly away. She didn't look at me again, but her friends did, their eyes filled with supercilious contempt.

I scowled and whittled away the rest of my break wondering exactly what she was doing in there. Her duty card had said "archivist", but I suspected there was more to it than that. Why would something like that require her to work in a security-locked building—among the *only* locked buildings in the whole project, so far as I knew?

It didn't make any sense.

By the time lunch break was over, after Ma had disappeared inside with the others and I was picking my way along the street once more. I was a little way from the others, so I was the only one who could see the errant branch that had caught in the doorjamb. Another inch and the lock would snap it shut, but there it was, open to the world.

I looked over my shoulder, saw the others making their way along the street, and made a snap decision. They wouldn't notice my being gone a few moments.

Casual as I could manage, I opened the door and secreted myself inside. I half-expected someone to be standing on the other side, waiting with their foot tapping and eyebrows raised: *No, no, no! The dirt stays on the outside! Now out with you!*

But there was only a long hallway with linoleum floors and standard beige walls. Not at all the spectacle of pristine white and chrome I had pictured. Not a lick of technology in sight.

I stood there listening a moment, heart thrumming in my chest. Mother Eden proclaimed there was nothing to hide, yet the lock on the door said otherwise.

Answers calling! I thought.

Hearing nothing, I proceeded along the hall. If I didn't find Ma, I was bound to run into something. I guessed the complex ran underground for some distance; there was no way all the labs I'd read about could fit under the low roof of this squat complex. There could have been endless wonders under my feet.

It was hard to believe that not long ago I had been so taken with the idea of coming here. Now it all seemed silly, the fantasy of a child I scarcely recognized.

It was time to get some real answers.

I rushed headlong down the hallway, passing doors and pressing my back against the wall every few steps like some kind of Hollywood secret agent.

I passed signs pointing to various departments marked *Admin, Duty Assignment, Coms, Amendments, Broadcasting,* and *Security*. But nothing like what I was looking for. Afar I could hear busy chattering and bustling bodies as droves of workers went about their business, but I was sure I was either in the wrong building or something was amiss.

Maybe I just had the wrong place. The research labs could be in one of the other buildings, after all. But that didn't fit. Even if they were underground, the kind of floor space the laboratories would need just didn't fit the layout of the Project.

What was going on?

They were supposed to be running a top-spec outfit here, pushing the forefront of knowledge, and pioneering new ways of life. They were supposed to be saving the goddamn world.

But so far as I could see, they were running some kind of social experiment. Hell, even that was dressing things up. The whole place smacked of a summer camp turned sour.

I kept on going until I came to the end of the hallway, then turned on my heels and looked back at the many doors I had passed. No elevator, no stairwells. Nothing.

They had cheated me, cheated everyone. The research efforts in the UN projects must have been overblown to the nth degree. If there *was* any research going on. From what I'd seen so far, they had a variety of innovative GM crops and a wicked-ton of fancy military gear, but there was little else to give any indication of revolutionary ways of life.

Dejected, I slumped along the hall toward the door. I was already focused on the best way to re-join Peters and the others when one of the doors caught my attention. *Surveillance*, the sign read. The door was ajar. There were voices inside, but still I paused and pressed myself up against the wall. I had risked coming in, after all. What did I have to lose?

"Look at those rats. You'd think we could just get rid of them." The grumpy male warble had a disgusted edge to it. "I don't get it."

A female voice, accented in the typical southern drawl

of the Project, answered in high-pitched tones. "Don't go speaking so harsh of them. They're less fortunate than most, after all. Bad luck in the duty lottery can get anyone down."

A grunt. "We're supposed to be building something better, here. Of all the billions of people on the planet to get chosen, we still get lumbered with enough slack-jawed idiots to fill the bunkhouses to the brim."

The woman's answer cut like glass. "We don't call them bunkhouses; you know how much Mother Eden hates that word. All's fair in Eden, remember? And watch your words. We all got to talk proper even when we're working, even when it's just us."

A long sigh, then the man's voice once more, this time threaded with the same affected drawl as hers. "Sorry, Jennifer, I forgot my manners."

I inched along the wall and chanced a peek inside. Half a dozen silhouettes were highlighted against a bank of hundreds of tiny wall-screen monitors. Each one showed a live feed of somewhere on the Project, inside and out. The parks, the fences, the washrooms, the streets, laundromats, library, alleys, and sidewalks. Every office and every home.

And from each came tiny voices, superimposed on one another to form a babbling cacophony trailing from the headphones of the surveillance room's six attendants.

They were watching and listening. Mother Eden truly did see and hear all.

I peered farther into the room, recoiling in momentary panic when the shadow of my head splashed across the beam of light falling across the floor. But the attendants didn't notice. The largest of the monitors held all their attention. It showed the Beetle, Peters, and the others on garbage duty.

"That's better," the woman was saying. "They're just as capable as the rest of us. But they don't see Mother Eden's wisdom just yet, so we got to be patient. Some people need a little nudge to see sense. We can't have everyone thinking they can go around saying whatever they please, writing things that can put dangerous thoughts into people's minds. We all got to stick together, that's what Mother Eden always says, right Mrs. Golding?"

My heart stopped.

A short silence held sway, interspersed with the scratching voices of the Project's hundreds of citizens, and then Ma's voice spoke up. "Right. We all got to pull together."

I frowned. She sounded just like them. The accent wasn't yet as developed, but the southern twang was growing thick.

"See? Some people see sense," the woman continued.

"I don't see it," the man grumbled. "Why do we got to be lumbered with those simpletons?"

The woman's silhouette chopped at the air with an open palm. "Like I said, they ain't simple! Hell, most of them are really smart, way smarter than any of us—though don't tell nobody I said that. Lot of doctors and professors down in the less fortunate parts of the Project. Damn shame, but fair's fair. The lottery speaks for itself, right?"

A general murmur of agreement ran through the room.

"I don't believe a word of it," the man said. "If they was so smart, they'd be the ones sitting here talking smack about us, and we'd be out there picking garbage."

"Ain't true! Don't be such a fool. Smarts don't equal power, not now and not ever."

"Bull. There's always some smartass pulling strings behind it all."

A pause. The answer came not from the woman, but from Ma. "It takes something else to rule. It takes guts. Like Mother Eden's got. Smarts don't equal nothing, cause with smarts comes all that worrisome talk about liberty and equality. And that ain't what we need now because we've all suffered enough. We need strength! And if that means we gotta walk over some people to get to something better, then I'm damn well gonna fall in line. Anybody that don't . . . well, there's where they end up."

A strained silence was followed by the woman's approving tone. "We got ourselves a winner here, Buck! I bet she's gonna be in Mother Eden's inner circle before the week's out! To hell with it, I'm putting in a recommendation soon as we get off this shift."

The man, however, sounded curious, if not grudgingly impressed. "You talk strong. But what've you got to say for fair's fair? Ain't your son out there today?"

Each of the shadowed heads in the room turned in Ma's direction, and my tongue stopped in my throat.

Ma answered without looking away from her monitor. "All's fair when times are tough," Ma said. She spoke quiet but strong. There was something alien to her tone, something dead and long-suffering. "Like I said, we need strength. Smarts takes longer to win over. And some . . . some people were made to be ruled."

I don't know what happened after that. It was all a blur. But by the time I'd stopped shaking I was back at the Beetle, and Peters was asking what had spooked me so bad to turn me white as a sheet.

Ma didn't come home after duties. I waited at the kitchen as the dappled sun tracked low in the sky, sheathing the clouds in streaks of crimson. Even after the last of the stragglers had dragged themselves indoors and the streetlights had burst alight to the sound of Mother Eden's evening street broadcast, I remained at the table.

Skin grimed, back aching, hands calloused, clothes reeking of rotting waste despite the overalls I'd been wearing, I sat and waited.

And waited.

Nothing.

I waited until the sky was black, the day's heat had ebbed to a relative chill, and even Mother Eden's voice had ceased to fill my ears. By then I was aching bone-deep, and my stomach was tying itself in knots; food plagued my every thought. God knew I'd need plenty; I had another six days of waste collection to get through.

But I didn't feel like cooking. Somehow, I knew that

fixing a meal here, in this beige plasterboard box, alone, would drive me too close to the edge. Instead, I struggled into bed without going out to the washhouse and fell into a restless torpor of tossing and turning.

Ma finally returned long after the late-night insects' song had died down to nothing. By the sound of her stumbling advance through the house, I could tell that she was drunk.

I even heard her giggling.

Then her bedroom door clicked shut, and silence enveloped me once more. I went back to tossing and turning. At some point, I fell into a shallow, dreamless sleep.

The next morning, Ma left before I woke.

I hadn't expected anything else. In fact, I was almost looking forward to returning to work, to Peters and the others, and unthinking oblivion. At least I had that. But what was unexpected was the note she'd left pinned to my bedroom door, scrawled in her arthritic, jagged hand:

Take a bath or you'll stink up the place. I'm having company over later.

Ma.

X

The 'X' was added in pencil. An afterthought.

I heard the tittering before I even got close to the fence. The street was alive with the echoes of at least a dozen feminine, demure cries of amusement, and they were all coming from my house.

The day had been a blur, but not at all the blur of cleansing labor I'd hoped for. Instead, it had been closer to a desperate struggle to stay conscious. Peters had called it a hot one, but that didn't begin to describe the sweltering kiln that had enshrouded me from dawn till dusk. I'd been slimed like an eel by nine o'clock and was dehydrated enough to have passed out twice before lunch. It had gone downhill from there.

I knew I wouldn't see out the week if I didn't head straight for the cot as soon as I got inside. My stomach growled and my bones creaked. My body throbbed as though I'd been beaten by a sack of bricks.

All I wanted to do was sleep. I hungered for it.

But that mad cackling beyond the living-room window stopped me in my tracks. Even over the din of all those squawking harpies, I could single out Ma's voice with ease. I knew it from many years before, when we'd had one of father's bosses over for supper. She'd laughed like that then—a laugh to impress, a laugh to win favor, a laugh for people she secretly despised.

I had the urge to turn on my heels and march off down the road. Exhausted or not, anything was better than going in there.

Then I caught sight of a pair of eyes amid the curtains of our neighbor's kitchen window. Suspicious eyes.

That started me off toward my own yard once more. Perhaps there was something worse than what lay inside: getting myself noticed. I sensed that doing so now would not be a good idea. I wasn't sure what happened to settlers who refused to conform to Mother Eden's little game, but I wasn't counting on it being anything pleasant.

Best case scenario: I'd be sent packing back to Saint Petersburg. And what would Father do when—if—he found out?

Thinking of him was now what kept me going. Not Ma; she was moving on. She didn't need me anymore. But Father, he was still back in Fremont, slaving away like a dog for a state falling to pieces, going home to an empty tenement flat that still had pencil marks of my childhood heights scratched into the bathroom doorframe.

What would he think if I threw away my chance at a real life—no matter what kind—after all he'd sacrificed?

I sighed and crept into the hallway. From the threshold I could see half the living room crammed with a parabola of chairs occupied by at least a dozen giggling women. All dressed in floral summer dresses, sipping glasses of iced lemonade, all squeaky clean and without a mote of fatigue about their eyes.

I couldn't imagine anything further from the pits of stinking grime I and the others on waste duty had been tramping through all day. At first I thought Ma was out of sight somewhere, but then I spotted her among the demure congregation, laughing along with the rest of them.

She was unrecognizable. Dressed in a floral white cotton slip, an elegant thing of subtle embellishments and sophisticated lines, she looked more alive than I'd seen her in years. Her face was full, her cheeks rosy, her back straight. Her bespectacled eyes were brimming with life. The frail creature I'd known since playschool had been subsumed by this picture of distilled vitality.

The women stopped in their tittering abruptly and turned my way. Closest to the door were the twins from orientation, ever serene and droopy eyed with their straight backs and plastic faces. They smiled as one, and a shiver crept up my spine.

I blinked and made an odd noise deep in my throat. So shocked had I been by Ma's transformation that I hadn't noticed my own advance into the house. Now that they were all staring, something even more shocking swelled in my guts: guilt.

Though this was my house, I was intruding upon betters; I in my garbage-stained overalls, they in their spotless summer outfits.

Ma's voice rang out in the silence. "My son." A pause. "He's on waste collection this week. Terrible luck. He has to work very hard, and late."

I could only blink.

"Yes," one of the other women said. "Terrible." Not a trace of emotion reached her voice.

Still they stared, women of every creed and culture, a full spectrum of tongues and faiths, all looking out at me. But now that Ma had voiced my place in Mother Eden's paradise, none of them saw me. I had blended into the background, suddenly become nothing but part of the decoration.

I nodded stiffly. "Excuse me." My voice went unheard. I stepped away toward the kitchen.

"Desh?" Ma said.

I darted back, grasping at the tone of her voice—the closest to real contact we'd had for days—and laid eyes on her, begging her to hold out her arms and send those wretched sirens away.

I saw only guilt. Another kind of guilt to that coursing my veins, to be sure, but still guilt. She glanced around at her guests, brushed her hair—newly permed, I noticed— and smiled, a horrific tightness that spread from her upper lip. "Do take a bath, won't you?"

I could only nod and retreat to the kitchen. I was ravenous, but I wasn't about to make a racket now. Grating my teeth, I went back to creeping about my own home. Black thoughts tumbled in the back of my mind; Ma's words had landed a vital blow.

I found a can of soup under the worktop and warmed it on the stove, swallowing to clear the lump in my throat, listening to the women as they returned with zeal to their chattering.

"Always a shame when families are split by duties," said a voice. I recognized it as that of the tight-lipped woman beside Ma. "It's a wonder, how some accept the way Mother Eden shows us, and some throw it all away. Always the young, it seems. They always rebel. As though we're some kind of evil."

A chorus of laughter followed, Ma's prominent among it all, now with a touch of hysteria floating above each chuckle. "Desh'll come around, I'm sure," she said. "Then he can start fitting in. I'm sure he'll see what's being offered once he gets a lighter duty, once we get a turn in the mansions—I mean, one of the finer homes."

Dead silence, one that seemed to stretch out for minute after minute but was probably no more than a few moments.

The stove hissed. The soup bubbled in the pot. Somewhere in the living room was the tinkle of a bone china teacup being set upon a saucer.

I could almost see Ma's face in my mind's eye: dawning comprehension of the truth I'd been so keen to force down her throat; a truth that could only be seen once the locals revealed their true selves.

There would be no turn in those fine houses nor a duty card with a pleasant shift in the coms office. Not for me. Not now that I'd shown my hand. Maybe not ever, not even if I played dead and plastered one of those plastic smiles onto my face. Hell, I could sit in a rocker by the window every night listening to the evening broadcast, and it wouldn't matter a bit. I'd never be one of them.

I'd been marked. But at the same time, I had vanished from sight.

I stirred my soup, took a sip from the steaming ladle, and burned my tongue. While I grimaced in fitful silence, another voice rose from the stolid cloud of tension in the living room, one that made my blood run cold:

"Now, now, y'all. Let's not ruin so civil a gathering at such a fair lady's welcome party with such ugly talk. I'm sure the young man enjoys the chance to flex those strapping young muscles of his. How men love strutting at that age. Let 'em enjoy it and put that steam to good use, I say. After all, we're happy here, aren't we, ladies?"

Mother Eden.

As always she sounded so sincere.

Professional liars always seem to be in earnest, sometimes even to themselves, I thought. *She has all these people parroting her own private mantra. Those twins are just swooning over her cockamamie life story. I can see stars in those eyes.*

I knew what I was supposed to do: roll over, smile just like them, and fall into line. Just how things had come this far so soon boggled the mind, but here we were. I was face-to-face with a person who had more power than heads of state, holding the keys to a life without sorrow, a life with hope. And so I was also face-to-face with somebody who was used to getting her own way.

How had she found such power in the first place? That in itself was odd enough to set my suspicion buzzing. Americans had become third-world citizens long before even this old-timer's heyday. So how had she ended up holding the conch?

My soup bubbled up over the pot and set about baking itself onto the stovetop. But try as I might, I couldn't bring myself to stir any further. My arm felt like a lead weight.

The women in the living room had gabbled in agreement, almost fighting one another to voice their agreement first. A dozen conversations had sprung up, drowning out the awkward silence.

I turned off the stove and ate what soup remained in the pot, all but falling into a chair by the table. I ate mechanically, needing the strength but tasting nothing, searing my throat, staring at the far wall.

Mother Eden, here, in my living room. Drinking lemonade with my mother, driving the wedge between us ever wider. I thought back to orientation day. How Ma's hand had felt on my chest, how her face had been warm and kind yet conveyed unmistakable menace. She had recognized an enemy in me and set her sights on my elimination.

It had taken her a handful of weeks. I had gone from a free man—poor and hungry, yes, but free, with all the rights that the outside world had given me—to a near-invisible untouchable. Weeks.

"Boy, is it stuffy in here!" a voice cried. "Too many beating hearts in one itty-bitty room." I recalled seeing a heavyset Asian woman; I suspected her of voicing such a complaint.

"My apologies," Ma said, flustered.

"Not to worry, dear." Old Tight-Lips again. "We all have to take a turn in these . . . houses once in a while." Her voice lowered a key. "Keeps the folks unlucky enough to always be getting lumbered with the labor duties from thinking the system don't work so well for them, somehow." Her tone took on a righteous edge. "It's our duty, so we do it without a peep—it's only neighborly, after all. We all gotta give something back, by and by."

"That's what keeps everything spinning around here," said the heavyset woman.

More gabbling agreement.

"I'm just glad we don't have to take turns in them pigsties out back, is all!" cried Tight-Lips.

An explosion of raucous giggling jarred me from my stupor. I looked down, saw that the soup was eaten, and staggered to my feet.

That really was the way of it, then. Mother Eden's clique of dull-faced robots enjoyed the leafy mansions and the breezy jobs; the untouchables labored in the folds of the Project's underbelly. And to keep their subjects placated, every now and then they took a spell away from their suburban fortress, walking among the people, visiting for tea and biscuits, as though the lottery had sent them there. As though they were taking their turn, just like everyone else—as though the lottery existed at all. It was all too easy to believe that one of the mansion folks' light duties was sifting through the Project's residents and picking out those worthy of joining their private community and identifying the troublemakers.

"Oh, I don't mind," Ma muttered. "It's only fair."

"Pish, dear. Don't you worry," said Tight-Lips. Though the disciple had spoken aloud only once, I could feel Mother Eden's will behind Tight-Lips' words, almost hear that rattling southern drawl behind the woman's faux-pleasant squeak. "Be patient, you'll be moving up in the world soon enough."

A few cheers and more laughter.

I was standing in the hallway once again, only wanting to get to my bedroom without being seen and hating myself for not having the confidence to simply stride past the living room to get the rest I deserved. My teeth ground, the skin of my knuckles stretched tight.

Then I was slipping back to the kitchen and out the back door, creeping along the alley that divided our yard from our neighbors'. As the giggling once again grew louder, I ducked down and shuffled along the front of the house. Soil slicked my overalls and came up in clumps in my hands. Then I was hovering just below the living room windowsill.

Though the window was cracked ajar, I couldn't hear quite as well. But from here I had a decent view inside without any chance of being spotted due to the cover afforded by Ma's net curtains.

"Well, you'll be here every now and then, by no mistake, dear," Mother Eden was saying. "But . . . well, you can say you won't need no moving truck to shift your possessions. Somehow we always end up back yonder in the finer places. Luck of the draw." There was a pause, and then she spoke again, her voice twee and sweet: "Some people are meant for the higher life, it seems. That's destiny for you."

Destiny [Eden-Speak]: See 'Subterfuge.'

I clenched my jaw, fuming. I could have surged through the window right then and wrapped my hands around her throat, all of their throats.

"That sounds . . ." Ma said. I could hear something in her voice, something hesitant, taken aback. Until now the bare truth of things had been safely veiled by the message of equality at orientation, the community-spirit bilge expounded during the evening broadcast, the oblique induction of those ready to stand on the shoulders of others for an easier existence, this poisonous charade of a tea party.

Now all of that had been given voice and dragged from shadow into the light, where there was no ambiguity to soften the blow. The grinning women sitting in my living room had unmasked themselves to one they had hoped to recruit: Ma.

And she had been caught off guard. I could hear it in her voice. Whether she was delighted or disgusted, I couldn't tell, but there was no question that the party was over. I could almost feel the pressure of those women's gazes fixed on Ma, even through the walls.

I swallowed, willing her to upturn her chair and storm from the room, to denounce the gathering as an insidious sham, link arms with me, and storm away with me into the desert sun.

But then her reply came, and that fantasy popped like a soap bubble: "That . . . that sounds wonderful."

A fresh bout of applause filled the house. "Well, I'm mighty pleased to hear that you're one to see things same as us," Mother Eden said coolly. "Lord knows there's always those who can't see it. Ain't pointing fingers, but your boy sure does seem put out by how we run things. Now, don't get me wrong, I'm sure there ain't no harm in it, but you can see how that kind of influence can get to disturbing the peace if we don't keep an eye on it."

"I've tried talking to him," Ma said, hushed. "He won't listen. But you mustn't judge him. We've just lost my husband, and we've been through so much before now. He's a good boy, he just needs time."

"None of us doubt that," said Tight-Lips.

"Seems a fine young man," said Ms. Heavyset.

"'Even the brightest sparks fizz and sputter,'" Tight-Lips quoted. Another oft-quoted line from *The Foundings*. I had to get my hands on that damn book.

"None of us would expect otherwise, dear," cooed Mother Eden. "Lord knows we've seen enough broken families to know what happens to folks."

She paused then and, despite myself, I leaned closer to the window as the other ladies leaned forward in their chairs. My nose squashed against the window.

A coy smile had touched Mother Eden's lips. "I wish I could give people the time they need to get over whatever ails them and see that how we live is proper. I wish I could give every doubter all the time in the world." She picked at her dress, drew a fine gossamer of stray fabric into the light, and flicked it away. "But we here are charged with a higher purpose. We can't afford to let those dangerous ideas run amok when there's so much riding on us."

"I will do everything I can, but he's got it into his head that there's something bad going on around these parts."

Mother Eden held up a hand, and Ma fell silent. "Ain't nobody pointing fingers, nor are they looking to drive any wedges between families that already got a load of grime in their gears. But we got to be straight with you."

She looked around at her companions, causing a ripple of head nodding to spread through the room. "You're one of us. Lord knows that. And we take care of our own."

Mother Eden cleared her throat, her brows ever so slightly furrowed. I sensed her distaste at so blatantly baring the truth of their subversion of the system. But her expression smoothed and she nodded to Tight-Lips. "Marlene ain't wrong. I just know you'll be a respected member of the community in no time. And I got every fiber of my being praying that your Desh is right there with you. We need strength like his, and I know young ones would look up to him, if we get any in the next shipment. But if he don't come around, well . . . Some of the neighborhoods can handle that kind of babble, but ours is, shall we say, a tad delicate. Folks from all over look at how we live, how peaceful we keep our streets, and they make an example of it. We just can't have any bad eggs getting in the way." Her smile widened in response to the terse quiet. "I'm sure you understand."

Ma's intertwined hands were writhing in her lap. "Are you saying that if I can't get Desh to come around, that I'll have to . . . to choose?"

All eyes were on her. Nobody said a word. Somewhere

far away, the desert winds were howling. "I'm sure you understand," Mother Eden repeated.

Ma's lips had parted, but she said nothing more. After a while of more silence and lip-smacking as people busied themselves drinking lemonade, Ms. Heavyset wafted a hand before her nose. "Well, I hate to be so crass, ladies, but I can't stand how stuffy it gets in these"—she glanced at Tight-Lips and stammered—"more modest dwellings. It's getting to smell like rotting garbage in here."

My heart skipped. Ash filled the space where my tongue had been moments before. As the cries of the other ladies' agreement rang out, I ducked low and plastered myself against the wall.

Sweat erupted on my forehead. Suddenly my clothes seemed stifling. In horror, I saw my own boot prints pressed into the soil, perfectly outlined, leading from the path to my hiding place.

"I'm so sorry, where are my manners?" Ma said, flustered. "I'll open the window a little wider."

I glanced around, praying for an escape route. A rock, a trash can, an errant cactus. But our yard was otherwise bare, uncultivated soil, freshly laid, awaiting a green thumb to bring forth the bluebells and crocuses that littered the mansions' lawns.

There was nowhere to hide. In any case, I'd be heard if I moved now. The laughter had died to a dull hubbub of general complaint about fresh air. Even a single footstep would alert them.

I was trapped. Pressing myself against the wall until the

back of my head ground against mortar, as though I could melt into the brickwork and become one with it if I pushed hard enough, I listened to Ma's approaching footsteps. She wouldn't see me. I willed her to shove the handle, walk away without so much as a glance outside, and just go back to her friends.

But she didn't. As her gnarled fingers appeared in midair above my head to grasp the handle, so too did her face, more vivid and animated than I could recall since the blur of infancy. She looked straight down at me, and her eyes met mine. She froze, blinked, then whitened.

I saw the cogs turn behind her gaze, and the realization that I'd heard everything crashed over her. I could only stare back and wait for her reaction. Either she'd give the game away, or she wouldn't.

But then I realized something worse was all too possible: she could turn me in on purpose. And, for a moment, I thought my own mother would do just that.

The lump of her Adam's apple slid up and down, her eyes fluttered to a close, and she flung the window wide. Then she was gone, leaving me fighting back tears with my heart buzzing, crouched in the mud, stinking of garbage.

Inside, Mother Eden sighed. "There, now ain't that better?"

❧

Extract #9
BINK — The one-stop web-com service, bringing the world together!

Jaimee991: I WON!! Just got my lottery ticket. Eden Project here I come!

Urbanduderox: _popping box of Xanax. Made redundant at the plant. What's the point going on?

HoustonGnrlHosp: Little grl needs home. 6 yrs old. Mother killed out shopping. Plz someone!

❧

Lights bobbing amid darkness. Cold singing beneath my bare feet, the chill of the wind against my skin. And, from all directions, interspersed with a few terrified shrieks, the wail of sirens.

I gasped, stunned, lost.

What was going on? How had I gotten here? Where *was* here?

I was standing in what I suspected were the dunes beyond our backyard. The lights I'd seen were quickly resolving into streetlamps, and the darkness beyond was becoming less total. Shadows sprinted back and forth, casting crazy duplicate figures in the swinging beams of distant searchlights. The screams were those of children and a few women. The proximity sensors around the camp had been tripped.

I must have leaped up and run here on impulse, driven by the flight instinct, before I'd fully gained consciousness.

Now that the fog of sleep was receding, I realized what the siren meant: we were under attack.

Ma.

I turned on shaking legs and ran across the sand, heading for the street. I couldn't see the house, but I couldn't have run far in my stupor. The screams afar were changing in tone, from surprise to outright fear.

By the time I'd reached the road and found my bearings, the gunfire had started. It came suddenly from the ether, rising up to a deafening cacophony in the merest of moments, so suddenly that I staggered as though struck by a glancing blow.

I gasped, dazed, ignoring the stabbing pain of sharp stones, still warm from basking in the day's sunlight, thrusting into the soles of my feet. The roar of machine guns was ringing out in every direction. Together with the sirens, they drowned out the rasp of my breathing, the rush of blood in my ears, even the screams of the others out there in the dark.

My neighbors' house emerged from the darkness—I could tell it apart from any other only because my neighbor and her children were huddled on the lawn, squealing like pigs.

I sprinted past, kicking the mailbox. Ignoring the burst of fresh pain, I erupted through my front door, bellowing, "Ma!"

The house was still and dark. Nothing stirred. The plasterboard walls did nothing to dampen the rat-a-tat of gunfire or the wailing sirens. I yelled once more, straining until my voice rasped and I felt something tear in my throat.

Ma didn't appear from the darkness. I surged into the hallway and into her bedroom, seeing even in the darkness that upon the mattress was nothing but a tangle of sheets. In my mind's eye ballooned a mental picture of my neighbors, paralyzed by fear on their lawn. And then there was my own unthinking escape into the dunes.

Where had Ma scrambled to in her own panic?

I turned on the light and ducked down to look under the bed, the dresser, the wardrobe. Seeing nothing, I returned to the hallway and searched the living room, the bathroom, the kitchen, turning on lights as I went, tearing up tablecloths, parting curtains, and pulling open cupboard drawers.

All the while, I screamed her name, as the sirens wailed and gunfire peppered the endless screeching. Ma wasn't in the house. I searched outside, having long since lost my voice, running the full length of the street, even passing the shuddering figures of my neighbors to search their house as well, but to no avail.

Eventually I stood back in our own kitchen, staring around in repeated, wide arcs, as though she would materialize from the shadows if I looked enough. Outside, convoys of armored trucks and Humvees tore past, manned by steely-faced men whose expressions resembled the serene gazes of Eden's flock.

In the distance, the searchlights had ceased their wild swinging and settled down to purposeful sweeping arcs, trained on the desert. The odd child's scream still rang out from the streets nearby, but the overbearing chorus of strangled, animalistic cries had abated.

Though I could see little through the quaint sash window, I had the distinct impression that the Project's counterattack had been swift and effective.

The noise died down over the space of almost two hours, by which time I had collapsed into a chair by the breakfast table, a nerveless mass, and the sun was thrusting its first fingers of daylight over the horizon. At some point I lapsed into a long thoughtless gaze. By the time I came out of it the sky was losing its last tinges of purple, replaced by perfect baby blue. Twittering birds perched on the lamppost outside.

On the lawn next door, my neighbor was standing stock-still, blank-faced and white-lipped, looking like a cyborg freshly reset. Far away, orders were being barked, and a hum of activity sounded from all directions, but the gunfire had died down and the sirens had stopped.

The attack was over.

But of Ma, there was no sign. She was just gone.

I made a pot of coffee and drank it throughout the morning as I sat there at the breakfast table. The armed men came around to patrol the streets every so often, and a few times they came to call at the houses of well-built men and took them away, though to where wasn't clear.

The street was deathly still for a while.

Then the time for duties came around. The second hand on the clock hung over the door struck twelve, the speakers on the lampposts outside emitted a prompt *bong*, and Mother Eden's voice rippled out across the desert sand.

"Morning, y'all!" She sounded upbeat, cheerful even. "Beautiful day! I just want to apologize for all that racket last night, but some folks just can't take no for an answer.

"I know some of you are scared, especially the young'uns, but we got everything locked down good and tight. Nothing can touch us, just like always. Now don't let all this get you down; we gotta just push on through, and we'll all be right as rain. So pull together, folks, and get down to work like usual. Everything's fine, you got my word on that."

A squeal of feedback, a crackle, and then silence.

I drained my coffee, refilled the coffee cup from the pot, and turned to the window. The echoes of the night-long screams still rang in my ears, and my neighbor's blank, dead-eyed stare flickered in my mind's eye.

How could Mother Eden expect normality after that, and so soon? The guards were still racing back and forth across the Project, and she expected people to drop their wailing children to go sit at their desks? Worse, she expected some to go picking through piles of rotten garbage.

Nobody would move an inch, of that I was sure. Mother Eden was wasting her goddamn time. As another truck raced past, I enjoyed a laugh at her expense. Not so wise and mighty, after all.

Then, all along the street, front doors started opening. While I looked on, mug frozen halfway to my face, people filed outside without a moment's delay.

And then everything was different. Though hair was uncombed, clothes were askew, and eyes were ringed by dark bands of sickly purple, the faces of my neighbors were content, calm, and carefree. It was as though the pall of shock had been whipped away in a single fluid motion.

I knew I should go, that there would be consequences if I didn't—in fact, I felt an almost visceral, unreasoning compunction to rise to my feet and march out the door—but my legs still felt like so much jelly. The coffee was helping, but I'd be a while yet in feeling right.

Then there was Ma. I couldn't just leave.

As the minutes ticked by, the few on the streets became a flood, all stiff-upper-lipped with their faces peaceable, as if the sound of heavy machinery in the distance was in fact the dainty twittering of songbirds. I'd be missed, and danger was still thick on the air. I couldn't attract attention to myself. Under siege or not, eyes were following me, watching carefully, waiting for a slipup—an excuse.

I struggled into my overalls after gulping down the rest of the coffee straight from the pot. I soon found myself standing back in the kitchen, staring dumbly at the other chair beside the table. The empty chair.

I scribbled a note saying I'd be back later, just in case

she came home, then scrunched it up and threw it in the trash on my way out.

I worried about Ma for the first part of the morning, but by lunchtime I'd almost forgotten about her. That wasn't long after Mother Eden's second broadcast, when the armed guards came around to herd up the rest of us.

Peters and I were loading up the last dripping garbage sacks into the Beetle when the Humvees careened around the corner. The two vehicles flanked a flatbed truck, which followed close behind. As the two of us stopped working to watch, the Humvees peeled off and circled us on opposing side streets, as though to prevent an escape.

The other guys on waste duty, strung along the street, froze at the sound of the engines' roars and shaded their eyes with their hands. We all stood there rooted in place until the flatbed had passed the Beetle and rumbled to a stop in our midst. The guards atop the circling Humvees, their faces obscured by desert headcloths, eyed us with pitiless gazes.

The driver's door of the nearest vehicle opened with a heavy rumble, and a guard swung out, his uniform decorated with a patch of pins and medals. He stepped into our midst and looked around. "Your services are required."

None of the "sir" business I'd been graced with out by the fences. Not now. We weren't citizens, clearly. Not while we held this duty. We were less than scum on the sole of his boot.

He turned on his heels to eye each of us in turn. The same cast-iron gaze as the rest, staring out from the depths of an identical mass of folded cloth. "You will climb onto the truck in single file, sit against the walls, and keep your eyes on the floor until told otherwise." A pause. "Questions?"

None of us were stupid enough to say a word. I dropped the garbage bag in my hands, joined the others in lining up dutifully at the rear of the flatbed, and climbed aboard. I caught Peters's eye at one point, but he only gave the smallest shakes of his head.

The others looked calm, but my hands were shaking. I kept my eyes set hard on the floor as the flatbed's diesel grumbled to life and we set off down the street. I could still sense eyes pressing in on me, burning a hole in my temple.

Why was I so afraid?

It wasn't the unknown. It wasn't not being addressed as "sir."

It was the air. The air around the guards. I was almost certain that these were the very same contingent I'd encountered at the fences; this was the same neighborhood, after all. Yet that comforting air I'd breathed in like nectar a few weeks before had evaporated. These men were cold and dangerous.

Every nerve in my body knew it. They thrummed like live wires.

Pain shot through my backside as we began to jolt over uneven ground, but still I kept my eyes glued to the sanded bed of the truck. I was sweating enough for a brook of perspiration to have forged a path between my shoulder blades. My own skin seemed ill-fitting, grimy and stifling, and the stench of diesel fumes was making me giddy.

I shook myself, determined to keep focus. My guts were squirming, and every instinct urged me to leap over the side and sprint for home. But I was going to see this out and watch for every detail, because now the ground beneath us had changed to rolling gradations of soft sand.

Dunes.

We were heading for the fences.

"Sit." That single word, and the force with which it was uttered by the guard standing over me, sent me crashing back to the floor like a punch to the solar plexus.

I blinked, saw blurred bands of faded desert hues, and then I was looking across the bed of the truck at Peters. He glanced up at me for a moment, flashed a warning bulge of his eyes, and then focused on a spot between his knees as though it fascinated him to no end.

"What—" I began.

"I told you to keep your eyes on the floor," the guard said. His voice was low, but the bass alone managed to carry genuine venom. That, coupled with his enormous presence—a slab of stinking muscle—sparked a primal urge to cower.

Despite myself, feeling shame creep into my cheeks, I realized that my bottom lip was quivering.

Like a dog, I thought.

I kept myself frozen until I felt the pressure of his gaze fade, and then I took a shuddering breath. What had happened? The last thing I remembered was trying to keep my senses as the sun's rays had beaten down on my shoulders, half drowning in my own perspiration.

Then a blank. I'd slipped away into a fog of confusion.

But I'd heard something. The clinking of metal. I shook myself, focusing on the jingle, and then recognized it as that of swinging gate, one made of chain-linked steel.

That was why I'd moved; I'd been trying to see over the side. We were at the fences. Somehow the flatbed had passed the minefield. And in my daze, my curiosity had gotten the better of me.

Around us was a medley of different sounds. Stamping boots, idling engines, shifting sand, hollering voices, and a steady rhythmic thumping I couldn't place. But I didn't dare look away from the cracked rubber between my ankles until the flatbed had drawn to a halt and the diesel had cut out with a stentorian rumble.

The underlying racket rang in my ears, pushing me further toward the same stupor brought on by the sun. The acrid smell of gunpowder, however, kept me alert. The air was thick with it.

"Your duties are suspended for the day," the lead guard

said. "Form up in two-man teams and file out along the side of the truck." He stepped out of sight, dropping down onto the sand. The suspension squealed in his absence, and the flatbed rose a few inches.

Wary, I glanced around at the others. I received similar wide-eyed stares in return. Then Peters reached across the bed and gripped my sleeve. "You're with me."

I didn't protest, just followed him and the rest at a low crouch toward the tailgate. I realized that my hands were still shaking.

No wonder I have the shakes, I thought. *Everyone else is a decade my senior, at the least. I'm among men, here— uncaring, work-calloused, and mean.*

I'd never felt so young in my life. The proverbial deer in the headlights.

Peters gripped my sleeve tighter after we'd dropped down onto the sand. "Keep your eyes on the ground," he said in a dire tone. "Trust me."

His hand lingered a moment on my sleeve and squeezed my arm. I didn't dare ask why, I was just thankful to be told what to do. The urge to look around would have been too great otherwise.

"This your first time out here?"

I nodded, not trusting myself to speak.

"Then learn fast. Line up, haul ass, and go home. Do anything else and you're meat on the roadside." His voice was shuddering, which set my own stomach aquiver. I hadn't thought him capable of emotion until now; he'd seemed as downright mechanical as the others in Eden.

Maybe not so taken by the sparkle of it all, but just as brain-dead.

Now, he'd come to life. I sensed for the first time a living, breathing human being beside me, thinking and terrified. And the others, too. Beneath that rhythmic thumping and the sound of the patrolling vehicles afar, their rasping breaths ebbed and flowed.

So there were people under all these masks, after all.

We lined up like we'd been told, and I tried to find something interesting in the minute sand ridges at my feet. The smell of gunpowder was stronger still, but out here in the slack afternoon breeze, there was another scent underneath, something sticky. That was the only word for it: *sticky*. It clung to the inside of my nostrils, taking root at the back of my throat.

"Listen up!" the lead guard bellowed. I couldn't help looking up at the sound of his voice. "You take a hold of these insurgents, one per pair, and you carry them over to that chute. You don't talk, you don't ask questions." He paused, then added, "You don't look at them, either. They're refuse now. Just more garbage. Same duty as before. Clear?"

Nobody said a word. I wondered what he'd do if anyone did. Nothing good, I'd wager. His beady eyes, still immersed in the folds of headcloth, seemed to be daring us to speak.

We were outside the fences. Beyond the guard was the rise preceding a ravine between dunes, but beyond that was nothing but sun-baked hard-top, right up to the distant craggy Altai peaks.

Despite everything, and the rolling in my guts, I still felt the urge to peer over my shoulder, around the side of the flatbed. How had we got past the mines?

"Get to it!" the lead guard barked and retreated to the nearest Humvee.

As one we all stepped forward. Then I saw the insurgents.

They carpeted the floor of the ravine, staining it and the surrounding sand with arcs of blood—crimson where it had yet to dry, and rusty brown where it had lay for some time. In places they were piled on top of one another, and in others a few had made it some way up the ravine walls. All were dressed in desert attire, faded by the sun and rotten with age. All were stained like the sand, riddled with ragged holes.

The world had grown far away. I might have gasped, I might have screamed, I mightn't have reacted at all. I had no way of knowing. Though I saw, it was all so much visual static, nonsense. I heard only muffled babble, and my legs were but jelly.

Peters was dragging me, I knew that, but for what could have been hours, I could only bear the brunt of the internal scream that had erupted behind my eyes. By the time I felt anything again, the others and I had moved down to the ravine's base, and Peters was punching me on the shoulder—no light jab, but a full-blown left hook.

"Don't look," he hissed. "Don't think. You're not here." His eyes darted to the trucks above us.

Though my back was to them, I knew they were still watching us. I nodded, numb, and stooped with him to the nearest body.

I'm not here, I thought. *I'm at home, back in Fremont. Father's home from the plant, and Ma's singing her radio tunes. We're dishing up a pot roast, and the cokehead neighbors have been out all day. Everything's fine. We're together.*

But as I grew close to the mass of rags at my feet, I couldn't help looking. And once I'd gripped a lifeless arm, the face underneath was unveiled. I don't know what I expected. I'd never seen a dead body before. But the inhumanity of the vessel before me was nothing I could fathom.

Here were ridges of thick brows, the curves of broad nostrils and red lips, the lids of an open pair of soft brown eyes. But whatever had once inhabited it had fled, leaving nothing but a slab of meat behind, pale and stiff. And the smell. There hadn't been time for decomposition, but death had been recent, and there remained a lingering charred aroma. My stomach turned as I realized it was the smell of flesh burned by high-caliber rounds. It reminded me of bacon just out of the pan.

"Desh, move it," Peters muttered, holding the legs, which were frozen by rigor mortis in the most awkward tangle. "Trust me, don't test these guys. They don't play the same game after an attack." He paused. "It's our duty. Everyone's relying on us."

I hauled the body upward, and together we stumbled

across the sand, half dragging an insurgent almost a head taller than either of us. How unbelievably heavy he was!

I fought an attack of hysterical giggling while we battled toward a low, concrete structure farther along the ravine, panting beside other pairs also carrying corpses. "Relying on us"! I'd never heard of anything so at odds with reality. To think that we were making an equal sacrifice as everyone else, taking up the unpleasant tasks of our own free will. To think that we were anything but servants.

Keeping my head turned over my shoulder, blinking through streams of sweat and trying to ignore the blood oozing from the body onto the sand, I struggled to hold back the laughter. Shoulders bucking, breathing stuttering, eyes weeping. I knew I'd never stop screaming it but one titter escaped.

Peters's eyes were wide with horror. "Desh, come on, man! Keep it together." He looked as though he wanted to beat me to the ground, but the mass of legs in his grasp was already too much. "They'll skin us both if you crack."

I nodded, hiccuped, and gave a heave that propelled us both stumbling on. After a few moments, the urge to shriek dissipated, and the concrete cube ahead had come within twenty feet. Other bodies had already disappeared inside, heaved into a metal receptacle in the wall, rolling end over end out of sight. The other pairs were dusting their hands—their eyes shards of flint and their expressions blank—and going back for more.

This couldn't have been the first time. Far from it. I

seemed to be the only one even remotely bothered by the carnage. Though the others had shown fear and dread, they were cold to the blood and death. To them, what the guard had said was true: it was just refuse, the same duty.

For the first time, I wished another new arrival had been assigned to garbage duty, if only to share my terror. The whole thing was made worse by the way we started queuing up, single file and orderly, waiting for our turn to dump our cargo. One by one, the masses of rags and flesh tumbled out of view, sightless eyes lolling, some blank and others frozen in terrible grimaces of fear and pain.

Then it was our turn. Peters and I shared a glance, then together we heaved and the body in our grasp was gone into darkness. I looked at the wall, at chipped concrete and weathered grouting, and wondered where the bodies were going. What was on the inside?

After what seemed an impossibly long time, I heard a distant thump. My guts spasmed, and I turned with Peters to collect our next body, willing myself not to vomit.

We worked like that for hours. The sun beat down on us without mercy, and the guards kept their vigil, watching us and the surrounding desert. I must have moved a hundred corpses with Peters. Between us and the others, it was at least twenty times that many. And that was only along this small stretch of the perimeter.

Two thousand. My mind couldn't grasp such an overbearing presence of death. The sights before my eyes were just too much to process. And, though it sickened me to my core, I too began to grow cold to it all. After the third hour of dragging bloodied cloth through the dunes, I found that the nausea was gone. No revulsion, no clenching guts. Nothing.

There was little else to do. Turn it off or lose everything.

No matter how many bodies were loaded into the chute, there was no sign of change, though the building was far too small to have held them all. I found myself wondering all the more what lay inside, desperate for something to focus on. Peters had been here before, surely he knew something. But he seemed to sense the question on the tip of my tongue; every time I met his gaze he flashed that same warning glare and shook his head.

A few guards set off in a Humvee and vanished into the desert for a while. They returned by the time we were finishing with the last of our refuse, and all that was left in the ravine were fading copper stains, soon to be obliterated by the sand devils and blustering wind. They reported an all clear to the lead guard.

A few had spoils with them. I guessed they'd been to investigate the insurgents' camp. Most of it was junk, jewelry, or food. But some had things that brought my horror flooding back: toys.

Children's toys. And comforters. And pacifiers.

They inspected and traded their loot and even began to play with the bright objects as though they were no more than five years old. Seeing that added a final unreal twist to everything, one I feared would push me over the brink and into the eternal twilight of insanity. Were they hardened militia or toddlers?

Eventually we all stood back in the empty ravine, staring around at the bare sand, too frightened to risk looking up at our captors for instruction. There was a pause and then the lead guard's satisfied voice. Suddenly he sounded amicable, respectful, even.

"Gentlemen, I've never seen such fine work. I shall pass on the word of your sacrifice to Mother Eden herself. Now, please step back this way. You must be awfully tired."

The others made for the flatbed without a break in their step. Aghast, I had to be dragged by Peters again.

It was as though none of it had happened. We were "sirs" again. Perhaps the harsh treatment had just been protocol, the result of deep-seated response from years of training. These were military men, after all.

I thought of chancing a smile at one of them, but Peters's eyes stopped me. Just as before, they were wide, bulging, warning.

I climbed into the flatbed and kept my gaze planted on the floor all the way back to the Project. I didn't care about the minefield anymore.

∞

The guards dropped us off where they'd found us, snapping off salutes as they roared away back toward the perimeter. We were left in silence.

I expected an explosion of chatter, cursing, and

indignation. Instead, everyone went back to the bags of refuse they'd left and started loading them onto the Beetle without a word. After a moment alone on the sidewalk, I joined them. We finished up the day's work in stifled silence, bowed and limping from aching muscles and borderline heatstroke.

Then everyone went home, each in their own daze, dog-tired. There was no energy left for fear, or anger, or anything at all. Peters gripped my arm after we parked the Beetle back into its charging station. "Try not to think about it," he said.

For moment I thought his hand might linger, but then he took it away sharply. Then he too disappeared in the direction of the bunkhouses.

I almost ran to catch up. Anything would have been better than going back to an empty house, even the infamous destitution Peters was all too happy to wax on about every day.

Then I remembered why the house was empty. I turned on my heels, heading for the White-Picket District.

She was home. The kitchen window and the front door were wide open to coax a breeze in the lingering heat. My body had jerked and clenched enough for one day, but I still managed to muster a sigh of relief from my depleted emotional reservoir.

I stumbled inside, not wanting to but needing to, and

found Ma waiting in the hallway. "You're back," I said.

She nodded, a slow, fluid gesture unbefitting her arthritic frame. "I am." She looked me up and down. "I'm glad you're safe."

I swallowed convulsively. Her face was smooth as alabaster, and her eyes had a sheen through which not an iota of concern penetrated.

Where had my mother gone? She had returned in body, it seemed, but in soul? This was another person altogether, born of Eden's foul mold. I wouldn't accept that.

I stepped forward and pulled her into a hug. "I'm not mad," I said. "I'm not going to ask about it. I don't care what happened or where you went. I just need to know you were safe."

Between my arms, muffled, a dry titter issued. "Oh, I was. Safe as can be." She was stiff and unyielding, her grip on my back perfunctory. "We need to have a little talk, I think, dear."

I pulled back. "You want to talk?"

"I do." She gestured to the kitchen table.

I scratched my head and caught a whiff of my own body odor. "Can it wait, Ma? I stink like a pig. I spent all day—" A lifeless pair of eyes flashed before mine. Had today really happened? It all seemed so unreal now, standing on a springy carpet with birds twittering on the front lawn. I shook myself. "I had a hard one. Can it wait?"

"No, I don't think it can." Somewhere deep behind

that enameled face, I saw a glint of sadness. "Please."

It was enough to take me off toward the kitchen. "All right," I muttered.

We sat facing one another. The scraping of the chairs and the chorus of birdsong outside seemed amplified tenfold. I waited until Ma had smoothed her blouse, fiddling with stray gossamers for a while. Then she folded her hands neatly in her lap and met my gaze. "They're moving us."

"Out of the house?"

"Outta the neighborhood."

I sat back, rubbing my eyes with my knuckles. "When?"

Her eyelids fluttered, and she leaned forward. "Soon. But as things are looking, we may not be going to the same place. I know this place don't sit right with you"—more Mother Eden speak—"but you're making waves that can't be ignored. It's time to make a decision."

"Are you saying that I either have to lie down and pretend I don't see what you're doing, or they're going to sling me into the garbage pile with the others who had something to say? Because that's not news to me, Ma. That's been clear from the word go."

"Desh, dear . . . my darling." Her eyes beseeched me.

I leaned back, exhaled through pursed nostrils, and fought back fresh tears. "Don't." I swallowed. "Don't."

"If you don't, you may find yourself rubbing shoulders with disreputable folks."

"I know exactly where I'm going, Ma. Let's be straight.

Those bunkhouses might be cesspools that make Fremont look like Shangri-La, for all I care. I'd sooner bed down with those people than sell my soul to sit pretty in those goddamn mansions."

Her face had slackened and grown gaunt. "If that's how you truly feel, we may not see so much of one another. I want to live a decent life, Desh, with decent people. I don't want to struggle anymore. And these people here have shown me kindness."

"They're showing you one hand while hammering others into the dirt with the other," I cried. "Ma, if you'd seen what they had us doing today!"

"Oh, it can't have been that bad. Don't be so dramatic!"

"They slaughtered thousands of people out there!" I bellowed. I was on my feet, fists planted on the tabletop, teeth bared. My heart thumped in my chest, driving a flood of blind fury. "We had to move the bodies, all of them. It took hours. And the way they looked at us, the way they spoke to us . . ." I took a deep, shuddering breath and forced myself to sit. "These are not good people, Ma. This isn't what this place was supposed to be. Mother Eden's twisted it into something where some people live like gods and others live like slaves."

"Desh, you're exaggerating."

"Thousands, Ma. Thousands of bodies."

"We've got to defend ourselves. Rotten insurgents attacking Projects has always been a problem. Everyone knows that."

"But these people, Ma, they weren't terrorists, not soldiers. They were just hungry, lost, without a home."

"We can't be a safe harbor for just anyone, Desh! We have a mission to uphold here. The human race depends on us."

"So we just turn guns on them? No quarter?"

Ma was still. "I don't want to talk about this anymore. Things are the way they are for a reason. Just leave things at that, can't you? All this fretting will only get you into trouble. Can't you just get along?"

"I won't turn a blind eye, Ma. I won't."

Suddenly she lurched across the table and gripped my hands. Her gnarled fingers clutched mine in a grip that reminded me that, deep underneath this reptilian doppelganger, my arthritic mother was still there. "I don't want to lose you, Desh. You're all I have left of my old life, the only thing to remind me of who I really am."

"I'm sorry, Ma. I can't. I just can't."

"We'd have a good life together. You'd get the best education, a good duty, a peaceful home. No more of all this hard labor."

"I won't live a lie," I said slowly. "They're building strata here, Ma. Rich and poor, aristocracy and peasantry, and . . . and slavery. I won't just abandon everyone in the bunkhouses."

"Desh, please . . ." Her milky eyes bored into mine.

I shook my head and, though I cursed myself for having to say it, muttered, "What would Father think?"

Ma whitened. Her hands fell away from mine. "I did

my time," she whispered. "I've suffered enough. Your father would understand."

"If he were here, he'd beat you to the ground," I snapped. "And me, for breaking my promise. I promised I'd take care of you, and I failed."

Her lips pursed and shuddered as though she was holding something in. Her throat undulated. "If you do this, there's no turning back," she said.

Chest pounding, mouth full of ash, I nodded. "I know."

And just like that, the spark of her old self faded like a flame snuffed out in the darkest cellar, and her face became plastic once more.

We sat in silence from then until the static squeal from the lampposts rolled in through the window, and Mother Eden's evening broadcast began.

Ma stood without a word, inch by inch, and ambled over to sit by the window to listen. Her eyes lingered on me a moment, then she turned her back.

The ache in my chest had spread into my throat and jaw, throbbing so much that my vision blurred. I sat watching her by the window for a minute, and then I stood and made for bed. I turned to say goodnight but found that I couldn't, nor wanted to. There was nothing left to be said.

She didn't turn around.

Extract #10
BINK - The one-stop web-com service, bringing the world together!

Harlequin71: _dwntwnDetroit Food bank depleted. All out until Monday. Emergencies only (if you ain't dead, don't bother).

UndrgrndRprtr: new delhi outbreak killing thousands, don't believe the press. haven't seen this bad since petyon milwaukee incident _LX27

MichaelHolmesAnchorage: out of water. Town well dry. FEMA hung up. Shit _endoftheline

The next morning she was gone, and on the doorstep was my relocation order to the bunkhouses. I'd expected some small measure of surprise but found that I felt nothing at all. Unfolding the envelope and reading it aloud, I padded around the house in a blind daze, trying to convince myself Ma was really gone by observing all her absent possessions. All her clothes, half our food, and the photo albums that had been her chosen personal item from outside the Project.

There was no note. The bed was neatly made.

I sat on her crisp sheets and lay down crosswise, inhaling. Her smell was in the air, like oatmeal cookies, and it felt like she was there in the room with me. Not the shell of a woman who'd been sharing the house with me since we arrived, but the real Ma, the frail and kind woman who used to work three shifts at soul-crushing jobs every day to pay the bills while I had been at Princeton and then still made time to ask me about my day.

I forced myself to my feet, fearing I'd stay on the bed forever if I didn't, and made my way to the kitchen. Eating bran flakes mechanically without bothering with milk, I read through the relocation order's small print. I had forty-eight hours to vacate the property and report to the bunkhouses. Duties were to continue as usual.

There and then, I decided that I'd be gone before the morning broadcast. The house seemed hollow now, taunting me with its wealth of space fit for a whole family instead of a single lonely occupant. The walls seemed more stark and bare than I remembered, too beige to look at.

I packed to the harsh echo of my every move and left with dew still on the ground. Nobody had yet risen, and a peaceful lull lay like a pall over the houses, the picket fences, the green grass, and the swaying trees. My footsteps echoed on the asphalt as I made my way toward the outskirts of the Project. I wouldn't have looked back, but something caught my eye.

My neighbor's face hung in shadow between her living room curtains, watching me. She made no effort to conceal herself, nor did she acknowledge our eye contact. She just stared, watching me leave, as though I was a dangerous animal that had been tormenting the neighborhood, finally banished.

I picked up my pace until I was beyond her sight, but still I felt eyes on me—not only those of my fellow arrivals, but others far away. Somehow I knew, just as clearly as I knew that one of those stares belonged to Mother Eden.

Quiet as the morning was, in my head I heard her jeering cackle.

Peters was waiting for me. Somehow he knew, too.

My chest fluttered at the sight of him. I hadn't expected to feel so relieved to see him—his big buffoonish face and ham-like hands—but the rush came nevertheless.

I descended the bank of scree that sloped down into the depression housing the sprawling ramshackle structures that comprised the bunkhouses. There wasn't even a road leading to their doors, out at the very edge of the Project, hidden from sight.

Peters greeted me at the lip of the crater, hands in his pockets. He was dressed in a vest permanently stained by sweat and a set of khaki shorts, lacking any trace of his usual chipper spirit.

I approached until we were face to face and dropped my bags into the sand. I worked halfway toward a legible sentence, but my wavering jaw was stilled by his hand upon my shoulder.

"My Ma . . ." I managed.

He shook his head. "What happened is your business. And here, that's how it stays. You shack with us, so we're your mothers, fathers, brothers, and sisters. Anything before now is just old memories."

I swallowed, looked past him to the corrugated iron rust pile spread out below us, and nodded. In my mind I fell against him and buried my head in his stupid chest. But I couldn't bring myself to do it. Somehow it didn't feel right.

Without another word, Peters picked up my bags and nudged me over the lip of the crater.

Peters took me through a winding labyrinth of metal bunk beds and lockers with practiced ease, weaving and ducking between and around wash lines, makeshift stoves, and overhanging lengths of perforated piping that I guessed passed for showers. Light thrust in from grimy windows in great shafts, revealing a soupy broth of dust motes and cigarette smoke. All was damp, mold grew thick on every surface, and meek fires crackled upon any remaining floor space.

Eyes were staring out at me from every mattress. Some were wide, young, and round as plates; others were weak and aged; many more were wholly indifferent.

Peters dropped my bag on a bunk against the west wall, tucked between a family of seven who huddled together under a reeking blanket and an elderly woman who had quite possibly been dead for some time, judging by the marble pallor of her leathery skin.

"I'll save you a lotta trouble," he said. "Put everything you got on the bed and stand aside. We share here. The little ones will divvy it up proper and fair."

My heart leaped. My last few possessions were in those bags. I'd left most of it behind. Other than clothes, it was a pile of sentimental tokens.

His lips stretched into a dry smile. "I know what you're thinking, but it ain't like that. There's no thieving here. We share." He glanced to the smaller sets of eyes among the seven in the bed beside mine. "We don't have the privileges the others got here. No regular schooling nor free use of that library you're so fond of talking down. We gotta take whatever we can to teach the young'uns that there's a world out there."

I hesitated, but the process had already begun.

Children were sliding into view from bedspreads, nooks, and palls of shadow, hypnotic gazes fixed upon my bags, drawn forth as though by unseen strings. They passed by without acknowledging me and, whispering in a tight huddle, spilled my last few worldly possessions onto the bed. Within moments they had dispersed, leaving my deflated rucksacks and a pile of dirty laundry in their wake.

Peters looked pleased.

"What?" I said.

"You're smiling."

I reached up to touch my face, felt the curve of upturned lips, then turned back to the site of my materialistic cleansing.

"I know it's not easy, but it gets better. Everyone here started out where you are now." He smiled back, a real smile so estranged from the overt falseness of the Project's china dolls that I couldn't have felt sad if I'd wanted to. "Get yourself stowed away. Duties in fifteen."

He made to turn away but then stopped. "A word of advice. Don't bother with the others now. You don't have to pretend anymore. You're invisible to them all from now on."

I nodded, and then something occurred to me. "How do they all know?"

"Everyone's got their own eyes and ears here and there. The one thing that ties us all together, besides the desert, is that there's precious few secrets in Eden."

I lay down, trying to ignore the bed frame's squeal of protest and the spur of broken spring digging into my ribs, and sighed. "Everyone knows about a nobody?"

"Everyone will know you're there, but no one will see you. That's how it is. We're tolerated so long as the duties get done, but we gotta fend for ourselves. As you might've guessed, we built all this with our hands. Sometimes the person next to us is all we have. Ask any woman around the Project. And who's to rule out a man or two?" He gave a long wolf howl, which rang against the dripping pipes.

I couldn't help but smile again.

I turned onto my side and lowered my voice. "Peters . . . how did she do it? How does one person take something so good and turn it into this? And why isn't anybody sending help?"

Peters's eyes flashed, and at last there was that twinkle I'd been searching for since we'd met at the crater—affection and sorrow in equal, agonizing measure—but his features smoothed before I could gauge anything by it. "Duties in ten," he said and was gone into the rusted labyrinth.

And that was my new life. For the next few weeks I settled into the routine of waking, working, eating, and sleeping. In between, I kicked ball with the kids, laughed over bubbling pots with old crones, and watched the Eden Project through a new lens.

Peters was right. I was invisible, though everyone knew I was there. I moved freely, without suspicion or hindrance, and saw the ogres in the mansions when their masks were off—ugly, conceited, vain creatures, quick to anger when not ensconced in the veil of false serenity the Project so often provided.

The work was hard, the sun hot, and the days long. I went from garbage collection to road sweeping, from working the fields to flushing the sewers. My body firmed and my appetite grew. Though I was now, in many ways, less than a person to the eyes of so many, I'd never felt so strong.

I even started keeping the bunkhouse log, an enormous dusty tome the size of a suitcase and older than anyone dared guess. Among its pages were the records of the bunkhouses from their foundations as a hollow in the sand where the first outcasts had sheltered from the wind. Dozens of keepers had kept it safe over the decades, but until I had arrived, nobody had the aptitude to do it justice. It had been consigned to the children's makeshift classroom, where it had been studied but never added to.

But I couldn't let that go on. The absence of media, of knowledge, of faithful recordings in the Projects, had stirred something in me. I knew I'd be good at it.

I read old passages to young and old when not making new entries, and while they listened, I too learned what lay hidden in Eden's past.

Between that and duties, there was little time for anything else. Each night the rickety bunk bed seemed like an all-embracing marshmallow.

It wasn't a happy life, but it was a life.

I seldom thought of Ma.

Extract #11
BUNKHOUSE LOG – THE FOLLOWING PAGES WERE STUCK TOGETHER

The others are gone. Vanquished, vanished. I am the last.

They call me "The Usurper." Quaint, you might think, yet the vehemence with which such a term is spat at me in the street fills my heart with sorrow.

People used to bring baskets of wine and cheese, begging for me to read a little of my work. "Just a poem!" they'd say, "Please, sir, just a paragraph from my favorite essay!" Now they throw rotten cabbage and grit. They aim for my eyes.
*   - Lutharo Bielshik*

They're making me write a book. No, I lie. She is making me write a book.

It may very well be my greatest work, I feel, yet it will also be the greatest lie I ever tell. For so long I've wondered why the others were removed and I was spared, why I linger on alone, surrounded by this twisted bastardization of endeavor. Now I know; I live on to further the lies, to set them in words for consumption by the masses. What will become of me when I finish and they don't need me anymore?

There's nothing I can do to change things, not alone. I've been keeping a log of everything going on around the Project for the poor children who live in these destitute bunkhouses. Perhaps they can learn some semblance of literacy before my fate catches up with me. But on those pages I can never include any truth of the evil going on here. I must reserve those secrets for these separate entries, which I intend to hide from view between select pages.

I will tell only the few I trust of this secret log. Perhaps they can learn from it and add secrets of their own when I am gone. For now, it is all I can do. To think such a young flower as Ms. Bateman could reduce me to a crawling cretin like this.

I must now search for glue in this hellish place.

- Lutharo Bielshik

My duty this week was a strange one: nutrition technician.

I sat on my bunk frowning at it all morning.

Peters was reticent when I asked and gave me a look that said "Don't ask."

So I chalked it up to an opportunity for a little break in the monotony and went along to the address on the duty card. It was a low, square building, not far from the fences. Bar the glimmering airlock set into its side, it was identical to the building Peters and I had tended to after the attack. Inside, it was very different from its concrete exterior—pristine, whitewashed, and sterile. Before exiting the airlock, we'd had to struggle into clean suits, face masks, and medical gloves.

And it was cool, by far the coldest I'd felt since leaving Saint Petersburg.

Of all my duties thus far, this one strayed out on its own by a mile.

I took my place along a spidery bank of panels and dials and monitors, so delicate and out of place amid the mid-twentieth-century low-tech frugality of the Project outside, and tried to take in all the labels in alphanumeric gibberish, funnel-shaped receptacles, rows of pipettes, and dozens of bubbling, colored liquids flowing through a vast complex of clear tubes.

"Where do the tubes go?" I asked.

Peters shrugged, flexing in his clean suit, and taking his own place along the complex array. "Who cares? Now hurry up; we gotta get started."

"I thought there were no secrets."

Peters rolled his eyes. "I guess some things are just too dull, Desh. Now come *on*. The pressure on this bastard spikes quick." He began inspecting gauges, muttering as he read from a small screen directly before his station, using pipettes to draw up liquid from vats in the array and depositing it in the receptacles. He glanced at me and shook his head sharply. "No questions today, Desh. Just get it done." He clocked my uncertain poise, hovering without a clue over all the steel and glass. "Just focus on the screen; it tells you everything. You'll pick it up. But do it fast."

I looked at the digital readout and saw one of the codes in large print letters. Peters's print was white; mine was flashing bright red. I grabbed clumsily at the correct vat, sucked up a random amount, and squirted it into what I hoped was the right receptacle.

For a moment the screen continued to flash, then there was a perfunctory *boop*, and a new code flashed up, this time in standard white.

"See, easy."

I nodded and set to work. I worked up a steady sweat keeping pace with the dozen or so others at the other stations, but once I worked up a rhythm, it quickly grew boring. Once that happened, my eyes started to wander. And soon after, my mind wandered, too.

My hands worked, my eyes read, but I stood apart, watching the liquid in the pipes flow away into the walls and disappear.

In truth, I hadn't thought much of anything since getting to the bunkhouses, nor had I pressed the others. I had watched the Eden folk go about their lives, but only vacantly, running on automatic. Had this duty not come around, I could have stayed that way, maybe forever.

But watching that liquid flow out of sight stirred me from slumber and set my old self blinking in fresh light. This building was so like the other beyond the fences, and the clean-room environment was so out of place with everything else. This place meant something, something big.

I tried to catch Peters's eye throughout the day, but he never seemed to notice, always conveniently busy, always deep in concentration.

What didn't he want to share?

Peters avoided me all week. The only time I saw him was when we rolled out of bed to get over to the concrete hut. Then his eyes were on his work and he didn't speak a word until sundown. By then he always seemed to have some obligation to fulfill and sped off.

I tried to take the hint and forget it all. What we had going was far from perfect, but it was a damn sight better than the lie I'd been living before.

I distracted myself with the log and read to the kids whenever I had a spare moment. At first I had only a few listeners, but soon enough I had a faithful congregation scrabbling for a good spot. Most of them had heard it all before from a half-blind tutor called Rosie, an ancient relic from a bygone era with eyes like clouded opals and a voice like crackling polystyrene. But still they listened.

Reading gave me purpose. I mattered, in some small way. But I knew from the start that it wouldn't be enough. In the end it was the log itself, the very thing that I thought might have saved me, that spelled my inevitable regression. Its pages, though marked by the near-illegible writings of long-dead keepers, most of which were blotted by ink stains or faded by time, held too many secrets.

The keepers had had all been curious, and they had never failed to pass on the tidbits of knowledge they acquired in the log's pages.

Slowly, over the years, a small but firm body of details on Eden's hidden workings had built up. Most of it was superfluous and inconsequential, mere mechanics of Eden's underground catacombs—what genetic aberrations were being tested on the desert soil, or the success rates of clean-energy developments by the Project's engineers.

But as I read to the kids and to myself by the last

glowing embers of each night's dying fires, I came to notice a single thread that had captivated every keeper since the beginning. For some of them it seemed to have become an obsession.

The very last entry removed any doubt: two words scrawled repeatedly across a full page spread, big and small, often so hard it had punctured the paper. In the center the words had been blown up, etched madly in capitals and underlined a dozen times:

THE FOUNDINGS

It made sense after a while. Of course, the real secrets of the Project lay with Mother Eden. All this time it had been absurd to think that a white, senior, American citizen could have risen to such giddy heights of power. There were simply so many South Americans, Middle Easterners, and southeast Asians, the crème de la crème of modern nations. They were the new money, the new enlightened.

How could a nobody from the dark depths of dilapidated Texas have forged her own totalitarian microstate? It was tantamount to the League of Nations having been led by a country bumpkin.

The horror of it was that the answers had been there, in *The Foundings*, not ten feet from me in the library. The librarian had even offered to loan it to me.

And now it was beyond my reach, out of bounds as

Peters had warned; I could feel danger-prickles rising up my neck in waves if I passed too close to a public space, whether it was the surveillance building or a goddamn toilet. I'd never even get close to a copy—though I had no idea what form any reprimand would take. In my mind's eye I was either vaporized by an unseen laser or hauled away with a black bag over my head.

In any case, the book would hardly be an accurate account. Most likely it was a mix of fairy tale, propaganda, and bleeding-heart autobiography—*Mein Kampf* 2.0, or *The Communist Manifesto* turned sour.

But I was willing to bet that it was all there, buried beneath the bullshit. Tyrants could never help showing their true selves. The ego always won. That was going to be her weakness.

On the face of it, it shouldn't have been that difficult, for it seemed that everyone not consigned to the bunkhouses had read it and lived by its every word. Perhaps I could pick up what I needed from the Eden folks' habit of quoting its passages alone.

The idea stuck for a while, but as the week wore on, and the bubbling tubes of vanishing colored liquid continued pouring away to who-knew-where, taunting me, I realized that I needed to study it—tear it apart and scrutinize every word under a microscope.

I was deep in the grips of obsession by Friday, and the others were upset despite my discretion. I did my work, kept my mouth shut, and kept on reading to the kids. But somehow they all knew something was wrong, as though they smelled crazy on me.

Halfway back to the bunkhouses, while the sun was sliding down behind the far-off dunes and a lively wind kicked sand around our ankles, Peters laid a hand flat on my chest and brought us to a halt. The others left us behind, pointedly not looking back. "Stop this," he croaked.

I started, jarred from a tired daze. "What?"

"Whatever it is you're planning. We've been good to you, and you could have a place with us if you just accept that this is how things are."

Tongue-tied by the venom in his voice and the bolts of lightning sparking in his eyes, I mouthed wordlessly. On the brink of audibility was the chatter of home, of fires cooking and sighing work-weary men and women resting their aching bodies.

Peters could hear it too; his eyes softened and his hand fell away to his side. "Desh, people like you don't belong in this place. Not anyplace, not now. The world's too small for your kind of smarts." He looked away and ran a hand through his prematurely-thinning hair. "You could put them all in danger. We're tolerated so long as we play sheep, but if we rock the boat . . . Every so often somebody like you comes along, and it always turns out bad, most times for us. They don't allow it. *She* don't allow it."

His eyes returned to me, once again diamond hard. "Leave it be."

He left me standing there with sand collecting around

my rotting boots, while the sky turned purple and the crackle of the evening broadcast rolled over me. From here I could see the peaks of the mansions, ensconced in glittering gilding and luscious greenery.

"I can't," I whispered. I followed him home with a heavy heart.

For a while, though, I did. There was little else to do. There wasn't enough to act on, no certainty, and I had no plan in any case. Itching to act, to do *something*, yet unable to do anything but watch, I festered like an open wound.

Peters kept a sharp eye on me, and I knew he had his spies among the bunkhouse ranks doing the same. I could feel their gazes on me when I went to wash in the sludge-thick spring out back, when I used the bathroom, when I worked on the log, even when I read to the kids.

I was a marked man all over again.

Somtimes it seemed he'd forgotten about it and tried to pass the time with me, but I took up whatever I was doing and moved on without a word. A few times he laid a hand on my shoulder. Each time I shrugged him off.

Pain was written in the rhythm of his stiff retreat, but I couldn't stop myself.

A few times I caught myself watching him, but each time I shook myself.

I can't afford to get attached, I reminded myself. *Mother Eden will only use it.*

In truth, I would have given anything to be with him; the loss of Ma had cut deep, leaving me a loose flag flailing in the wind. But those whispering doubts were right: Mother Eden would turn any affection to poison. I had to be alone.

Duties continued to change over, which kept my hands busy and my mind sane. The days slipped past, each the same as the last, marked only by blistering afternoons and the occasional rush to water and shade for those who collapsed.

I couldn't tell when I started writing the letter to Father. Life had become such a blur of unthinking day-to-day passings that I had no reference, no way to measure the breadth of time it took to push out those few words, each one an agony, like tweezing shrapnel from a deep wound. All I knew is that one afternoon I held the finished piece in my hands, scrawled on a scrap of stained exercise book paper—the best the bunkhouses had to offer bar the pages of the log. Every word had been painstakingly scratched out with the nub of a pencil older than Rosie, for there wasn't the space or spare paper for mistakes or redrafts.

I read it over and over. Each time my skin came up in gooseflesh. Laid bare, it chilled me deep, the waking nightmare I'd been living poured onto the page.

Yet I'd been clever. I hesitated to congratulate myself for a job well done, but soon enough I relented with a wry half smile to my own subconscious cunning. There was nothing overt about the Project's secrets, nor a word about my being a modern untouchable, nor even a passing mention that I hadn't seen Ma in weeks. Yet it was all there, buried in subtext. Maybe nothing specific, but I knew Father would see it for what it really was: a cry for help.

I'd stopped reading. Even given the HUD a rest—the computer too. I'd taken up a lot of manual labor roles and was spending a lot of time giving back to the community. Ma was happier than ever. Her arthritis was eased by excellent health care and good food, and she was moving up fast in the Project.

She didn't even have time for her radio tunes anymore.

We both missed him with all our hearts.

It was in some ways a grotesque caricature of our new lives, but perhaps it would get the message across without tripping the attention of the censors the Project surely had in place.

Father knew that I wouldn't stop reading—even if I had to resort to dusty old physical books—or surrender the web unless there was no choice in the matter, just as much as he knew I was about as inclined to manual labor as a dog was to take up paragliding.

But the details I knew really mattered were those about Ma. She had loved those show tunes too much for it to pass under his radar. And though my father had loved her to death, I suspected that he had always known about her desire for a comfortable life, no matter the cost. He'd known what she was capable of.

"What you got there?"

I glanced from the page to the depths of Peters's searching eyes. He was eyeing the paper in my hands as though it could have leaped across the room and decapitated him.

I considered lying, but what would that have done? He'd find out sooner or later. Without a word I crawled from the musty confines of my bunk and handed it over. He read it right there in front of me, with a slowness that could only have come from lack of practice. How long had it been since he'd actually had to read anything?

After a while he dropped it back onto the bed. We both watched it tumble end over end, dancing upon a draft and settling by my boots. "Don't bother," he said.

I picked it up and smoothed the creases for the thousandth time. I stared back at him but found that I didn't have anything to say to him. I knew it was a long shot, damn near futile, in fact.

Peters's eyes said it all: "Even if they let that letter through—and why the hell would they allow scum like us let out a peep—what do you think your pa could do about it? Come storming in with a flight of gunships?"

But I didn't care. I was sending it, and that was that. I needed to, to make this one small gesture, if only to prove to myself that I wasn't beaten.

After a long stalemate, Peters's shoulders slackened. He made his way around my bunk, out of earshot of my ever-mute, ever-staring neighbors. "Just don't get your hopes up," he muttered.

I got up and met his eyes. "There's one thing missing."

He eyed me warily. "What?"

"Ma's signature. I want her to read it before I send it. I want her to see that he'll know what she's become." I stroked the last free scrap of blank space at the letter's foot. "And she's going to sign it."

Peters's sigh was thicker than molasses. "I guess I don't need to tell you that you'd be a goddamn moron."

"Probably not."

Peters scowled. He was silent a while and followed me to the bunkhouse door. A light breeze caressed my face, drying off the slick of sweat on my brow. My arms ached from the day's toil, but it was a good ache; not pain, but a satisfied thrumming. My belly was full of stew, nothing fancy or contrite, just laced with beans, greens, and heavy spices, pure no-nonsense man-fuel. I was in good company, and I'd just finished reading a few passages of the log to my still-growing congregation.

I wasn't afraid of this place anymore. There was no point in being afraid.

"All right, what you got planned?" Peters said. "Just gonna waltz up and knock on the front door?"

I touched the bulge in my pocket where the letter lay neatly folded. "Yep," I said.

Extract #12
BUNKHOUSE LOG

This place is poison. Mother Eden came

to visit Bielshik three weeks ago. They sat and drank tea. He made jokes, she laughed. He told me after that he had gotten off lucky. The next morning, he was gone.

Now all the old scientists are gone. Thank God he told me about these secret pages. At least something of him, of all of them, will live on. I must make a note to pick my own successor from the others, lest the same happen to me.

But already I am maligned. The others knew I was Bielshik's favorite, and they only tolerated him because he was under Mother Eden's wing, working on her puerile book. The Foundings, they're calling it. What bile.

They can all sense that I'm not taken by it. They all think I'm up to something. They've started calling me Sneaky Sik. Funny, right?

- Sik Mendez

Khaled came back today after weeks of there being no sign of him. He doesn't recognize me. All he does is recite The Foundings.

That's how it works now, it seems. There's no public execution, no pitchfork-wielding mobs, no violence of any kind. If you make waves, they pin you on a board somewhere and keep a close eye. Then they pay you a visit and you have a little chat. If you don't listen, then some time, one day, you just

disappear. Then some time passes and you come back different. I'm still gathering information, but I get the feeling that this is all part of a cycle that's been going for a very long time.
    - Jorgia Andersson

The neighborhood of the mansions was deathly still. Ringing silence hung thick in the air, pressing in from all directions. It was an eerie place after the ruggedness and ramshackle functionality of the bunkhouses.

Nobody noticed my approach. Why would they? I was little more than a broom on legs. The bell for duties rang elsewhere with the same jarring aplomb as usual, launching residents across their lawns like spring hares; here, there was only a pleasant jingle, barely audible above the gentle rustle of the breeze and the twittering birds roosting amid the trees' luscious foliage.

A few people were emerging from their grand abodes through mahogany doors with a light spring in their step, but there was no great rush about them. These few peppered the streets of only the smallest mansions.

I'd been on garbage duty often enough to know that not everyone was equal, not even here. Certainly, even the smallest dwelling was lavish with all the comforts of wealth and made the ordinary mainstay homes across the Project look shabby and downright ugly by contrast; comparing them to the bunkhouses wasn't worth the time it would take to recover from the corresponding fit of insane laughter.

But they paled in the wake of those in the nexus of the district's leafy embrace. Those were true abominations—towering marble behemoths, three stories high and surrounded by security-gated ten-foot walls. And dead center in the middle of it all was a single structure that would have dominated the skyline were it not for a clever screening of cycads. I'd puzzled over it whenever we'd driven past in the Beetle. It was simply too large to be a home, yet it didn't seem to serve any practical purpose, either.

Peters had relented one afternoon when we'd been parked out front on our short lunch break. "They call it the club."

Looking at it now, it wasn't hard to see why. It smacked of a Victorian gentlemen's club; through the open sash windows I could hear sitar music and the clink of glasses overshadowed by the occasional titter of "civilized" discourse. But at the same time, I knew that no man ruled here. This was Mother Eden's throne.

Ma would be inside, of that I had no doubt.

I walked up through the gates, left ajar for the many folks from the bunkhouses who were on gardening duty—a considerable task, for the lawns stretched all the way around the building—and then walked along the graveled driveway.

It was cooler here, somehow, even away from the shade of the trees. Of course it was. Decent folk like these simply wouldn't allow the kind of heat everyone else dealt with.

I grinned to myself despite the heavy beat of my heart, scaling the granite steps and lifting a brass knocker the size of a human head. The weight resounded against the stop, and I heard a stirring inside.

Behind me I could sense the gardeners focusing on their rakes and trowels, feel their sideways glances and their silent pleading for me to turn tail while I still could.

But then the latch clunked and the door swung open on inch-thick hinges, revealing a composed alabaster female face with a long, bulbous nose. She observed me as though I was curious amoeba. An Asian visage trussed up in the finest garments of white and ochre tones. She had the unmistakable rigid posture of a house servant.

I recognized her at once. It was my old neighbor, the woman who had so often peeped through her curtains. "May I help you?" Her icy tone, bearing no trace of her native intonation, emulated that southern drawl to a tee. She enunciated every syllable.

I almost recoiled at her transformation.

My plan momentarily forgotten, I stood lame and silent until one of her waspish, preened eyebrows arched toward her hairline. Then I cleared my throat and stepped forward. "I'm here to see my ma."

After a beat the woman's other brow ascended to join its twin. "The members of this establishment are not wont to entertain unexpected visitors."

The gardeners were all watching. I knew they were. The rustle of leaves and rustle of trowels had become few and far between. I stepped even closer and laid my hand flat on the door, placing a foot over the threshold. I hoped to God she wouldn't try to slam it on me. "She sent for me. I know she's here."

The woman eyed me with suspicion. Her stare—identical to the way she'd looked at me from behind her drapes only a few months before—brought forth ugly memories that I quickly squashed.

"We have business together. Go and ask her if you want."

A shadow crossed her face, I guessed from the mere thought of disturbing the sainted mansion folks. She relented with a tightness about her lips, stepping aside to allow me access.

I stepped over the threshold, stifling a smile. The combined pressure emanating from the watchful gardeners was cut off as though by a switch with the closing of the door. The boom resounded in the cavernous space in which I now stood, echoing away to infinity in the recesses of countless rooms.

Rich mahogany trim surrounded gleaming stone and sumptuous crimson carpets. Vibrant shrubs and ferns adorned every corner, and wall-screen monitors plastered the walls; most showed picturesque landscapes from across the globe—I recognized a few from the Project commercials I used to watch, so often voiced over with messages of the UN's grand humanitarian mission—but others showed quotations in shimmering italics. From every direction came the dull murmur of conversation, but besides the woman there was nobody in sight.

"This way, please," she said in clipped tones. Her upper lip curled as she observed my grimy trousers and tattered work boots. "Wipe your feet, if you would. And kindly refrain from . . . touching anything."

She led the way to a winding staircase and we ascended to the second floor in terse silence. I had no idea how bad I smelled until now. The air was so fresh and cool; by contrast my skin seemed to radiate stifling heat and a heady musk of fetid, dried sweat.

She led the way along a corridor that seemed to stretch for at least a quarter mile before opening onto an elaborate ballroom, alive with bunkhouse help and dignified mansion folk. I craned my neck for a better view, but then we broke off into one of the many side rooms, a forty-foot library with a crackling fire at the far end.

"Please wait here while I inquire on your mother's whereabouts." The woman left me standing in the center of the room, alone. The look she turned upon me as she took a last glance back was of the purest contempt. In moments all I could hear was the crackling flames in the grate.

My guts were alive, squirming around like a bucket of snakes. Desperate to keep myself composed, I focused on my surroundings. I spent a while reading the italicized text on the wall-screens until I realized they were quotations from *The Foundings*. One read: "And the poison that was Machine was banished from Eden—that which made genius into dullard, and good citizen into revolutionary.

Thus, the dominion of the Good People was restored."

The radio silence. The anti-technological fervour. The confiscation of my HUD.

I suppressed a shiver. Noise was brewing nearby, and I couldn't help but suppose I was the cause. I set to observing the hardbacks lining the shelves. There were enough in this room alone to outstrip the Project library.

On a whim I pulled out a copy of *Brave New World*. Flicking through, I saw that these volumes were just as "edited." As the noise afar grew louder, I pulled out *Brave New World*'s twin, *Island*. It was immediately clear that, besides the very last pages, the entire manuscript had been removed, leaving only the leather casing.

I thrust it back and moved on. It was all I could do to not let fly a peal of manic laughter. I kept reading titles in an effort to keep my nerves at bay, all too aware that the noise outside wasn't so far away anymore. It was a bad joke. Here the foundations of all the world's knowledge and wisdom had been brutalized and put on display, like the dismembered body-part trophies a serial killer might hang on the wall.

Hume, Wittgenstein, Chaucer, Steinbeck, Wolf, Marx, Hardy, Pasternak, Hemmingway, Tzu, Confucius, Marquez, Plato, Russell . . . all of it hulled out and sanitized, now only so much otiose tree pulp and cowhide.

Except one. A single volume brimmed with the hearty sheen that comes with meticulous care, set in the center of them all, hidden, yet unavoidable. Its title seemed to leap from the shelf.

"*The Foundings*," I muttered. My heart skipped and my mouth ran dry. The fear that had been skulking under my skin leaped forth, and I set to pacing with a fretful grunt. It seemed I had been seeking a copy for countless days. And now, when I had almost given it up as hopeless, one had fallen within reach.

A thought occurred to me: had I concocted this visit on the pretense of cajoling Ma, while subconsciously hoping that the book would be here? It was hardly likely. How could I have guessed that I'd be left unattended within feet of it?

Yet now that I was here, it seemed right. The mansion folks' weakness, after all, was their bulletproof confidence that their subjects were so many helpless sheep. And now that my eyes lay upon it, I realized that I'd been looking for it from the start.

I started to reach out, then hesitated. The noise outside was closer still, mere feet away, a ruckus that spat ice into my veins. Would they notice its absence before I could escape? Had they left me here with the sole expectation that I would pinch it, like an inveterate addict, unable to help myself? In my mind's eye the door opened to reveal a troupe of waiting china dolls, all laughing with gaudy derision at the fool who thought he could stand against their divine leader.

My pacing was finally stilled by the sight of the great portrait hanging over the fireplace. At least ten feet high, alive with deep rouges and vibrant sky blues, it depicted a desert scene, complete with dunes half concealed by a vicious sandstorm. Upon a sandstone bluff, from the perspective of one who groveled at her feet, was a young woman dressed in a white robe. The painter had cast her in such a pall of dramatic beauty that her features seemed to glow with preternatural perfection, with cheeks like apples and skin clear as a baby's. Her long, flowing auburn hair and the hem of her cloak had been set billowing around her by the storm, and her eyes stared beyond the picture's frame with a diamond-hard countenance.

It was her. Mother Eden. Or how she had been, a long time ago.

Though there had unquestionably been flattering artistic embellishments, it was clear that the subject had been quite beautiful and, despite her stoic expression, almost innocent.

She couldn't have been much older than I was now.

I swallowed, overcome by a sudden certainty that I had to know the truth, whatever the risk. As the voices reached the other side of the door, I had just enough time to yank *The Foundings* from the shelf, stuff it into my jacket, and turn to face the portrait.

The latch clicked, the hinges squealed. Then, nothing.

I waited with gooseflesh crawling up my neck, exposed and defenseless with my back to my guest. I wasn't sure *The Foundings* had been secured, that it wasn't producing an obvious blockish shape mid-chest.

To just stand here facing away was altogether too suspicious in itself. But if I turned, the book might fall, tumble out onto the floor at my feet, and seal my fate.

After what seemed too long an interval, receding footsteps reached my ears—heels clacking on granite. The house servant had been wearing heels. That meant I wasn't alone; she had been dismissed by whomever I still had for company. I listened for movement—a rustle or breath sounds. But there was only the ringing silence.

"Ma?" I said.

No reply.

Turn around, I thought.

I ached to rush over and pull her to my chest. The child within cried out for its last known comfort. But our last meeting was too fresh in my mind. I willed myself to keep form and remember that until I could find a way to shake her from the talons of the mansion folks and break the spell they had over her, she was one of them.

"Ma, I've come to show you something. I know you might not want to see me, but it's important."

I paused and waited but still received no reply.

She's not your mother, a voice whispered at the back of my mind. *And she never will be again. Look at you, still clinging to the hope of rescuing her, like an eight-year-old. Face it: she's gone. She's happy here, without you.*

I touched a hand to my pocket, where the folded letter rested against my chest. "I have a letter for Father. I want you to see it."

Still nothing. I sighed and took a moment to still my trembling larynx. Adrenaline was making me stupid and clumsy in thought. What had happened to my surefootedness?

It had seemed so easy to stroll in here and flaunt my encoded communique under her nose when I'd been lounging in the bunkhouses. But now that I was here, among the wolves, the very air seemed to gnaw at me.

"Ma, talk to me," I said. "Just say something."

I'd grown cold to how things had been. The bunkhouses had given me a blanket to throw over my head and forget about it all, but now it was all flooding back. I thought I had accepted it all. I thought I'd learned to live with my new life. But I was wrong. I just wanted my mother back.

"Please," I said.

She wasn't going to answer. I stared into the fire and let my hand fall away from my pocket. Standing there with the flames licking up toward the gilded mantelpiece, I thought of the bunkhouses—of home. Time passed, and I began to wonder whether we'd stay standing like that forever.

Then, a voice: "Boy, do I hate that painting. Artist never could get my good side. Look at that nose. Like a damn powder puff."

My blood ran cold. The graveled texture of that southern drawl sent me spinning on my heels before I had time to think.

Mother Eden was standing just over the threshold, dressed in an elegant sequined gown that highlighted her regal posture. A lupine smile was spread across her lips. The face was a ruin of the flawless beauty of the portrait subject, shrunken and pale. But the cold steel of those eyes was just as intense, just as merciless.

Her smile widened when I failed to suppress a convulsive swallow. "I'm afraid your Ma ain't available to meet you for such an impromptu visit. She's got a previous engagement, I'm sure you understand. But if you need a message passed, I'm all ears."

My mind raced, yet my thoughts could gain no traction, crushed by the suspicion that Ma had refused to see me—I knew she was here, somewhere, I just knew. I had let down my defenses in front of this devil woman; terror swelled at the thought of having my letter confiscated before I could even mail it. All the while I also bore the nagging fear of my thievery being discovered.

The Foundings rested heavy in the folds of my jacket. Suddenly I imagined it wasn't quite as inconspicuous as I'd hoped. And I had whirled to face her. Had I dislodged it? I didn't dare check.

That predatory smile of hers grew wider still. "It sure is a shame you couldn't settle with us here. Your Ma's slid right in, making a big name for herself, in fact. Already a big shot. Got herself a nice following. Before long she'll be running the place!" She advanced into the room, tracing her fingers over the sumptuous fabric of a chaise longue. "Such a shame greatness like that don't run in the family."

She eyed me with a victorious glint. There wasn't going to be any letter delivered. Most likely, anything I mailed would end up hanging like a trophy over her bed.

I said nothing, just kept circling the room, passing inch after inch of extravagant luxury. It was too much, after the raw simplicity of the bare bunkhouse walls—too much color, too plush an image, too fine a cultured splendor. I was drowning in it.

Mother Eden had given up the chase. Standing with her hands planted on a thick throw rug hanging over an oxblood wingback, she followed my progress as a lion watches a panicked gazelle, that immobile smile etched into her granite wrinkle-ridden face.

"Don't go thinking badly of us. I know it must sometimes feel that you got a bad run of luck, what with those pesky duties you keep getting lumbered with and being put in the . . . less plush environs we got to offer."

Bunkhouses. They were the bunkhouses. She knew their true name just as well as I did. Who was she trying to fool?

"You all right, dear?" A twinkle of joy flashed behind the faded silver sheen of those predatory eyes. "You look a little peaky."

I looked down at my hands and saw that they were twisted into bone-white fists, shaking and gnarled, and thrust them in my pockets.

Bunkhouses. What was wrong with saying it out loud?

But by not saying it, it rang louder in the air around us than if she had bellowed into my ear. Another jab, another bamboo shoot pushed under my fingernails.

Her mouth said: "But things turn around. You never know what might happen tomorrow." Her eyes said: *Look what I did to you in just a few short months. And there's nothing you can do about it.*

"One piece of advice." She ran her fingers sensually

through the soft tufts of the throw, and a little note of coquettish satisfaction escaped her throat. My skin crawled at the sound of something so sexual emerging from such a wrinkled creature.

I wondered how many men had fallen under her spell when that body had been abound with youthful vim and bounce and those wasted hips had been rounded and full. Judging by the portrait over the fireplace, I bet she'd had everything that stood up to whizz wrapped around her little finger.

Even now, she batted her lids at me, and incredibly I felt a stirring in my gut as my body responded. There was still a glow about her, beneath the liver spots and whitened masses of loose skin. "Those who get along often find their luck changes, sometime overnight."

Luck [Eden-Speak]: Reward for selling one's self to the devil.

The stirring in my gut was moving south. Unbelievable.

What kind of monster was she?

I forced myself to keep moving. "Don't bother. I'm fine where I am."

She shrugged as though my words were irksome flies alighting on her shoulder. "Just friendly advice, is all."

"Does everyone get all this advice?"

Something far removed from the inner minx was hiding in the fold of that flawless gown, but I didn't know what it was. Pleasure? Fury?

"No, my dear," she said, tilting her head to the side. "I

gotta confess, you're something special. We don't get a lot like you around these parts. And the last of your sort to be among us . . . well, they haven't been around for a good long while."

I backed up, inching toward the door. "Guess I wasted a visit."

A real smile blossomed on her mouth. "Think on it, you hear? A mind like yours could do us a heap of good, if you could just see this place for what it really is."

I stepped out into the corridor, keeping the arm cradling *The Foundings* turned away from her. "I thought I did. Turns out all I knew is what it's supposed to be."

A nod. Nothing more. "Just think on it. We got a lot of years ahead. Don't go picking any sides just yet. Be a shame to wind up on the wrong one if anything ugly ever happened."

I glanced along the corridor to the ballroom, where elegant folks still floated back and forth amid classical oil canvasses and trays of canapés, then turned back to the puppet master. "I better get back to my cage."

I was too choked to say a word to anyone when I got back to the bunkhouses. Peters watched me try reading to the kids and looked only too ready to step in and kick up an impromptu game of tag-ball when I failed to utter a single cohesive sentence. When he left, guiding them away to the bluff out back, he offered a consoling smile before disappearing.

I loved him for that. But I was still shaken, more so than when I'd been outcast. When the fissure between us had still been narrow, Ma had been furious and disappointed with me, but she had tried to make me see sense, at least as she saw it. She had still cared.

But this was different. After the coldness of our time apart, she had been within earshot, within sight, maybe, and had turned me away. Worse, she had let her new master shoo me away in her stead.

I returned to my bunk as the game outside began in earnest. In my peripheral vision I caught the wary glances of a few stragglers scurrying away to join in, as though I had become ridden with some fresh contagious disease.

I let the last of them trail out and then slipped onto my bunk. I gazed at the cover of *The Foundings*. Without real interest I picked it up and flipped to the first page.

Later, it was hard to believe I could swallow up a book so fast, to feel every word cut a little deeper. It seemed like no time passed at all, yet what I learned changed everything. One moment I was moping in the pre-dusk haze; the next, it was morning, the book's back cover lay facing the ceiling, and my nerves burned like wildfire.

The Foundings read like a biblical epic from page one. From the darkness had sprung the One, the Savior. A young warrior princess who had led the Lost and Helpless from a state of damnation into the light.

It went on like that for a good long while. Drivel upon drivel. There was scarcely any mention of the UN or the other Projects. Eden Prime might as well have sprung from the desert, struggling to find its way. From the crowd had emerged a woman who had taken a straggling community on its knees and brought it to greatness.

And so it went.

Even when four hundred pages of dense text had whizzed by, specifics were a rarity, and the melodrama had yet to ease up any. But between the lines, there was a treasure trove of trivia—mashed and brutalized, maybe, but information all the same.

And along the way, I learned.

Extract #13
The Foundings

[**vs. 1**] *In the beginning there was sand and the sky. Through the ebb of eternity it had gone on unchanging, and men appeared only in passing, journeying through the blazing desert between far-flung lands.*

. . .

[**vs. 37**] *Change came to the world. The sky sagged with clouds and the sand knew rain, while the distant oases of men grew frail and wilted. And so the mightiest came together to bring life to the sands, sending their vanguard into the wastes to* *bring about new order.*

A handful were chosen from the world's heaving multitude, great men of science handpicked, and lesser to support them by games of fortune and chance.

[vs. 38] *These few Chosen were sent out under the sun's fire, and there they made a home between the dunes. Elsewhere, other islands of mankind's great nations sprang forth upon virgin earth and pushed back the coming damnation.*

. . .

[vs.50] *And for a time it was good.*

. . .

[vs.63] *Dates did spring from the earth, and channels brought water and new life to where there was none. Plenty befell those wise souls who looked inward and kept their own house.*

. . .

[vs.66] *The old metropolises did decry their own decadence, yet damned they stayed, and the great plagues and droughts of the earth did strike down upon them, for their roots were fouled, and their bloodlines muddied by those inferior.*

. . .

[vs.70] *In time many islands of new life flourished, and among them was a shining star where the great Genghis had once ruled: Eden Prime, a beacon to which all others did rally.*

[vs.71] *Yet a plague slumbered even in paradise, for the chiefs of Eden were unwise and naïve. When kingdoms fell and blood was spilled and hungry heathens came wandering to pilfer and drain all that was good in Eden, they did welcome the Fallen with open arms.*

[vs.72] *While the Fallen did give their thanks, their thirst was unquenched and their greed only multiplied, as did their numbers. Soon great droves wandered the wastes in search of Eden, their ravenous mouths slavering and their eyes alight with envy.*

⁓

Pain in my shoulder.

A grunt. After a moment I realized it had come from my own mouth. I dropped *The Foundings* and blinked tears of exhaustion from my eyes. I was nearing the end of my second read through. A dark figure loomed over me, beating on my arm.

"What?" I managed.

"You didn't show for duty," Peters grunted. There was no sign of the understanding glint from the day before. Instead, he was harried, sweat-soaked and breathless.

I shook myself and stretched aching limbs, stretching fingers that had become no more than claws. "I'm sorry. I got caught up. You can get lost in this, really." I grunted, then murmured, "No wonder she has them all so hypnotized."

He fumed. "No, it's lunch break. I ran my ass off back to make sure you hadn't gone on some suicide run, and I find you here"—he spun on his heel and slammed both fists against the bunk frame, triggering a chorus of metallic squealing—"goddamn reading!"

"Did anyone miss me?"

"No. Not yet."

I sighed and lay back, on the verge of jumping off the sheets when my eyes fell on the book once more.

"Desh, move your butt! We got one rule to live by, and I'll be damned if I'm gonna let you break it. We do our duties, and they leave us in peace." A pile of my stinking garments showered over my ears, followed by the stinging slap of work gloves against my cheek. "Move it!"

Peters paced in a fit of frustration, which turned to bug-eyed speechlessness over the next few beats when I remained sedentary upon the mattress.

"Did you know her name was Olivia?" I said at last.

He started forward. I swear he meant to hit me. But something stopped him. Over what felt like minutes of silence so taut you could have plucked it and played a tune, his glare melted. "What're you talking about?"

"Mother Eden. Her name was Olivia." I flicked through the volume to a leaf I'd folded at the corner, one of many. "Page thirty-five." I hefted *The Foundings* up to shoulder height. "Full to the brim and spilling over with bullshit, but it's all in here."

"Desh, you can't be messing around too heavy with this crap. We can swallow you not being happy about the way things are, but you're liable to get us all put under the microscope if you go down this road."

"It's too late to turn back now."

Especially with what I know now, I thought.

I saw a scuffle erupt behind his eyes. His lids fluttered and his brows twitched. Then, slowly, he lowered himself down beside me, placing his hand on the page. When his fingertip brushed mine, I didn't pull away. "Tell me."

I talked, he listened.

Neither of us showed for duty that afternoon.

∞

I mailed my letter. I knew it was hopeless, but I wouldn't give Mother Eden the satisfaction of knowing she'd beaten me yet again. Peters and I showed for duty prompt and early from then on. We knew our day's absence hadn't gone unnoticed.

Nobody said anything, but I could feel distant eyes on us again. Had I been alone I might have slipped, but Peters kept me in check. At the same time, his vehement aversion to *The Foundings* began to ebb.

We met in the middle.

By day we played it safe, did our work, and watched for any scrap of useful information on our daily rounds. By night we studied *The Foundings*.

We cross-referenced the log. We eavesdropped on the

mansion folks' mindless chatter. We probed every elder under the bunkhouse roof, careful to keep under the radar. That didn't take much—the old-timers all but fought one another for a willing ear.

I stopped counting the days. For a while, I forgot about everything but gathering more intel. Piece by piece, prospecting like men panning for gold, we sifted out the lies.

⸎

"One question we haven't got a hope in hell of getting an answer to anytime soon," Peters muttered.

"Only one?" I grunted, hauling a sack of grass cuttings from the gutter. I already knew what he was going to say, but we had to keep our heads down during the day.

Also, the novelty of having someone, a kindred, had yet to wear off. I liked hearing him talk, simple as that. I wasn't alone after all.

"How did she get started? No offense, but Americans ain't . . . aren't . . . exactly the glittering angels they once was . . . were. Even when she first got here, she must've been just another face."

We both hauled rotting plant matter onto the Beetle's back. We were on garbage duty again.

He looked over his shoulder to check that the others were out of earshot. "How did she end up holding it all in her hands?"

I could only stare back at him and try to hide the secret

relief swelling inside me. The danger of our collusion seemed dampened by his every word. Not because of what he said but because of how he said it. His southern accent was fading. It was a long way from being gone, but his face often creased into lines of concentration, squashing the affected Texan drawl. Underneath, I thought I could hear his natural accent returning.

I'd never asked where he was from. South American definitely, but probably from the richer northern states—Brazil, Columbia, maybe Belize. And that in itself stabbed at me like a fiery dagger—that he might have hailed from one of the new superpowers. His people were the twenty-first-century gold-standard citizens, holding all the keys, all the money, all the power. He could have been in the upper echelons of the mansion folks without lifting a finger if he'd but played along.

Yet here he was, reeking of moldy leaves and two-day-old sweat in the desert sun.

I never answered his question. How could I?

There wasn't a shred of evidence to tell how a low-caste runt from the deep woods of East Texas had poisoned the well of what could be one of the civilized world's true hopes. Not in *The Foundings*. Not in the log. Not hidden in words of gossip or the memories of the most ancient old-timers.

It had been all but wiped clean from the pages of history.

"You see it now, don't you?" I said.

"What?"

"That we have to do something. We can make a difference. This can't go on."

He was quiet for a while. "I don't know. You've shown me a lot lately, Desh. Pulled all the wool outta . . . out of . . . my ears. But we can't do anything about it. It's just as dangerous as ever."

"That's why we have to do something. This can't go on. This isn't a life."

"We gotta . . . we have to . . . make one. I saw you before. You can be just as happy in the bunkhouses as the rest. You just have to—"

"Forget? Give up?"

"Adjust."

I threw a bag into the Beetle with a curse, and something made of glass shattered. People never bothered to separate their cuttings properly. It was beneath them. "I can't. I thought I might be able to, but I'm never going to just lie down and accept any of this. And I know you can't either, not anymore."

"I don't know, Desh. I just don't know."

I watched his flickering brow carefully and decided to let it go. Grumbling, I climbed into the Beetle in search of broken glass.

We decided that our time was better spent worrying about something more immediate. There were a dozen other riddles clamoring for our attention. We worked without a word for the rest of the morning, heads down, thinking hard.

A hundred bags of refuse passed under my eyes, and the thick muscles of my arms thrummed with a steady burn. How hard they'd become. How calloused my hands. Not boy's hands, not the hands of a nerdy introvert. They were man's hands.

Midday became early afternoon, and we ate up the miles round the Project's edge until the heat became too much. The day was hot even for Eden, blistering, in fact. The air undulated close to the ground, smearing the desert into a rippling medley of yellows and browns and blinding blues.

We took shelter under a date palm, sweat streaming off our backs, our necks gritted with salty residue. I fought off a giddy spell and gulped water until I could see straight again.

A few others had taken shelter elsewhere, under awnings and down alleys. But the majority were slaving away with only more fervor than usual, determined to be good citizens.

Peters wobbled to his feet to join them, but I guided him back to the palm's trunk with a firm hand. A week before, he would have fought me to the ground to get out there and push himself until he hit the dirt. Now he just laid there, brows furrowed. Twitching every now and then, a part of him clearly wanted to stand, some reflex action at work, the result of long years of servitude.

His grip was almost too hard, a desperate clasping. My

desire had grown restless and unyielding, and each night I lay awake thinking about him, wondering if he thought of me, too.

In any case, something had awakened in him. *The Foundings* had changed him, more than it had changed me.

We sat recovering for a few minutes, swigging water and blinking the stinging sweat from our eyes. Even when the others seeking shelter lost their nerve and went back to work, we stayed in the palm's shade. We received no shortage of derisive stares from those throwing all they were worth into loading the Beetle.

Then a shadow fell across us and Peters was on his feet. I peered around his hip to see a dignified Indian man in his mid-fifties. His eyes were dark, shimmering slate and his jaw thrust out a surprising distance from his skull. Dressed in the standard white robes of a Project citizen, his status couldn't have been clearer. He was not a mansion denizen, but he was a privileged superior, to be sure.

He clutched a bag of garden waste. His stare cut through the air like a honed blade.

I sensed Peters wince.

"Sahib," he muttered and gave a small bow.

"May I ask what y'all are doing on my lawn?" the man said delicately. Each syllable lacerated my ears. For a man no larger than either of us, his certainty of dominance was jarring enough for my inner primitive to accept it out of hand. He might as well have been twenty feet tall.

Still, I wasn't about to move on in any hurry. I was willing to keep up my duties to stay out of trouble, but I wasn't going to get myself killed hauling trash.

Peters, however, was already stepping forward, shoulders hunched. A part of me died, seeing him like that, groveling out of habit like a whipped animal. All sense of his newfound defiance had melted away in an instant. The Texan drawl spilling from his lips was butter thick. "Lemme take that for you."

The man held the bag out of reach with a lazy sweep of his arm. "I asked what y'all were doing on my property."

I stood slowly, taking in our surroundings with fresh eyes. I hadn't realized how much ground we'd covered over the morning. If I'd known that we were stopping in so affluent a neighborhood, perhaps I would have sought a more inconspicuous rest spot. But I had been near delirium. I wasn't sure I would have noticed a herd of elephants on parade.

The others had thrown themselves back to work with renewed zeal, intent on impressing the ruddy-faced citizen. The stink of their thoughts hung heavy in the air: "*Show your worth, move up the ladder. Become a citizen!*" Mother Eden's propaganda from the evening broadcasts.

They'd never be citizens. They were marked. If they slaved away every day until they hung in tatters, the most they would ever achieve was a few more spells in the newcomers' district.

Peters's mouth hung ajar. A pained noise escaped his throat as he grasped for words that danced out of reach.

His tortured eyes darted to mine. In the end all he managed was to reach for the bag once more.

The man simply held it higher aloft. "I'm. Waiting." His acidic tone sent Peters flinching several inches closer to the floor.

A few of the others, despite themselves, had stopped to watch. The man ignored them—as always, the vermin of the bunkhouses were invisible from the astral plane of the Enlightened Citizen. It was only Peters and I who had become suddenly visible. "Pardon me for saying, gentlemen, but I'm not sure lazing around on my lawn is the best way to get your duties done. Maybe y'all had best get to clearing up all this mess. We can't have dirty streets now, can we? Would be bad for everyone. A good citizen would be glad to do his part."

A leering smile had grown on his lips. He watched us with those shimmering-slate eyes as he waited for a reply, a coiled viper ready to strike.

I cleared my throat. Those eyes turned on me, threatening to pierce my skin, but I held his gaze, circling around Peters. The man made to pull the cuttings farther out of reach, but I seized the bag and pulled it from his grip. Just short of violent, nothing he could use against me. "The sun isn't safe. It wouldn't do any good for tomorrow if we roasted ourselves today," I said, finishing up with a curt, "Sahib."

His lip curled. "I know you," he said. "One of our newest arrivals, am I right? You've made quite a name for yourself, son." The threat was veiled in words only; his face contorted into an ugly sneer.

I didn't reply, just took the bag and walked over toward the Beetle. I made a point to keep pace as I left the shade and the sunbeams struck the back of my neck, puckering the skin and sending fresh sweat gathering on my brow. "Thanks for your hospitality. The shade is most appreciated. My friend and I will be moving on, now. Duties to fulfill, you understand."

"Of course."

Peters was nodding, stumbling off the lawn. He'd only taken a few steps when the man's voice filled the air once more. "Wait."

I turned on my heel. Peters was being beckoned by the steady upward curl of the man's index finger.

Not good. My guts tightened as I locked eyes with Peters, who had been so close to the curb. Forlorn, he locked eyes with me, but I could only look on as he turned on his heel and returned to the shade of the palm. "Yes, Sahib?" He clutched his gloves in both hands, kneading the leather with nervous fervor.

I yearned to rush forward and pull him away, the same impulse that provokes one to save a moth from incinerating itself upon a scalding bulb. But I didn't move an inch.

This was something he had to deal with on his own. This was his fight. Meanwhile, the others kept up their merciless pace, wheezing and panting, moving away down the street, leaving us behind. I bet half of them would have heatstroke before the hour was through.

I stood in the middle of the street and watched. Whatever happened, I decided I wouldn't interfere.

"Do I know you?" the man was saying. His tone made it clear what he thought of Peters: shit on the polished heel of his elegant loafers.

"No, Sahib."

"I thought not. But may I be so bold as to make a request? One citizen to another?"

Peters hesitated but nodded. "Of course, Sahib."

"My daughter asked me an important question this morning. She asked why some people always end up manning the control stations, why some are always getting rest shifts, and why others always seem to be collecting everyone's garbage."

Silence exploded across the lawn, striking me full in the face, stretching out that long moment before he continued in the same serpentine sibilance. "Course I told her just how it's all down to fair chance. We're all in it together. It's important for the young'uns to know that, don't you think?"

"Yes, Sahib," Peters muttered. I imagined the same images were flashing through his mind's eye as those passing before mine: the dirt-stained faces of the kids back in the bunkhouses, skin and bones bound in faded tatters of cloth.

Then the man gestured to his living-room window, through which a watchful pair of eyes in a plump brown face observed them. From the chubby earlobes, half obscured by plaited locks of shining black hair, were a pair of diamond earrings. The girl couldn't have been more than eight.

Her father waved to her with a cheerful smile. Rows of perfect white teeth glared out between the depths of a well-groomed beard. "But she's set on pressing me for answers. She's no dummy. Of course we're all equals here, of course we are! But some just belong in certain places. Don't you agree?"

Equals [Eden-Speak]: Wretched drudges and their magnanimous masters.

"Yes, Sahib."

"We all have our lots in life."

Peters's voice, tiny, hardly there. "Yes, Sahib."

"That's why I need your help. She's so young, she hasn't the years to understand. She needs to *see* something real, see what it means to have our places here." He stepped forward with hands clasped, back arched some. "If you'd be so kind, would you grant me one favor, for my little girl's sake?"

I couldn't bear to watch, but there was no chance of turning away.

"Of course, Sahib." Peters nodded. "Anything for a citizen."

"Kiss my shoes."

A second wave of silence rumbled in my ears, louder than the first. A heady punch of disgust flooded my head as I watched Peters meet the man's gaze. He vibrated in a full-body shudder. "Sahib?"

"Kiss my shoes." The man's tone had fallen flat, dead.

"For my little girl."

Peters glanced at the pair of white orbs peering out, then turned back to the Sahib. They remained frozen in place for what seemed an age.

I willed Peters to sock the Sahib in the jaw and stamp on his balls until he cried for mercy.

But he wouldn't. I knew he wouldn't, because I could feel more than the little girl's gaze upon us. And with our fellow Beetle-loaders out of sight, that could only mean spying neighbors. This wasn't the area to make a stand.

Peters was a nobody. It had to stay that way. I doubted two bunkhouse men going against the grain would be tolerated for long. No, he had to stay invisible if he wanted the others safe, and I could tell by his rigid stance that he knew it.

The bearded man smiled. "If it'd make you uncomfortable, of course, I understand. Just a friendly request, is all."

"No, no." Peters's voice was thick, as though his tongue had grown too large for his mouth. Each word seemed to cling to his lips like molasses. "No, Sahib . . . I want to."

Then he began the long descent to his knees. I keened like a dog, watching him kneel on the manicured lawn and lean forward, his face scarlet and his eyes filled with murder.

The man looked in at his daughter and gave another wave, smiling and nodding down at Peters as though pointing out a delightful and instructive spectacle. The girl's giant peepers blinked once, stared for a good moment longer, and then vanished from the window.

"There, now," the man said, "that's mighty fine of you, sir."

Peters stood without a word, somehow salvaging an admirable amount of dignity while keeping his eyes on the ground.

The man nodded. "You be about your business, now." He turned and strode back toward his front door. Over his shoulder, he threw a last word over his shoulder, laced with venom: "*Citizen.*"

He disappeared inside and slammed the door.

Peters waited several moments and then sagged. His breathing labored, his jaw pulsating, he turned on his heel and made his way out of the shade of the palm, joining me in the sunlight.

We turned and followed the Beetle's trail in silence. There was nothing to say. For the rest of the afternoon we worked in the sun with everyone else, risking sunstroke and not caring. Stony faced and hunchbacked, Peters didn't show a sign of life until the evening gong announced the end of duties.

He volunteered to wheel the Beetle back to her charging station over by the dumping ground. I rode shotgun. The others had stumbled off in search of the bunkhouse by the time we parked, and the engine died with an electric whir.

We sat watching the sun fall from the cloudless sky. "I'm in with you until the end," Peters said finally.

I nodded. Another minute of silence. We need to get a message to the outside."

"I thought you sent your letter."

I grunted. "I'm not holding out any great hope. Anyway, that's not what I meant. We need something more direct. We need to find out how they're duping the UN."

"That won't be easy, Desh."

"No. No, I think it might get us both killed. Maybe a whole lot of other people." I paused, waiting for him to object, but he didn't. I swallowed. He wasn't going to be there to check me anymore. There was nothing to hold me back. "That's not all. I need to get into that bunker out by the fences. The guards. There's something about them. The only problem is there's no way to get within a hundred yards of them."

Peters turned to me. "That ain't true." His speech was caught in purgatory between a Texan drawl and a warm South American lilt. "Remember the other bunker? The clean room with the tubes?"

I blinked. "What about it?"

"Come on, Desh, you know as well as the rest of us there's something wrong with that place. Loading up all those psychedelic chemicals . . . gave me the creeps."

"So?"

"So, I'm betting those tubes gotta go somewhere."

I looked out through the windshield again in the direction of the fences. "What do you have in mind?"

Peters wiped his lips. I bet the taste of that son of a

bitch's loafers would never leave his mouth. "Easy. Just wait until the duty rolls around."

"And then?"

"Then we tear this fucking place apart."

❦

Extract #14
The Foundings

[vs.112] *In time the gates of paradise were barred by the churning droves, and the Chosen of Eden did suffer hunger and thirst of their own.*

[vs.143] *And so the shining star's radiance withered, and discontent reigned. Time passed, and the droves at the gate grew bold, but the fools at the helm of Eden's destiny took no heed and gave that which they did not have to give.*

[vs.144] *Yet all was not lost, one among the lessers' ranks was wise and saw the forthcoming doom. A young maiden from a fallen nation of states united in centuries past, Olivia Bateman. She passed unseen under the leaders' gaze and drew fellow citizens with minds untainted to her side, and over time their influence grew across Eden.*

[vs.156] *The naïve leaders of Eden drew*

inward and grew jealous of the wisdom of young Olivia. Soon their ranks were closed, and those who sought to right their wrongs came to know them as the Syndicate.

[vs.159] *As Olivia and her faithful companions were wise and merciful, there was a time when they went to the Syndicate and begged them to see the light and to guide Eden back to strength. But the Syndicate looked only outward, blind to the woes of their flock, corrupted by compassion and sympathy for those who destroyed themselves.*

We lucked out the next day in stopping for lunch outside Ma's old workplace again, parked in the shade of the same alley. I knew I was going to try for breaking in again before Peters had even cut the ignition.

I was going deeper. I was getting answers if I had to drag them into the light kicking and screaming. If there were labs in there, I wanted to know just *why* I wasn't cut out to chip in. If a thousand Einsteins slaved away down there, then fine; I'd be happy to work on the Beetle for the rest of my life, and I'd be all too happy to have them put up in the mansions if it meant all that space and luxury gave them just one more idea, that little boost that could make all the difference.

But so far all I'd seen was a bunch of lazy folks in blue

robes coasting along with non-jobs, and those in white . . . well, I'd never actually seen any of them do anything.

I feigned a dizzy spell and jumped out around back before Peters could say a word. I didn't think he'd disagree that we needed to know what was inside, but I couldn't risk him trying to stop me.

I slipped out of the alley in the shade and crossed the street, glancing every which way until I was secure behind the fire door Ma and her friends used on their break. I'd driven past while on garbage duty often enough to know when they would file out, giggling and gabbling. They sent the door banging back on its hinges right on cue, oblivious to the world, and then I was inside.

White everywhere. I'd forgotten how white.

I didn't waste a single second, not this time. I ran down the corridor on tiptoes and was about to search for a stairwell when I peeked into the surveillance office and saw it was empty. Flinching and sweating, but still too pissed off to stop, I slipped inside and jumped into one of the swivel chairs, taking in the monitors papering the entire wall.

I swept my gaze over every one of them before I realized I was wrong; the monitors didn't quite cover all of the Project, after all. None of them showed a single image of the bunkhouses, nor Mother Eden's private mansion or the fences.

Bizarre. Why would they forgo installing surveillance in the very areas they would need it most. Surely they would keep tabs on potential dissenters amongst the proletariat, as much as they would keep watch over the Project's perimeter?

I stared at each feed until overcome by fear of discovery, and then rooted around for anything else of interest. It didn't take long to find a data terminal, the layout shockingly pedestrian. I guessed most of the blue cloaks were middle-aged and wouldn't be savvy with the modern sprawl found on HUDs; they'd be stranded in the yesteryear world of primitive touch devices.

I navigated to the "Archives" folder and began rooting through an index of thousands of video files, frustrated to find them marked only by alphanumeric designations. I clicked the first few, but they were only a few seconds of footage, mostly of unidentifiable silhouettes walking the streets at night. Scrolling through endless meaningless files, I had only their creation dates to go by. Eventually I started clicking at random, staggering each by a few months.

As my concentration began to wane, I struck lucky on a recording made three years before my arrival.

I looked down on two women being recorded simultaneously in different rooms, the separate feeds splitting the screen down the middle. For a moment I thought they were actually recordings of the same woman at different times, but then I recognized the china-doll twins. It was some feat of imagination to accept it was really them, but there was no denying it, either.

They looked so young, and feminine, and afraid. Their faces were both wet with tears, their cheeks pinched into crimson grimaces of terror, their red and blonde locks tussled and matted. They couldn't have been further removed from the hulled-out manikins that haunted the Project's streets today.

A calm, emotionless voice spoke out from offscreen. "Helen," from the left speaker, then from the right, "Patty." The two girls looked up with identical expressions of venom in their eyes. The same calm voice continued, Mother Eden's voice: "I just can't understand why you're being so disagreeable around town, darlin'. Things are the way they are for a reason, and they ain't gonna change any time soon. You best just make the best of it, help us make the world a better place! Your sister's already realized the truth for what it is." Both sisters twitched and cried out, blind to each other. "Come, child. Join us."

Both screamed as one, "I'd rather die!"

Mother Eden, still offscreen, sighed. "Take her back to her cell. We'll pick it up tomorrow."

The recording ended there. I immediately scrolled farther through the archive, clicking away, looking for more entries of the twins, but all I got were duds.

I made myself step away from the terminal and head back out into the corridor. I glanced around to make sure I was still alone, then delved farther into the building until I found a stairwell. The door squealed from misuse. I descended the dust-covered steps two at a time.

So there had been others. The secret log pages weren't the fantasy of some paranoid scribes, after all.

Somehow it felt like the biggest secrets would be the

farthest underground. I kept going until I dared descend no farther and threw myself against the nearest door. It crunched in protest, but after a few persistent impacts, it shunted inward. I took a deep breath and dashed through. Stale, dusty air swirled around my head, and I squinted until I'd adjusted to the scant light.

I was in a huge white space, maybe the size of a football field, stretching away into blackness. Before me were workbenches laden with vials, culture banks, centrifuges, animal enclosures, terminals and monitors, 3D printers and wall-screen visualizers, and mazes of ceiling-high blocky towers that I guessed were gene sequencers. It was a genetics lab, for sure. But dust lay over everything, and the whole place had the feel of entombed decay about it.

Every door I'd passed on my way down had had the same rust around its frame. If every floor was as large as this, there were miles of labs down here. At least, there had been. This room hadn't been used in many years.

A clatter rattled down from far above my head, echoing off the far wall. Lunch break was over, it seemed. My pulse stepped up as I turned and headed back to the corridor and up the stairs, kicking dust over each step to smear my prints.

All the while, my mind turned over. The lab could have put hundreds of scientists to work with all the equipment they'd ever need. The propaganda had been fond of parading the research being funded: energy, hydroponics, genetics, antibiotic, life extension, carbon trapping, solar efficiency, fusion . . . If there really had been labs for each one, Eden Prime would have been the nexus of thousands of researchers' work.

"What the hell happened here?" I whispered. "What did you do to this place, you bitch?" My voice bled into silence amid the concrete stairwell.

I reached the white corridor once more, waited until the distant mumbling had trickled away into the surveillance room before running once again on tiptoes. I slipped outside and made a point to keep walking right out into full sunlight as though it was my rightful place to do so.

I refused to glance over my shoulder, just in case there had been some security measure designed to pick up on suspicious terminal activity. I half expected to be tackled to the ground and couldn't help but tense my shoulders against the coming impact. But I reached the other side of the road and headed into the alley.

When I jumped back into the Battle, I could tell by the look Peters gave me that he knew where I'd been. He kept quiet, lest the guys hanging on the side of the Beetle overheard, and we went through the motions for the rest of the workday. Even when we got back to the bunkhouses, we stayed quiet, cooking around the fire and reading from the log to the kids. After lights out, once the snoring had started in earnest, he whispered, "So what's the deal?"

I let my thoughts percolate for a while to the tune of the crickets outside. "There have been others just like us. Plenty, I'm sure. They turn them, down there underground." I paused. "I found the labs, too. Gathering dust. This whole place is a front."

"Anything we didn't know?"

I turned onto my side, catching the whites of his eyes in the gloom. Strange that there had been no surveillance in the bunkhouses. I couldn't make heads or tails of it. But the fences, maybe there was something there. The surprise body-moving duty we'd had danced in front of my eyes.

I sat forward when a memory of our duty in another bunker, one all too similar, jumped into my memory. "That bunker we worked in, with the tubes. There weren't any cameras in there, either. There's something up with that. It must be important, somehow."

Peters grunted. "Lucky for us, we'll be right back there soon enough. Perks of having a rigged lottery."

Our plan was twofold.

First, we had to get back into that bunker. How we'd go about following those pipes was something we were going to have to work out on the fly. Getting in there was all we could aim for.

Second, we had to get news about whatever we found out to the masses.

I toyed with the idea of forming an underground resistance. It was a romantic notion, and it stuck fast to my thoughts like a limpet for days. But as soon as I voiced it to Peters, I knew just how terrible an idea it was.

From what we'd gathered, there had been such things before. The log hinted at a few forming over the years, and *The Foundings* spent a whole chapter on Mother Eden's triumph over the Syndicate. She'd be waiting for signs of it, and I was willing to bet we'd all disappear overnight if she so much as caught a whiff of a brewing brotherhood.

We couldn't risk it. We were on our own.

Like Peters said, all we had to do was wait.

～

Extract #15
The Foundings

[vs.177] *While the last of Eden's wealth was spent and desperation took root in the souls of its good folk, they turned to Olivia and begged her to purge their crumbling paradise of foolishness, and those closest to her—her inner circle—soon became trusted disciples, and they too spread her message to the masses.*

>

[vs.178] *And so Olivia and her disciples took the only course of action left to them, and after a single night of revolution, the sun rose on a new Eden free of the Syndicate's poison. Eden's gates were scoured clean of the wandering droves, who became one with the desert and were silenced.*

[vs.179] Such was her wisdom that the leaderless people of Eden demanded Olivia take the Syndicate's place and guide Eden back to its true purpose. Under her watchful gaze, Eden's strength returned. In time, folks flourished once more, and hunger and sickness became unknown to even the lessers.

[vs.192] Olivia saw that preserving Eden's true mission required an end to the meddlings of science, and saw to it that Eden respawned without interference. Such was her success and so great was the bounty as consequence that the people recognized her divine place as leader.

[vs.200] So it was that the Syndicate was vanquished, the endless droves were returned to whence they came, and Olivia Bateman was placed up on high by those who saw her infinite wisdom. From that day, she was known as Mother Eden, and for the many years since, all has been good in the land.

We went back to work for another two weeks without further development. You could almost say things went back to normal. But not quite for Peters. Something had changed in him.

"You gotta stop studying that thing," Peters said.

I closed *The Foundings* with a snap, sending a puff of

dust sailing from my bunk. "Good literature is hard to come by."

"So's good toilet paper."

Fresh guilt grimed my insides. When I'd arrived, he'd been happy. He'd had a place in Eden, even if it had been at the very bottom of the pile. There was bliss in ignorance, after all.

But now he was different. Bitter, humiliated. It was evident in the way he carried himself, the twitch in his brow. He'd stopped playing with the kids. A great swell of pity choked me up when the morning duty bell shrilled and I had to watch him struggle out of bed like an arthritic pensioner.

But there was no sense in the guilt. The same thing would have happened to him if I'd never come here. Maybe he wouldn't have been conscious of the sheer ugliness behind the Sahib's act, but was that better? For him to have remained a catatonic herd animal for the rest of his days?

It didn't matter, in any case. What was done was done.

"I'm serious," I said. "This thing reads like a goddamn fairy tale. Rose-tinted fancy. I can see how they all believe it. All you need is a wad of wool pulled over your eyes, and it's all smooth sailing."

I'd already opened my mouth to continue when Peters stole my words. "We're like children," he said. He was laid flat out on his mattress, arms folded behind his head, staring at the rusted iron of the bunk over him. "So long as Mother Eden plays the part, taking care of all of us, none of us have to bother with a single thought. Just sweet lullabies, like the one in your hands."

I blinked, taken aback. "You talk like an English Lit student."

"Who says I wasn't?"

What did I know about him, anyway?

Not a whole lot, actually.

"What the hell happened to you?" I said.

He frowned. "What are you talking about?"

"When I got here you were ready to lie down and take whatever came your way, to let anyone walk all over you." I flailed, fingers curled into talons. "I almost thought you were happy." I paused. "I thought you were an idiot."

Peters didn't smile. "It's a long story."

"We've got time."

He shook his head. "Desh, I was hiding. And now I'm not. You brought me back, and I'll thank you to my dying breath for that, but some things haven't changed. And one of them is this: in Eden, the past stays in the past."

"What's that supposed to mean?"

"As much as it might shock you, you're not the only one with family troubles." There was a trace of bitterness to his voice. I recoiled, a trifle wounded.

I reached out for him. I needed him now. I didn't care what Mother Eden did. There was no point pretending we could ever have anything real, anything romantic, but I wouldn't deny myself any longer.

But he backed away, his frown deep. He sat up and swung out of his bunk and walked away along the aisle, heading for the door.

He had almost turned around the corner when I called out, "Bullshit." I had no idea possessed me, but suddenly I'd lost all control. I was on my feet, fists bunched.

Was I angry at him? No.

But the words came flying out nonetheless, laced with acid: "You're on a revenge kick. I might not be fighting just for some fancy ideals, but at least I admit I'm fighting to get my Ma back. You . . . you're fighting for someone just as much as me. Sound like somebody leaving their baggage in the past to you?"

He paused but didn't turn around. We stood in silence while the others cowered in shadow. Eventually I stood slack beside my bunk, all the fight drained out of me. "I'm sorry," I said.

I saw his shadow pause just beyond the threshold. He grunted, then said, "Yeah."

After that, we read *The Foundings* together without fail.

We pulled our duty cards when Monday rolled around, and I cursed when I saw we were on sewer duty, out by the public parks. Public. I had to snort at that word. Lying out on the grass there was tantamount to painting a bull's eye on our chests. I threw my card into the dirt, and ran a hand through my hair. It'd be at least another week before we had a chance at even one objective. And my letter to Father had gone unanswered. I hadn't expected anything else, but that did nothing to soften the blow.

Peters, however, barely reacted.

When I asked how he could be so calm, he turned eyes

the tone and flavor of tundra on me and said, "I'm in no hurry." There was no trace of the Texan accent now. His voice was thick with native twang, a curdling low-pitched growl.

I realized the balance of power between us was shifting. This was as much his vendetta now as mine.

⚬

Extract #16
BUNKHOUSE LOG

I knew something was wrong. But I never knew how bad it was until now. I don't know who'll ever read this; I can only hope somebody comes after me, like I came after the poor bastards who've written between these pages thus far. Allah, be merciful. It's hard to believe what they've written!

From what I can gather from the other entries, there's more to Eden's perimeter than they let on. Something to do with the fences, those bunkers, and the guards protecting us.

I don't have anything more. Maybe one day someone will.

– Nadia Hadad

⚬

I dreamed of home, a few hours caught somewhere between sweat-stained sheets and the kitchen back in

Fremont, eating dinner to the sound of sirens. Father was back there. I saw him at the same table, under the same flickering lights, staring across at two empty seats.

Then I was lying in the dark, the night stink of the bunkhouse filling my nose. Someone was lying down beside me, slow to keep the springs from creaking. It was too dark to see, but I knew the beat of those breaths, the rough touch of those calloused hands.

"Do you want me to go?" Peters said.

"No. Stay."

He settled and traced my jaw with his fingertip. We lay there like that until our skin had melded together from the heat and I couldn't tell where his body ended and mine began. Heat, hands, darkness. Our mouths met in a clumsy fusion, all chapped lips and sleep-dry tongues the texture of sandpaper.

I swallowed audibly.

He drew back, hovering over me. "You sure this is what you want?"

"Yes."

"What's wrong?"

"I'm scared," I muttered.

"Me too. I've wanted this, but couldn't bring myself to. But now . . ."

"I know." I took his hand and placed it against my cheek.

We might not get another chance.

Our lips met again. This time it was gentle and warm. Piece by piece, night clothes fell to the floor. My shaking fingers grew steadier. Soon it was his face in my hands.

For a brief while, I wasn't afraid. Then we slept, and I dreamed no more.

 espe

"Desh!"

I yelped as Peters jabbed me hard in the shoulder, shaking me from a sweaty, uncomfortable mid-afternoon nap. "Whassit?" I mumbled, blinking in the light.

He was standing over me, panting, a heady musk coming off him in waves. He was dripping. He must have run halfway across the Project. "I couldn't wait for the duty cards. I knew Anders had to hand them out this week, so I snuck out to grab ours off him at the depot."

I jolted upright and slammed my head against my bunk post with a resounding *gong*. Cursing, seeing stars, I slurred, "How could you be so stupid? What if somebody saw you out after curfew? How . . . you idiot!"

The giddy smile on his lips didn't shift an inch. He was waving something in front of my face. "It's on! It's on!" He kept saying it even as I pushed his hand away and swung out with a spate of cursing.

"Keep your damn voice down!" I hissed, gripping his sleeve. I dragged him jittering along the aisle, where we wouldn't be overheard. Then I rounded on him and blinked sleep from my eyes. "Now, *what's* on?"

"We hit the jackpot, Desh." His voice had leveled to a tenor that laid my annoyance flat on the ground. I locked eyes with the piece paper in his hands. I took it, studied the print in disbelief.

"You're smiling," he said.

I looked at him. "I bet." Then I looked back at the duty card, shaking my head. "It's too good to be true."

"Don't question destiny, Desh."

Who the hell speaks like that? I thought. *Peters, you stupid fool, you're a bona fide mystery. If only we'd met elsewhere.*

I wasn't about to question this, not now. It had been almost two months since we'd decided to go looking for answers. Over a month since I'd stolen *The Foundings*. And three weeks of slaving away at dead-end duties with eyes pressing in from all directions.

But now all that was over. Peters was right: we'd hit the jackpot. The card had all the names of the guys and gals in our bunkhouse scrawled in neat rows. Ours were beside one another, tagged dead center, next to the words "nutrition technician". The same duty we'd had a few weeks before, in the concrete bunker.

"We've got a lot of planning to do," I said.

Peters's face had morphed into the kind of expression I imagined Japanese kamikaze pilots had worn as they headed for Pearl Harbor. Dead, shark eyes, haunted by unfeeling determination. "It's time," he said.

I nodded, trying to ignore the upset in my gut, hidden behind a veil of excitement.

Only one thing bothered me: we alone were on nutrition duty; everyone else in the bunkhouse had been assigned garbage collection.

✳

Extract #17
BUNKHOUSE LOG

I guess I should write something between these pages, too. It might be the only record left of me after I disappear like the others. I'm pretty sure they'll be coming for me soon. It seems the others before me who realized the truth just stopped writing one day. The gaps in the dates are huge, sometimes years. I'm guessing a handful of people wake up and smell the bullshit every so often, and we vanish soon enough. Then Bateman's gestapo wait until the next troublemaker comes along.

All I have to add is this: the labs are a lie. The research being done here stopped years ago. The underground complexes are used for something else—the white-robes aren't working on anything to do with climate change or saving the goddamn world. They're up to something down there, and it stinks of danger.

I think it has something to do with the tubes. They're everywhere, but nobody knows where they go. Nobody that'll talk to me, anyway. The tubes might lead to the answers. If only I could get down underground, follow them . . .

It's not much, but it's something.

Incrementally, our knowledge might grow. Maybe one day one of us will benefit from these tidbits enough to make a difference.

But not me. All I can do is hide this log. Good luck, whoever you are. Know I was here.

- Huple Cartwright

I thought I was going to throw up my breakfast as we came in sight of the bunker. All my tough talk had evaporated into a shuddering medley of nerves and burgeoning diarrhea. It took an iron-hard squeeze on my elbow from Peters to shore me up.

"Keep walking, Desh."

"I'm fine," I muttered.

"You look green."

"I'm *fine*."

I expected him to pester me to the door, but instead his voice pirouetted into something frighteningly close to paternal. "Just take a breath. We're close now."

I glanced at him, ashen mouthed. He was at least a decade my senior, but I hadn't really noticed until now. I'd thought of him like my idiot little brother most of the time. Even a week ago I would have told him to shut the hell up.

Now those words hit me off kilter. Having him there made me better, stronger, a feeling my own father had never managed to inspire in me, decent a man as he had been. Peters was more than a friend, now. We were in this together until the end.

The big iron door was looming closer. We hushed up and fell into step with the others on nutrition duty.

None of them said a word or even acknowledged us. They were from the White-Picket District, after all, our social betters. It was early, and the duty was a dull one. To them, and everyone else, it was just another day. None of them knew of the riot tearing away at my insides.

We passed inside and began suiting up. My hands were shaking as we got to work, and Peters rightfully showed no mercy. He only had to pinch me twice, but my arm ached for a good while afterward. From then on we settled into a steady rhythm, heads down. The talk died down as the drudgery set in, and the hours ebbed at the usual snail's pace.

The screen beeped, I sucked up the correct liquid, and deposited it into the indicated tube. Repeat *ad infinitum*.

Where do you go? I thought in desperate agony. *I know you'll lead me to answers. Where do you* go?

The adrenaline remained in my system for over an hour, keeping my mouth dry and my mind hopping from disaster scenario to consequence. But even that excitement couldn't stand up to such repetition.

Beep, suck, plonk. Beep, slurp, plonk. Beep . . .

By the time our break came around, the lunch bell startled me from a reverie. I cursed inwardly, looking around in surprise, and found Peters's gaze trained on me, not three feet away. He was milling at his station as the others departed, making a big deal of clearing up a spill. He gave the tiniest nod.

I followed suit, fiddling with my pipette, acting as though the head had come loose. I shook all over but kept my eyes down, and sure enough everyone else filed away, hungry enough to be in a hurry but zombified enough to be blind to anything around them.

After the gushing of cleansing air cannons, a lot of grumbling and squealing of plastic against plastic, and finally the sharp *plunk* of the vacuum seal, there was nothing but the bare concrete walls and silence. We were alone.

For a moment I kept on fiddling with the pipette just in case someone came back; then I stripped off my helmet. Peters was already rushing headlong up the conveyer toward the tangle of bright tubes at the end, where they met a gap in the concrete and disappeared from sight.

I ran after him, cursing and stumbling as I stripped off the rest of the suit, and together we peered into the black hole. Such an unspectacular, utilitarian sight, yet behind it lay answers.

"How long, do you think?" Peters said, bending down to inspect the aperture.

The break was scheduled for half an hour, but I wasn't sure we had that long. As soon as the others had refueled and filled their lungs with fresh air, one of them was bound to notice we weren't among them.

"Twenty minutes, tops. Fifteen to be safe," I said. "We need to be walking out of here by then."

"Well, let's get on with it."

We settled down to peer into the hole, and for a full minute all we did was stare. Now that we were here, I wasn't sure what to do. I had assumed everything would make sense when this moment came.

What was I hoping for? A gold-plated scroll proclaiming Mother Eden's darkest secrets?

There had been plenty of daydreaming to lull me into a false sense of ease and security. But this was just a hole in the wall. We were going to have to go at least a little further. Maybe a lot.

Peters straightened up. I kept looking into the gap dumbly a while longer, hoping it might dispense pearls of wisdom. "Well?" I said. Time was already slipping away. We might not get another chance at this. "What do you think?"

Peters's foot flew from left field and collided with the gap. I winced instinctively, expecting to hear the cracking of bone.

Yet the only sounds were of crumbling plaster and Peters's satisfied grunt as his leg sank into the wall. I blinked as the perfect round hole was obliterated in a shower of fragments.

It *was* plaster! Or, at least, some brittle material blending with the concrete. A clever ruse to keep out prying eyes.

The pipes had to go somewhere, and pipes broke. Things went wrong. They would have needed a maintenance hatch. Why hadn't I thought of that?

A breeze colder than any air-con blustered out and lifted my fringe. Inside I could hear dripping water and the rumbling echo of shifting air that only comes with great underground spaces.

"Good thinking," I muttered as Peters hauled his leg back into view, sheer white and trailing a cloud of dust.

"Some of us aren't as blind as you."

"I see just fine."

Peters grinned, tearing away great chunks of the faux wall with another swing of his boot. "Not what I meant. You can't see the wood for the trees, bookworm."

I looked again, saw the hairline join where the strange substance blended with the concrete, and took a lump of it in my hands, tearing it clean away in a great strip. Maybe he was right.

A thought occurred to me. "What are we going to say when the others get back? I hate to say it, but they're going to notice."

"I'm making this up as I go along, chief," Peters said, bringing the hole to a size large enough to climb through with a final swift kick. "Your turn to have a bright idea."

I cursed as he stepped through. "We'll cross that bridge—"

"Uh-huh."

I ambled through the hole, gripping the cold curves of the tangle of pipes to guide me, and stepped forward into darkness.

"Where are you?" I said. My voice rang hollow and dead, echoing back from God-only-knew-how-far away. I sensed enclosing walls by the way those echoes barreled back from only dead ahead. I guessed it was some kind of tunnel.

"Over here." A few feet ahead. "It slopes down. It's gentle, but it's there."

I took a few steps and found that he was right. A downward gradient gave the smallest of nudges, like a fist pressed lightly into the small of my back. We both scuffed our way forward, careful not to stumble with the added impetus, and within a few more steps the light filtering in through the hole behind us dwindled to something akin to distant starlight.

Ahead, Peters wheezed in laughter. "Hey, maybe this goes all the way to China."

"Easy, boy," I said. "Keep your head."

The gradient flattened out after a while, and then we were hurrying at a trot. The pipes thrummed in my hands. It was pitch dark by now; we had only them to warn of an upcoming bend or corner. The last thing we needed was to crack our skulls by running headlong into a stone wall.

"Time's running low," Peters hissed. "We gotta hurry."

"Just keep going!"

"Got any bright ideas about explaining all this yet?"

"It'll come to me. Just keep moving!"

Panting, breathing in cold musty air, we hurtled along the tunnel, passing under the Project and all those lying, alabaster faces. It took the sudden end of the pipes to bring us to a stop. One moment we were going on as before, the next we were grasping thin air.

I dug in my heels and skidded to a halt before I could stumble into Peters. "Where are you?"

"Here."

"What the hell happened?"

"It just stopped."

"I know, but why?"

"I don't know." I could hear him feeling around. "There's nothing. The pipes just run right into the rock." The sound of flesh slapping wet rock filled the air. "There's no gap, nothing."

"What?" I gasped, staggering forward, groping until his hand caught mine. His slippery fingers brought me to the wall so that I could feel for myself. "There has to be something!" I said, scrabbling up and down. "There has to be." Panic reared its head, and before I knew it I was pounding uselessly on the rock, snarling. "Damn! *Damn it*! What's the point of the pipes don't go anywhere?"

"Desh."

"We have to get back; we'll be missed."

"Desh."

"I've got nothing, still, but I'll think of something on the way up—"

"Desh!"

"What?" I bellowed.

"The tunnel keeps going."

I sighed. "What's the point? The pipes end here."

"Do they? Why bother digging more tunnel if there's nothing else down here?" He paused and then said, "What do we have to lose?"

I didn't bother answering, just hauled myself up and fell into step with him. There wasn't time for wallowing or doubting. I just ran. There was now half an inch of water on the floor that made our progress all the more hazardous. I kept my hands held out every step of the way, waving up and down lest the walls converge on us or we came to a bend. Peters was ahead as before, and now his ragged breath sounds and the crash of splashing water were all I could hear.

We couldn't have had more than five minutes to get back. Not enough time to resurface if we turned back that second. To hell with it. Might as well write off the possibility of that. There was no going back now.

I was about to call for Peters to slow down when he started screaming. Terror gripped my heart as I ran into his back—his *lower* back. He had somehow been lifted three feet into the air. I gripped him around the middle, yelling, "What the hell's the matter?"

He writhed in my grip. Then he began screeching. "Desh, Desh, something's got me! Something's got me by the arms!"

Before I could reply, he started to move forward, nearly torn from my grip by an irresistible force. I tried to haul him back, but he kept on going as though my arms meant nothing. He had stopped screaming now, and the stentorian echo was beginning to die down.

As the chaos of noise gave way to grunting and some kind of mechanical whirring, I realized we were sliding at quite a pace along the tunnel. "What's going on?" I bawled.

Peters grunted. "Some kind of . . . metal grip wrapped around my shoulders!"

"Can you break out of it?"

"What do you think I'm trying to do?"

"Well hurry up, I can barely hold on to you. If we lose each other in here—"

"I know!" he roared, panting and thrashing above me.

My grip was slipping. I wasn't going to be able to hold on to him. "It's okay," I panted. "It'll be fine."

"Desh, don't let go. I don't know where this thing'll take me."

"I'll find you, just keep fighting it!" My hands stretched to the point of peeling away my fingernails, but I fought back the urge to cry out, pulling with everything I had.

Something solid met my shins with a stunning crack, and Peters was torn from my grasp. I crashed to the floor to find not stone, but something soft and yielding. I sank into a mass of what felt like cloth and leather, filling my nostrils with a rancid stench of sweat and something sweet yet rusty. Fighting in the dark, I scrabbled through an ocean of stinking rags, succeeding only in sinking further.

Peters's desperate calls were already growing distant. Try as I might, I couldn't gain even enough traction to lift my head clear and call out to him. Raw panic told me that I really might drown. Whorling in feral fury, I finally gave a final great heave and sailed through the air, landing with an unceremonious crunch on bare sandstone.

Blinding light flashed before my eyes and a wave of nausea put me in danger of a concussion, but I was on my feet before any ill effects could hit me. If I was going down, I'd get as close to Peters as possible.

Somewhere far away, a tiny voice, frighteningly childish: "Desh?"

"I'm here. I'm all right! Where are you?"

"Over here. Hurry. Desh, the light . . . the . . . what the *fuck* is this place?"

I skirted the mountain of rags carpeting the floor, toeing its edge with the cap of my boots, then took flight along the tunnel once more. I no longer had to wave my arms quite so wildly. Peters was right, there was light. Not enough to see by yet, but enough to push back total darkness. It was growing brighter with every step.

A distant and absurd part of me wondered what the others were thinking right now, back at their stations. Would they think us playing truant? Would they try to look for us? Maybe a snitch or two would report us. Maybe they wouldn't notice at all.

The light was still growing, a deep orange splashed against the slick brown walls, illuminating the way ahead. It seemed to be coming from the floor. Unencumbered by blindness, I started to sprint.

The pipes hadn't ended at the wall. I could see that now. In fact, they had snaked up to the ceiling and budded into an intricate web, densely woven over my head. The liquid was noticeably different even in this light, a lifeless brown so dark it looked almost sticky.

Peters had come into view, struggling like a bug trapped on a collector's pin. I had a sense of a much larger space up ahead, and Peters's renewed screaming sent a slick of apprehension spurting in my bowels.

"*What the*—" Peters screeched. "Desh . . ." He was blubbering. "Hurry. Hurry!"

My breathing ragged, my legs screaming, I slowly gained on him. The tunnel shrank back on either side as I entered a cavern the size of a football field. The walls were smooth and worn by time, the ceiling some hundred feet above my head. A dense network of chutes and glass tubes hung like a rusted chandelier from the concrete roof, surrounded by metal struts thrusting down from the surface.

After a moment's confusion I realized those struts were the base of the perimeter fence, cutting across the cavern. And the concrete was the foundation of the bunker where we had disposed of the insurgents. Now I knew where all those bodies had gone, for the chutes began directly below that concrete slab.

They had all ended up down here.

At the base of the chutes were dozens of mechanical arms set on overhanging rails, each tapering to mean-looking claws. One such pair of metal hands gripped Peters's shoulders, twenty yards ahead of me.

It held him fast in its clutches, but he had succeeded in wriggling free of one of the fingers. He was still being carried inexorably onward, toward a distant steel complex.

We were suspended twenty feet off the cavern floor by

a metal catwalk. Despite the adrenaline in my blood, the sight of what lay below us stopped me dead in my tracks. The pile of rotten rags I had collided with was but a pinprick, for clothing carpeted the entire cavern floor. Tattered and faded by long exposure to the sun, marked by streaks of dirt, I recognized the clothes of countless desert wanderers. All of it had grown sodden in the damp, half buried in lichen and mold. Endless thousands of coats, shawls, pairs of shoes, headscarves, shirts and trousers, piled so thick that not an inch of bare ground was visible.

Their owners were nowhere to be seen.

"Desh!" Peters bawled. He was farther ahead now, closer to the metal contraption I'd spied.

Smaller sets of arms had descended from the ceiling and converged on Peters. They were stripping off his clothes, dumping them with almost human distaste over their skeletal shoulders.

Peters didn't seem to notice. He was too busy fighting the claws on his shoulders. It wasn't until he was bare, and the last pair of miniature hands stripped off his underwear, that he yelped. A long, "Fuuu*uuuck!*" ricocheted throughout the cavern.

I set after him again, feeling unreality wrap closer around me. My footsteps echoed from afar in the great expanse, and I started choking in air that seemed alive with acrid bitterness.

It was as though a thousand slices of toast had been burned in there before the whole place had been sealed up, though the smell lacked distinctness. It was too clinical, too clean. Only the essence of ash itself remained.

I was within twenty feet of Peters. Then fifteen. Ten.

I leaped and caught him around the midriff, then we were both racing toward the complex ahead, a cast-iron cube with an ominous black doorway.

"Desh, I'm not—I can't . . . What the hell is in there?"

"Shut up and keep fighting!" The dark hole loomed closer. We made no progress.

"It's got me. I can't—" Peters gave a blood-curdling roar of frustration and then fell slack in the metallic grasp. When he spoke again, his voice had wilted to a toneless murmur. "You gotta let me go."

"Don't be an idiot. *Fight*, damn you!"

"You have to let go. If you don't, we'll both end up in there."

It might be nothing. It must just be a shed, cried a voice in my head.

It isn't, and you know it, said another.

"I won't!" I cried.

"Desh," Peters turned to look over his shoulder. His eyes met mine. "Let go."

Five feet.

"No," I said. My voice cracked.

His eyes glazed for a moment, then he delivered a sharp donkey-kick to my stomach. My lungs sandwiched together as all my breath came sailing out in a hoarse whistle, and my hands unclasped instinctively. I crashed to the floor just inches from the concrete, raising my head in time to see the darkness swallow Peters.

Then, with cruel speed, an iron door slammed down and sealed him inside. I staggered to my feet and threw myself forward, crumpling against the door. I sucked air, spluttering until I was strong enough to cry out. "Are you all right?"

His faint voice answered as though from the bottom of a well. "Fine. Can't see. The arms let me go, I can hear them moving away. They're leaving through some hole in the ceiling."

A moment later the arms came sailing from the top of the cube, rising out of sight.

"Can you see anything?"

"Nothing . . . wait. There's a vent or something to the right. Move around, we might be able to talk better."

I scrabbled around the catwalk until I came to the side of the cube. It looked just the same from this side as it did from the front, bar a grating set about chest-level into the wall. Peering in, I couldn't make out much of anything except brief glimmers of movement. "I see you," I lied.

A scuffling. "Yeah, I see you too. Sort of."

"What's in there?"

"Nothing. Just bare walls. The floor's all grating. And the walls are . . . crumbling. Just comes away in clods in my hands."

My throat quivered in disquiet, but I tried to keep my voice steady. "All right, forget about that. Just focus on getting out of there."

"Did you try the door?"

I shook my head even though he probably couldn't see it. "No chance of moving it. Hard iron. There must be another way out."

"Not that I can see."

I looked over my shoulder at all the clothes laid out far below us, Peters's now among them. Something bad was about to happen. I had to get him out of there. I hammered on the grill. "All right, enough playing. Get your ass out of there right now!"

His answer was flat and frank. "I'm open to suggestions, Desh."

My lips moved but no sound emerged. A rumble was building under our feet, and it seemed the cube's interior was growing brighter, the same orange shade as the light under our feet. "Just ... feel around. There has to be something!"

He didn't reply, but I heard the scratch of his fingers moving over metal. He went away, looping around until he was back in front of me. "Nothing." A pause. "It's getting hotter, Desh. I mean . . . hot."

I almost choked but wrestled myself under control. "What do you mean?" I already knew exactly what he meant.

"Hot." An unspoken understanding passed between us. It was an oven, and it was waking up. "The light's getting brighter. Guess I know what the grating is for. Fire's stoking."

I stifled a whimper and looked desperately at the iron cube, hoping that reality couldn't be so very cruel, that perhaps some trapdoor would appear from the ether. None did.

Peters was talking constantly, whistling in the dark. "The tubes are in here, Desh. They're everywhere, built into the walls. I think this is where they start. They're all covered in the crumbly stuff. Wait a second, let me get a better look—"

"Don't worry about that, just keeping looking for a way out!"

He ignored me. There was a horror in his voice so deep it seemed devoid of any emotion. "It's ash, Desh. I think I know where it came from. It's . . . people. All the people they've thrown down here. All the refugees." He didn't sound scared anymore, just toneless and detached, like a surveyor reporting on a housing project. "They let them come, they mow them down, and we mop them up and throw them down here. Then they burn them up and feed what's left into the pipes." He gave a bark of lunacy. "Why the hell would they do that?"

I was sucking air through trembling lips now. "I don't know what to do . . . tell me what to do."

"Nothing you can do, chief." He gave a small, wry laugh. "Luck of the draw. Mother Eden's philosophy. Seems the bunkhouse folk lose every time. You might even think the game's rigged."

We stood in silence as a clanking started up, inhuman and deep, while the orange glow grew brighter still. I could feel the heat now, radiating out through the grate. It must already have been over a hundred degrees in there.

Peters sounded fainter, too addled to be afraid. "Listen, I'll tell you what you can do."

I rested my head against the grate and let my eyes fall to a close, ignoring how the fins burned my forehead. "What?"

"Keep going. These tubes go somewhere. Find out where, and tell them. Tell the others. Tell everyone."

"I can't."

"You have to. If you don't, nobody ever will. It takes an asshole as big as you to rock the boat this far, but your kind are far between. Who knows how many people are gonna die if you don't tear this place down."

"I can't do it alone."

He gave a small laugh. "You've done all of this alone. I was just along for the ride. You opened my eyes again, Desh, and I'm not bitter about how it's ending. I wouldn't trade a minute of this for a lifetime under that witch's spell." He gasped, and I heard a clatter. I guessed he had fallen to his knees. "Now get going."

The clatter suddenly spooled up to a whine akin to that of a jet engine, and I leaped back from the grate. "Peters!"

"Bye, Desh."

The orange glow became a blinding medley of coronal inferno in a fraction of a second, and a wave of heat seethed through the grate. My left shoulder burst into flame as an arc of flame blasted out over the catwalk railing, searing my face, missing me by inches.

I fell back, rolling to put out the flames, screaming for Peters.

When it was over, the whine died down, the heat dissipated, and the cavern was deathly silent. After a full minute the iron door slid open, revealing nothing but walls studded with pipes, covered by a thick layer of fresh grey ash.

Eventually I stood up, alone in the great silent expanse. The roof over my head now seemed lower, looming, as though it would suddenly fall down on my head if it was but jarred. It was a long way back along the tunnel, and I wasn't sure I would make it even if I turned back now.

Who was to say I wouldn't get grabbed by one of the metal arms as well? There was no saying why I hadn't been grabbed in the first place along with Peters. And if I got back to the hole in the wall of the concrete bunker, what would happen then? What could I do to stop every one of the others running to Mother Eden's heels to turn me in?

Despite all that, I turned toward the way I'd come. I had to go back, even if it meant death, even if it meant being thrown into the flames or spending the rest of my life in a dungeon under the mansions.

Only the echo of Peters's voice stopped me. *"Tell the others. Tell everyone."*

I wasn't going to let him die for nothing. It was possible nobody had ever got this far before, and there was no guarantee any future newcomer could follow in my footsteps.

This might be our only chance. I had to take it.

I lingered a moment longer in silence, my eyes on the puffs of ash still falling away from the oven's grills, then I set off at a run along the catwalk, following the tubes.

The liquid was still a mucky brown, but it appeared to be growing brighter at each intersection with smaller tubes jutting from the rock. I recognized them as the very tubes being loaded with the chemicals by our coworkers up in the bunker. I had helped load these tubes, as had Peters.

I felt little of anything now. An emotionless pall had fallen over me. Or maybe I was in shock. Did it matter?

I kept moving until I left the cavern behind, following the tubes into yet another tunnel. This one began a steep upward gradient so great that I had to scrabble on my hands and knees. I felt the ache in my thighs, but it seemed distant, unimportant; the fire in my lungs and throat were all I had to remind me I was flesh and blood, a vital perspiring creature that lived and breathed.

Once this was done, whatever happened, happened. When it was done. But for now I would fight to the end. Mother Eden had played God long enough.

There was light ahead. No orange glow, but the white sparkle of purest daylight. I had been underground a mere half hour at most, yet I felt like a trapped miner surfacing after a month buried. I lapped at that sunlight, bathed in it, like a man dying of thirst in the desert.

The tubes shot out onto the surface ahead of me. Their destination was finally within my grasp. I put on a spurt of speed, and with a last ditch effort hauled myself over the lip of the tunnel and rolled panting onto a horizontal bluff, ragged and broken.

Tears erupted from my ash-streaked eyes. For a handful

of seconds, hysteria overtook me. I whimpered, yipped like a frenzied dog, and tore at my face in an effort to stem the fat teardrops. With supreme effort I expelled a short burst of breath and took control. There was no time for that. No more. I was so close.

I rolled up onto my haunches and blinked in the blazing sun. It was just after lunchtime; sweat popped out in beads on the back of my neck in seconds. The thick fresh air clutched at the back of my throat.

The sudden transition out into the heat brought nausea and memories of the iron oven with it, but I wasn't going to give in. I struggled forward, disoriented, until I gripped something metal and wiry. Sagging against it, I felt a lattice pattern press up on my cheek.

It was the fence. But before me was nowhere I had seen before. In every direction was ample screening provided by dunes, date groves, and rocky outcrops. Everywhere were half-cylindrical buildings that looked like army barracks, and the ground was of mud torn up into a ruin of tire tracks and meaty boot prints. Armored Humvees and trucks were parked here and there, and lounging around, shirtless, were the guards.

This must have been where they lived. The assembly of tubes headed straight into their camp's midst, fanning out and vanishing into each of the barracks. This was their terminus.

In times gone by I would have stayed here, canvased the place for an hour or so before considering the best way to sneak in. But not now. Like a thing possessed I walked in a crouch from the fence and made a beeline for the nearest of the barracks. Either I was caught, or I found my answers.

Emotion had abandoned me. I was a machine viewing the world from outside—though with a beating heart and a sweat-slickened brow—a spectator. Only a moment's hesitation stalled my progress when I reached the barrack's open canvas flap, and then I had ducked inside, not caring whether I'd been spotted.

It was empty. Two dozen steel-framed bunks of the same make as those in the bunkhouses—though sparkling new and free of rust—lined both walls, with a trunk at the foot of each, leaving a central gangway that led clear across to the other side. Every bed was neatly made, the sheets turned down, fresh and pressed.

Every compartmentalized personal space was identical, down to the smallest detail, just as identical as their owners. I felt my gaze drawn to the other end of the room, where the gangway ended, opening out into a small kitchen area, encircling a steel dining table and a few scattered chairs.

Upon the far wall was a bank of nozzles, like those at a gas station, set on extendable cantilevers. Leading into each one was a glass tube filled with brightly colored liquid. Below each nozzle was a stack of bowls and a rack of spoons.

Hypnotized, I approached. My feet weighed a thousand tons.

The nozzles swam closer, closer, and then I was

stepping around the table and taking in the maze of tubes converging from the walls. There were no cupboards, no refrigerators. No sources of food or water. Just the cutlery, bowls, and the nozzles.

It was food. The liquid was food.

Countless desert wanderers, nameless droves seeking shelter and salvation—all had ended up here. The next meal of a witch's vanguard, providing the men outside with the strength to renew the cycle.

"You made it." A voice I recognized, calm and flat, somewhere behind me.

I paused, but no slick of fear stirred in my gut. I was past that. The muscles of my face had tightened to a rigid mask, but still a distant flicker of a smile reached my lips. I turned to find the captain I'd first met all those weeks ago at the minefield.

Up close, I was reminded just how enormous he and the other guards were, how thickly muscled and dead in the eyes. Everything about him and his kin was heightened, unnatural.

"We didn't know if you would get this far. Some of the others couldn't handle the caves and cracked. Some go crazy when they see the dispensers." He nodded to the nozzles.

"You're copies, aren't you?" I said. "Clones?"

He nodded.

"And the citizens?"

"No. They're just devoted. They were all normal people, once."

"Just like me, huh?"

He smiled, but his shark eyes remained dead and black. "No. Not like you. You're one of the others."

"Bunkhouse folks?"

"Them?" His smile widened. Still, the eyes were dead. It was all conditioned reflex, and all the more frightening for it. "They're citizens as much as everyone else. They just don't know it yet. Most come around in the end. The others, well they just fade away." The smile melted. "You're different."

He tilted his head as though I was a curiosity under a microscope. "I'm impressed. There hasn't been one like you for a long time. No wonder you got her attention." He let that sink in. When I didn't reply, he continued, "A few of us had a wager going. We're not supposed to do that kind of thing . . . actually, we're not supposed to be capable of it, but I'm told some impulses are hard to program out of the human genome."

I blinked. "What kind of wager?"

"On how long it would take you to get here."

"Here?"

"The end of our trail."

A nugget of truth bubbled up to the surface then: it had all been arranged, all facilitated. Finding *The Foundings*, the concrete bunker, Ma's departure, the caves, right up to here and now. I was just another puppet.

I took a breath and nodded. What could I do but accept it?

"My men bet it would be years. Some bet you'd go

dark, give in."

"And you? What did you bet?"

He stepped forward. "Suffice it to say, I just made a lot of money." He laid a hand on my shoulder. "Come on, she's waiting."

⁂

We took a Humvee out of the sheltered depression housing the guards' camp. Whole regiments of them lined the dirt track all the way to the first of the screening date groves, staring in through the windshield.

Before they had all been lounging around, minding their own business. Now it was undeniable that they had been waiting for us to emerge from the barracks. They had known I had been there all along.

Of course they had.

This had been set up from day one. Every encounter, every interaction.

Their stares were a thousand infernos reduced to embers by extreme distance, like the cold touch of starlight on my skin.

The captain steered us from their midst and accelerated under the canopy of tall dates. Soon we were passing a hidden gate in a wall clad in jungle camouflage, and then we headed out toward the Project. Neighborhoods I recognized drifted by, but he drove fast and my mind was sluggish; I couldn't figure out from where we had sprung.

For a moment I saw the roofs of the bunkhouses flash

upon the horizon, and a riot of snakes slithered in my throat. I had been holed up there with Peters only a few hours ago, yet it seemed like an age. I could have had a life there. We both could have.

Or could we? If this had all been a setup, it was doubtful we would have been left to our own devices. Even if I had conceded to my new life, there would always have been that nagging doubt, all those maddening questions. If I hadn't gone looking for answers now, I would have at some point—maybe not for years, decades, but eventually I would have. And somebody that dangerous couldn't be allowed to roam free.

And so they had triggered my pursuit.

We drove in silence and soon reached the first of the mansions. I sensed a great many eyes peering out through net curtains and from behind garden hedges.

I turned to the captain. "After the raid, when you took us out to the fences," I said, "and you made us move all those people . . ." I steeled myself. There was no going back now. "All of that was for me."

He didn't answer. There wasn't even a little twitch on his face this time.

More mansions slid by, dotted with toiling bunkhouse-gardeners on the lawn and brown-robed maids shuttling back and forth between sash windows. They all watched us, servants and masters alike.

I sat back and watched Mother Eden's clubhouse appear directly ahead. "You killed hundreds of people to teach me a lesson?"

"I and my men do as we must," he said. "Whatever is necessary, for the good of the Project." The cadence of it was chillingly mechanical. There was no thought behind those words. Each empty syllable bore the hallmarks of conditioned response.

The guards were copies. Did that mean their minds as well?

We passed through the clubhouse gate and headed up along the driveway. There were no gardeners here, not today. Nor could I see a sign of activity about the entire grand palace. It was all shut up, dormant, waiting. Every window pane seemed to be a pair of eyes in itself, staring down at me as we pulled up and got out amid soup-thick silence.

The captain led me around to the front door, and it popped open to reveal my old curtain-peeping neighbor, her face a picture of satisfaction as she laid eyes on me.

The captain stopped on the top step. "This is as far as I go," he said.

I turned to him. "Do you have a name?"

"Does it matter, sir?"

I could have laughed at that. *Sir*. "Humor me."

He backed away down the stairs. "I'm Michael."

"Let me guess: you're all called Michael."

He popped the Humvee door open. "She's waiting."

"Enjoy your winnings," I said.

He didn't reply, but his eyes lingered on me a moment longer. Somewhere beneath an immovable slab of ingrained servility, something might have stirred. Then he was climbing into the driver's seat and his eyes left me. The Humvee roared away in a cloud of dust, leaving me standing there with the coy maid.

She had a certain twinkle in her eye, something victorious. She stepped aside to allow me entry, and together we walked the echoing halls of the mansion.

In a detached and distant manner, I considered strangling her and running. She was a wisp of a creature who barely reached my shoulder. I could snap her neck before she could utter a sound.

But what good would that do? The place might be empty, but we certainly weren't alone. I knew there were cameras here, somewhere. Probably everywhere. The isolation was all part of the show, just another magic trick in Mother Eden's repertoire.

"You knew I had *The Foundings* last time I was here, didn't you?" I said.

We climbed the marble staircase to the upper floor. She didn't answer.

"I've never seen you in the bunkhouses. How is that? You're a servant, so I'm betting you're not a citizen. No white picket fences for you."

That coy smile remained. We advanced down that long corridor leading to the ballroom, but I knew where we were going. The library door where I had come to see Ma was open and waiting, amid a sea of other doors shut fast.

"There are certain advantages to my position," the maid said, her voice so smooth it could have passed for a whisper of wind. But behind it I could sense joy, and malice.

A servant she might have been, but she was no innocent.

We reached the library and I stepped inside, leaving the maid behind. A moment later I heard the door close behind me, and the *wsh-wsh* of her retreating footsteps.

Mother Eden was waiting beneath the portrait of her younger self, sitting primly before a crackling fire in the grate, a cup of tea to her lips. She took her time in swallowing, smacked her lips, and said, "Ah, Deshun, what a delight! Come and sit. You must be tired after all that digging."

I advanced into the room knowing that my every move was being watched. I wondered how close to her I could get if I made a beeline for her throat. Not very close, I decided.

"I figured out the real trick to making a home for yourself in this place," I said, sitting on the sofa opposite her.

"Is that right?" she said brightly, leaning forward to pour redolent tea from a steaming pot beside her. I watched for frailty, hoping some would spill out onto the saucer, but her hand was as steady as her iron gaze.

She pushed the cup toward me and lifted her own cup to her lips. "Do tell."

I flicked my head in the direction of the departed maid. "I didn't figure out until just now. Your help gave me the final nudge.

"It's not fitting in, not being happy or aiming high, not

looking to make a better world or even fighting for the 'good of the Project.'" I took a sip of tea, hating every delicious drop. "It's not quite *shadenfraude*, but sometimes it isn't far from it. It's something more selfish than that. It's the willingness to climb over anybody else to get yourself high and dry." I took another sip of tea, enjoying it this time; I had that freedom still. "That's the secret of all places like this. There's this goodness to most folk you can never quite get rid of, even in the harshest of times— especially then. That certain sort of naïve kindness that takes you off guard when a stranger sometimes offers it. We talk about it like it's childish, but it runs deep in us all. Even when we're being pushed and shoved, herded and taken advantage of, most people will bow down in the distant hope that the cruelty will turn to kindness—the kindness they would show.

"You know, I heard one of your following say it all in a nutshell. 'Some people were made to be ruled.'" I couldn't help laughing at the recollection of my own mother saying those words.

"Then there's a few who can turn all that on its head, the kind of people who end up standing in line to get into this place. The little gardens, the picket fences, the marble floors, the servants and luxuries; it's enough for people like that—like *you*—enough to make them forget about all the people they're standing on to keep their heads above water.

"But you make one fatal error. Your man out there, Michael, told me the people in the bunkhouses were all citizens, they just didn't know it yet. Well, you're wrong.

"You might think you have this whole place wrapped around your little finger, that you've beaten the system and set yourself up a little empire in the desert. But what I see is a social experiment gone all to shit. But it just happens to have shown one thing beyond any doubt: people are good." I sat forward, brushed my cup aside, and steepled my fingers. "I'm going to show them the truth. Somehow, sometime, I'll show them all. Unless you kill me. And I know you're too bored to do that." I searched her eyes for the fear I sought. "I'll show them who you really are, and you'll see that there's a limit to what people will take."

Though I didn't see a wink of emotion behind her steely gaze, I stood. I wasn't playing her game anymore. "When they see what you are, I'll get to watch them tear this whole goddamn place to pieces."

Mother Eden was still for a time, and then she leaned forward and poured herself another cup of tea. She swilled it, tasted it, sighed, and smacked her lips some more. Then her eyes rose to meet mine. "Quite a speech, son," she said. "You've been worth every lick of attention. It's been so long since anyone's said anything to me but 'baa.'"

She laughed at that, and I knew then that it was the first real laugh I'd heard from her, a high-pitched squeal that rang painfully in my ears. It took her a few seconds to recover, and then she said, "But before you go off hunting glory and truth, why don't you take a seat?"

"I have nothing to say."

"But I do." She looked disappointed for the first time. "You wanted answers. Well, child, all you had to do was ask. But seeing as you didn't take the initiative, I figure I'll come out and tell you off my own back. A little education. See, just like everyone else, I got a story to tell."

Adrenaline set my fists shaking and cemented my jaw shut. It took a whole lot of willpower not to run for the door, but eventually my knees folded and I sat back down.

Mother Eden's story began. "Don't worry, I ain't gonna start with *once upon a time*. You already got all that from my little autobiography." She paused. "Did you like it?"

"Literature that hasn't been butchered is hard to find out here," I said. "I'll take what I can get."

"Course you will," she said curtly. "They always do. In fact, I had the whole thing put together for folk such as yourself—hell, it was one of your kind who wrote it."

"Bielshik?"

"Oh sure, Lutharo was a real card. Hell of a scribe. Quite prominent here early on." She laughed fondly, her eyes rolled skyward with nostalgia. "He thought helping me out would win him some points, wipe the slate clean. Poor dear. Shame his crimes could never be written off."

I gritted my teeth, stiffening.

"But his magnum opus stuck around. It's been real useful. Means all citizens get a look into what it means to be an upstanding member of the community, but the motivation for getting it written came from having to go through these shenanigans over and over. A person can explain themselves only so many times before they just gotta get it down on paper." She shrugged. "Anyhow, you know the rest. You know I was just like you, once. Long, long time ago . . . There were a whole lot of us, chosen special by the bigwigs. All of us young, spry, and full of spunk, thought we could change the world, we could do anything!"

"The Syndicate," I said.

"Well, none of us knew that name till much later."

"When you invented it, you mean. When you turned against them."

"They turned against me!" Snarling fury burst forth without warning, serenity dissolving in an instant. Before she became herself again, her eyes briefly were windows to a blazing inferno, in which I saw Peters's shadow writhing, burning, along with the countless others who had defied her.

Then she was a sweet old lady once more. She raised her eyebrows as though the outburst had come from elsewhere, perhaps an unruly neighbor, and took a sip of tea. "I don't expect you to understand. It was different in those times. We weren't all equal then. There was a glass ceiling that no amount of hard work for the Project could break."

I almost balked with sheer incredulity at the irony, but she wasn't going to stop there.

"To tell the truth, I didn't come to Eden to change the world. I was just a girl looking for a way out, like a lotta other people. I won my place by chance like everyone else, and I couldn't believe my luck. But when I got over here, I found it all backward.

"See, we got a mission here. The strongest powers all over the world are funding us out here from their own pockets. And if we fail here, everywhere could fail. That's the whole purpose of all of our lives. And there's too much at stake to let it all go to hell because of some misplaced sense of charity."

I sat back on the sofa. "I know all this already," I said. "I read your book."

"Right you are. But you need to know why."

"I know that too. You saw an opportunity to lord over a bunch of people trying to make a difference, to play God when all mankind is in danger of collapse, and when people got in your way, you got rid of them. Sounds pretty simple to me."

She finished her tea yet again and refilled it with mechanical fluidity. "You and your kind always like to think that way. But the truth is, I only ever had the mission of this Project at heart. Without me, there would be no Project, no mission. This whole operation would have failed decades back."

I shook my head. "You're crazy."

"What do you know about the Syndicate?"

"They were the original leaders of the Project."

A thin smile appeared on her face. "Funny how the mind doesn't bother to probe anymore into that, ain't it? What do you *know* about them?"

I said nothing.

"They were good folk, mostly. I'd never say a word against their intentions. Nobody ever knew a better bunch. But there was one problem about all them that doomed us all from day one: who they were. Not a pragmatist among them. Not a one."

Pragmatist [Eden Speak]: One with the capability to rule and subjugate.

"They were scientists, mostly. Engineers, psychologists, biochemists, sociologists, geologists. All academics, world leaders who could make a difference. The UN put it all in their hands. 'Because they had the potential to do what we couldn't,' they said." A wicked smile twitched across her face. "That was the big mistake. Some fickle disease had infiltrated all the governments backing the Projects: the idea that the world was falling because of old-time materialistic consumerisms. But remove the politicians and the bureaucrats and put the power in the hands of the eggheads, and things would change. Things would be better.

"But there's a reason people like that should never have power: they don't want it. They don't know what to do with it. Given the chance, they'd spread it to anyone who asked for it, spread it so thin that nobody's in charge at all. And they're too soft to make the tough decisions. Oh sure, it's all expounding wisdom and leading their followers to a bright new beginning when times are good, but throw 'em a curveball and . . . well, we got thrown a doozy."

"The refugees," I said.

She nodded. "They didn't see it, didn't see that we

couldn't help. That wasn't our purpose. Soon as Bangladesh was hit by the floods and Ulan Bator ousted the survivors of the Xinjiang massacre, there were millions of people wandering around the desert. We're well set up here—the UN always took precautions to make sure we weren't gonna be bothered. But against some endless river of hungry mouths and grabbing hands . . ." She shivered. I could see the shadow of all those desperate souls behind her disgusted eyes. "If we was ever gonna help anyone, we had to keep our doors shut and everyone knew it. And nothing's changed, even today. But they wouldn't see it. Saps, the right lot of them, holding out their hands and giving anyone a bed who came our way."

Her nose wrinkled. "For a while it worked, until some of those refugees left. Then they told whomever they bumped into about us, about the suckers who gave bed and board to anyone who asked for it. That's how the others got their name." A wicked smile flickered and then died. Her lips formed the words bitterly: "'The Blessed Syndicate.' Funny how you can turn something like that into a phrase people scorn nowadays, ain't it?

"Anyway, soon they came in their droves, and inside of a year we had damn near a hundred thousand clawing at our gates. Still the others gave, and then we was starving just as much as they were. Folks got angry, people got sick. Some died." For the first time in memory, I saw genuine emotion wrack Mother Eden's body in a visceral ripple. "They betrayed us."

A sick satisfaction spewed into my veins at the sight of

her distress.

She scowled. "That's why I had to rise up and try to make a difference in my own way." She took a sip of fresh tea, and her eyes swam with affection as she looked up at her portrait looming above us. "That's why I had to save us."

"How?" I said. Despite all the rest, this was the real question that had plagued my mind since I'd gotten here. How had a nobody broken that glass ceiling?

"The same way all governments are saved. Through the people. We met under their noses, we plotted, and we took action. Soon as we took out the radio mast connecting us with the outside world, the 'Blessed Syndicate' didn't know heads from tails.

"No matter how smart they were, there was no big voice among them—that was the danger of putting all the power in the hands of the smartest. The whole system tore itself apart, and all we had to do was watch. Then I and the others rose up, took control.

"And there was a point when we looked out at the refugees, at all those clawing hands reaching through the fences. We could've given them what we had, sparse as it was. But that would have been a mistake. It would have been the end of us. It takes guts to save us all; someone willing to do the wrong thing, to do everyone else right. It takes someone like me to pay the ultimate price."

"The slaughter of innocent people, you mean," I spat. "It takes people like you to leave all those people to rot in the desert, or have them shot and thrown into the catacombs—melted down to feed those guards!"

She smiled. "Our strapping protectors weren't always there. Standing sentry was just another duty, one of which I got my fair share. But after I took the hot seat, I saw there was always a weakness in some people: no matter how much they saw the truth, they just couldn't help themselves, opening the gate to all those hungry mouths. So we took steps. It wasn't easy, but we got there. All the labs were already here, all the equipment, all the smarts— we just had to put them to use."

"I thought you killed the Syndicate."

"Not at first. They were the smartest the world had to offer. They had their uses. Only once they were done, when we knew they'd never fit in, did I cleanse us of their filth."

I sat back. "I don't understand. You destroy the coms, you kill thousands, and still the UN sends new recruits and supplies, regular as clockwork. They don't send anyone else out here to check on the Project. How has it stayed this way for so many years? How is it you keep the whole world in the dark?"

Her face didn't change at all. "They don't care. That's the God's-honest truth. *They don't care.* Nobody ever expected this place and those like it to work. It's a fad, all wool pulled over folks' eyes to keep them sober, working, and hopeful while the rest of the world uses up whatever's left in a mad scrabble. We all want to hold on to what we have, even if it means sacrificing our futures.

"So they keep the commercials going, keep the lottery

running, keep sending the new recruits. Because we do what we were supposed to do, what the posters say: hope for the future, hope for civilization, even when there is none."

I swallowed. "And the guards? What about them?"

"We found that over the years, no matter how well you train people, they always find some way to turn against you."

"You mean they show their conscience?"

She straightened. "Not how I see it. We need a certain kind of trust out here if we're gonna survive. That's how it is. You need truth from the cradle. And once I got it right, I had to replicate it—a stable model, sure win, safe bet."

"So you cloned them?"

"Damn right. Why not? They get the job done, they keep us safe. I wouldn't complain. You'd be dead without them, starved months back."

"It's not right. You can't do that to people."

The corners of her mouth puckered with contempt. "I've been doing this for longer than you've been alive, son. I've saved thousands."

"You killed tens of thousands."

"Yes, I have. Tens of thousands of nobodies, to save those of us worth saving."

"Who are you to judge who's worthy?"

"Why don't you look out the window? See for yourself. See who put me here, who keeps me here."

I went to the window and looked out down through the gardens, which had been empty mere minutes before.

Where before there had only been windswept asphalt and errant leaves, there were now endless droves—the whole Project crammed against the walls, staring through the gates.

They all saw me, all saw her. Staring lambs waiting for the final decision.

"You see, they keep me in power," she said behind me, her voice tickling my shoulder. "Most people, they sense it, they sense the wrong in it all. But it don't matter. Most people just want to be told what to do, they want an easy life, they want to forget—they don't want to think for themselves."

"There's enough down there to throw you off, to show you the good in us."

"We'll see," she said. "Why don't you go down and share the truth?"

"Watch me," I hissed.

We turned as one in an absurd dance, pirouetting through the room. I really could have killed her then, crushed her with my bare hands. There was nobody watching, I knew that now. They were all outside, waiting. There might have been cameras all around, but there was nobody manning the stations; even the guards were probably down there.

But I couldn't. What good would it do? There were a dozen people just as bad in her circle itching to take her place and show how committed they were to the Project. To win, to ever change anything, I had to unmask them all in front of everyone.

We passed into the hall and onto the staircase, descending amid our own echoing footfalls, making our way toward the enormous mahogany door and the crowds waiting beyond.

There was a collective sigh of relief as we stepped out into the light. For a moment I thought it was for me a swell of gratitude welled up, but then it clicked: it was for her.

I knew from the first moment that this wasn't what Mother Eden had advertised. This wasn't my chance to whip the cover off her lie and lead the masses to a new beginning.

This wasn't how it was supposed to be.

We were greeted by utter silence. I had pictured spewing stentorian secrets about the monster atop her marble castle to a chorus of gasps. But there was no surprise in all those eyes, just that same maddening, blank stare.

Those who had not completely fallen under the Project's spell seemed to have been shepherded to the front to witness my downfall. Among them I sensed sympathy, but none were brave enough—or stupid enough—to let it show.

The rest bore a blankness so much worse than open hostility. I felt as though I could be strung up and burned alive right in front of them, and they wouldn't have batted an eye.

"I don't understand," I muttered into the dirt.

I didn't fight Mother Eden off when she gripped my shoulder with her gnarled talons. Maybe, in her own way, she was trying to be comforting. "It never does to try convincing people like y'all, Deshun," she said. "Never has, never will. No fault of yours, just the way you are. And our citizens are ready to live with it." She stepped down beside me, looking out over her flock. "Look at 'em. All of them come out here just to support you. No secrets, no subterfuge, no letting you scheme on your lonesome, pretending these people are brainless bananas that need looking after."

She looped her arm around me. "You really think you're the first to get this far? You really think you were saving people? Look at 'em. We all chose this, a better life, one where we get what we deserve."

"This doesn't prove anything," I said. "So you brought everyone out here. They don't know what I know." But all my confidence had drained away.

"Why don't you tell them? Go ahead. Destroy all we've built here."

I mouthed wordlessly for a moment and then fought from her grasp. I dashed forward over the lawn, sweating out of sheer hysteria, Peters's voice screaming aloud in the back of my mind: "Tell them, Desh! Tell them!" My gaze slipped among them, over features of every tone from palest chalk to darkest ebony, pinched Asian slopes to bulbous African peaks and cragged Caucasian valleys. I saw my pals from duty on the Beetle who I'd sweated with day in day out, straight jawed and slack cheeked; I saw those who looked down on me daily, including my old wench of a neighbor and the Sahib who had humiliated Peters; I saw the twins and their eternal lupine leers, all the more victorious and supercilious than ever.

All the world's races and cultures amalgamated into one, a perfect synergy, united by a common goal: the Project. For that fleeting moment as I raced headlong toward them over the pristine manicured grass, I saw just how doomed my plight really was.

I stopped in front of them, breathless, only able to wave in the direction of the mansion. The gates were ajar, yet the crowd didn't dare move an inch farther onto such sacred land.

I had no idea what I was going to say until I opened my mouth. But when I did, the words simply emerged, full formed and gushing.

"I know what you all think," I said. "That I'm some dangerous animal got out of its cage. I bet I've looked like one most of the time. But you have to know the truth."

Mother Eden swept across her own lawn at a leisurely pace, sidling toward the gate. I fixed her with a shaking finger and thrust it in her direction. "*She* is not what she says she is. She's a liar. Every night she comes on that intercom and bleats a heaping pile of crap into your ears, and all of you gulp it down like it was chowder. It's all a pantomime to keep you scared and safe wrapped up in your little lives.

"But this Project has failed. We're not working toward

a better beginning or to save the world. We're using everyone else's misery for our own gain. She and those like her"—I picked out a few, notably Mother Eden's trusty circle of disciples and the twins, from the crowd—"are using the nations we used to call home to give a few lives of luxury, while most of us are reduced to slavery.

"It's easy to think that you're all being kept safe by those fences, the guards, the lottery system and all those duties, until you try to leave. Go ahead, just try it—you won't make it as far as the dunes before you run into the minefields. How many times has Mother Eden's broadcasts mentioned those?"

The face of the masses didn't change a mote. True, somewhere in the deep depths of the crowd I sensed outrage and fear from those whom Mother Eden's disciples had chaperoned to the gate, but their ire was but a drop in an ocean of apathy.

If blowing tumbleweeds had been a thing of the Gobi, a whole herd would have just come rolling down the street.

I was left gasping as Mother Eden came strolling up and stood at a respectful distance, as though a fellow customer at Kmart waiting in line to be served at the checkout.

Only the thought of Peters kept me going. He had given his life so I could stand there. I couldn't fail him. Though I knew it was useless, I pressed on. "Once this place was the sharp edge pushing forward. But now it's just a shell. There's nothing being done here but covering up a great lie. I've seen what some of you have glimpsed and what the rest choose not to acknowledge. The raids are just people looking for a place to sleep, and once the guards have finished shooting, they boil them down into slurry, for feed. Our brave protectors eat those people."

That got a reaction. Smooth expressionless faces contorted into troubled frowns. I might as well have been a child inappropriately exposing itself. There was little outrage among the outer tiers of the crowd, just exasperation at the sheer guile of speaking out of turn. I was disturbing the peace.

As before, those in the middle were beaming derision in my direction, as though their furtive glances alone could buoy me up and keep me from crumbling. All those young and elderly folk I had read to from the log, and the men I'd sweated beside on duties, all reduced to sheep encircled by rings of watchful predators.

"The duties, the lottery, the fairness. It's all a lie! *A lie!*" I pointed to the wolves on the periphery of the pack. "Most of them will never see anything but marble over their heads ever again!"

My voice rang hollow, returning as a repeating echo marred by the desert wind. Still they stared. I waited for the consternation to boil over, for the underclass to realize their fate and tear down the great lie.

Yet it didn't happen. My fantasy had been just that: a fantasy. Something to keep me going. It couldn't have been more obvious, now.

"They . . . she . . . it's all a lie!" I screamed.

Some of them must feel it! Rage, horror—something!

All they had to do was speak out and the nightmare would end. The time was now, this critical mass where people could be heard instead of disappearing, fractured and hunted.

But none did. I stood before a sea of people willing to throw morality and the fate of civilization to the wind in exchange for a slice of comfy living—even those for whom life wasn't so comfy at all; it was just easier than the alternative.

"It doesn't have to be this way!" I screamed. I pointed to those on the periphery of the crowd. "These people might speak pretty about 'saving the world,' but they'd walk over your corpses if it meant keeping things the way they are.

"None of us is innocent here. So many of you help clear the bodies and blood, watch your friends disappear and come back as shells of themselves—and the rest, well, you sit in *her*"—I pointed at Mother Eden once more with more venom in my voice than I thought possible— "pocket."

"Don't be the ones history remembers as cowards who gave it all up for plush living, while the world went to hell. Be the ones who saved it. That is our mission."

Wind. The blustering sand. My own jagged breath sounds. Somewhere far away, an impatient infant set to weeping.

Tears splashed on the lawn at my feet, but I scarcely noticed. It was too much to bear, and my throat thrummed from the strain of sheer disbelief. Vomit climbed my throat. "You can't do this. *YOU CAN'T GIVE IN!* People have shed blood for this place for so many years, before most of us were We can't let our last chance slip through our fingers."

The last breath of fight drained out of me then. I had succeeded in two things only: first, in forging pain on the faces of those I could have called friends, had I not insisted on ostracizing myself; second, in cementing silent victory on the faces of everyone else.

But I had failed wholly in dividing those living in fear and those with intent to live as best they could at all costs. The gradient of sympathy to apathy was too gradual, and remained so. After all my talk, there was no way to distinguish sheep from predator, friend from foe.

The crowd had won. They were more united than ever now, in their discomfort at watching me make such a fool of myself.

And just like that, my great reveal was at a close.

Mother Eden spoke up. "It's all right, folks. Mr. Golding has had a difficult time, and we have to stay strong for him. My thanks go to every one of you for coming out here to show your support." She gave my shoulder a squeeze, and I no longer had the strength to suppress a wince as her nails dug into my flesh. "Don't worry, dear, we all find it tough some time or another. But we'll get you to fit in right and proper, don't you worry. It just takes time. And we have all the time in the world."

She turned back to the crowd. "Folks, you've been

angels. I thought it necessary to get this tomfoolery out in the open and settle any little quibbles. Now that Mr. Golding has said his piece, I'll give the floor to anyone who wants to voice any grievances. Of course, this ain't no different from normal, but I want to make sure while we're all present and accounted for." She swept her hawk gaze over them all.

This was it. The final humiliation. Once it had become painfully clear that not a word was to be spoken, she nodded with curt grace and bowed to them all. "In that case, I feel it might be best to put an end to this excitement before we all go wasting a fine day. Beautiful weather, folks. Hell, let's take the day off duties and soak up some rays. We all earned a little R and R after this here escapade. Chop chop!"

She clapped once, a tiny gesture that commanded thousands. The crowd fractured and flowed away from the gates without a moment's pause. Within hours balance would be restored; those in the bunkhouses would smart for a while, then revel in their day off and forget everything—me and my worries, even Peters. And the rest would return to their plush homes and lives of sweet sedentary relaxation.

Their footfalls were gone before I could even search for a single face among them. They were gone, and it was just me and her standing there on the lawn, before her enormous three-story Victorian manor.

"What now?" I muttered.

She smacked her lips and mused with a twinkle in her

eye. "Now? Now you get what you always wanted, Desh. You get to go to your cage."

I had no idea how long the darkness lasted, nor when it started. At some point I was standing on the grass with Mother Eden, and at another I was lying horizontal in a pall of perfect black, silence ringing in my ears.

Peters was there, his warm embrace all that I had in the cool dank interior of my eternal night. I could hear him breathing right beside me, feel the rise and fall of his chest.

Then I'd turn over and he'd be gone, nothing but a fold of the cheap rough blanket I was left with. For a while I'd weep, then I'd lay motionless for endless years. Then I'd laugh, a hysterical hyena bark that echoed off the walls and made the air shudder with its very hilarity; I'd laugh because I'd remember that I hadn't even known his first name. All the time we'd spent together, everything we'd shared, and I'd never bothered to ask.

Then I would realize that I hadn't needed to know, because it hadn't been important. I'd feel closer to him than ever, and I was sure he was beside me still. Then the cycle would begin all over again.

All the time I was in the cell, I moved from place to place. Blink my eyes and I was standing out in the desert looking over a carpet of bodies. *Blink*. Peters by my side, running his finger along my forearm until it came out in gooseflesh. *Blink*. I was back in Fremont at the kitchen table, Ma singing her show tunes and Father resting his feet after a twelve-hour shift. It was cold, dank, and dangerous. But we were free. *Blink.* Darkness again. Sooner or later I always ended up back in the dark.

After a few round trips I realized what had been missing from my failed exposé outside Mother Eden's mansion, what I'd been looking for amid all those faces.Now it couldn't have been more obvious: I'd been looking for Ma.

And I'd failed. She hadn't been out there with the others. Oh, she'd been watching, all right. I was sure of that. But she hadn't been part of the crowd.

∾

The darkness went on so long that I forgot what it was like to see my own hand in front of my face. But at some point I opened my eyes, turned on my side with my face screwed up, half blinded by piercing daylight, and Mother Eden was sitting before me.

"I wanna thank you," were the first words out of her mouth.

My tongue made a rasping sound as it parted from the roof of my mouth. "For what?"

A golden arc of light cut in through the door, and a shower of dust motes were pouring over her cardigan. Her hair was curled into a tight perm, and by contrast with the light her skin was thin and translucent. She was just a little old lady. A frail ball of cotton and wrinkled skin.

"It's been a long time, Desh. I was beginning to think the world had run outta interesting people." She laughed, the high-pitched and stertorous giggle of a school girl. "I was beginning to think it was just my lonesome self. Boy, are you a breath of something sweet."

I didn't feel so sweet. My breath passed over my furry teeth in a puff of night stink, and I whined as I struggled into a sitting position, my skin rubbed raw by the coarse blanket. Beneath that two-inch layer of synthetic fabric was bare concrete; by now my shoulder blades had gone permanently numb and my spine cried out at every movement. "So I'm your prisoner now," I muttered. "That's the tyrant's method. Hold up a sacrificial lamb to the masses, make an example of them, and then make them disappear."

She tittered again and shook her head. Vortices of dust motes whorled around her permed locks.

How beautiful dust could be when you had nothing else.

"Oh no, my dear," she said. "You'll see the light of day soon enough. We have great plans for you. It's been so long that I forgot I ever questioned how we run things here. Our ways keep life going, sure, but are they the best ways? The most peaceful? The most efficient? Hell, how are we to know without some bright young thing to show the holes in our big plan."

"Looks like it worked out pretty well for you."

She gave me a measured look. From deep in those aged eyes a brief flash of ire seemed to raise the room temperature a degree or two. "I gotta admit, you made bigger waves than anyone. We've never had to make quite so many . . . adjustments to so many folks around the Project."

Adjustment [Eden-Speak]: See 'Brainwashing.'

"I'll take that as a compliment."

"Yes. Indeed." Another dangerous look, more concentrated than the first. "You showed us something: we can't keep growing in numbers and live quite so apart. We gotta lay it out straight from here on." She bounced upon her stool, excited. "Oh, phooey, it's been too long since something real good came up to sink my teeth into. There's so much to do, so much to get in order. And it's all thanks to you, Desh. You've sparked a revolution!"

Just not the one I'd hoped, I thought. *I took a dictator and turned her into a god.*

"So what's the plan?" I murmured. "Screenings fresh off the Skyrail, straight to the bunkhouses for anyone who shows any symptoms of having a personality?"

"Oh, you." She waved her hand coquettishly. "No, no, I'm talking a real policy of honesty, here! Give people the choice to work toward something better, straight to their face, instead of all this cloak and dagger."

"And when they refuse?"

"Well, anyone's welcome to stay with us. Of course, there's the matter of squaring up for bed and board—"

"Bet they can pay in the form of manual labor, right?"

"You betcha! Nothing like a day's hard labor."

"Sounds wonderful. But I'm betting if, say, they

wanted to leave—"

"Well." Her lips twitched. "Shameful thing, us being so cut off out here. It's a rare thing to hear from the outside world, so kind as they are sending us all these supplies. We can't just let anyone wander the dunes. It ain't safe. And there's the chance they could leak our location to unvaccinated refugees. We can't have that, as you know, Desh. This is a secure location."

"I see." I flexed my neck, the taste of ash in my mouth. What had I done? "And I suppose you won't be continuing with the duty lottery?"

"The beauty of the truth: we don't need it! Anyone willing to live proper can contribute without being bothered by all that messing around moving back and forth and working duties not suited to their status. We can leave that to the rest, those who maybe can't see the wood for the trees but still need a place to eat and sleep."

"Sounds perfect," I said. "You get a substrata of slaves to do your dirty work, and you get your mansions to yourselves. No more pretense. Straight feudalism."

"Don't give me that liberal crap, young man. We're living the best we can, and that's all."

She stood and moved toward the door. "One day they'll write stories about what we did here."

"Yes," I said, "they will. You'll go down with everyone else who wrote history in the blood of innocents."

"Poetic," she said, heading for the door. "You are a hoot, dear."

A guard appeared beside her and started closing the

door. I stood up. "What are you going to do with me?"

Kill me? I wanted to say. But I couldn't bring myself to do it, not because I was afraid of dying, but because I was afraid the answer was No.

"There's a whole lot to do and little time. We have new recruits on the way, after all!"

Before I could say a word further, the door had clanged shut, and I was surrounded by darkness once more.

❦

It turned out my prison wasn't quite so deep a hole after all. Over the next few days, when the hatch in the door banged open once every few hours and a plate of stale food was thrown in with a little water, it was accompanied by the sound of scuffling feet, begging and cursing.

It was a stark change from the utter silence of before. Mother Eden hadn't lied. Change was afoot. I had a vague sense of upheaval even behind an iron door and several feet of concrete. The sheer volume of arrests—I assumed they were arrests—defied belief. A sizeable portion of the Project must have been hauled in.

Pride boiled over into maniacal laughter a few times after that. So I had made an impression. Even if it hadn't been enough to spark public uproar, it had been enough to prompt a manhunt.

I wondered whether Mother Eden had had any choice in her little revolution.

But then that laughter turned to tears when I realized

that all I'd done was help root out the best folk, such that those left would be an even more degraded caste of robots.

As the ache in my back turned to numbing, bone-deep agony, and the air in my cell turned sour, the whimpering outside turned to roars of defiance, then cries of pain, and eventually, silence.

Still, I remained in darkness.

❧

"Good morning, sir." A sedate feminine voice reached into the void. I ascended from the far depths of sleep. The voice repeated every few moments: "Good morning, sir." Insistent, monotonous, smooth as date leaves. "Good morning, sir."

Ungodly comfort, softness all around me. I smelled fresh linen and lemongrass and the pink smell of freshly washed skin.

This wasn't the boiling, fetid heat I'd known since arriving at Eden, but comfortable, swaddling womb-warmth. I could have been lying inside a giant marshmallow.

My eyes were gummed together by sleep, and I had to pry them open with knuckles that smelled of soap and ointment. Blinding whiteness awaited my sensitive retinas and I cowered for a while under that marshmallow, which turned out to be Egyptian cotton sheets.

That voice kept on bleating. "Good morning, sir. Good morning, sir."

I looked over to the side table for the source and saw a sleek digital display, some kind of alarm clock integrated into the wall. I reached over with difficulty and shut it off. Almost immediately another voice started speaking, this one intonated with genuine human expression. "Ah, Mr. Golding, you're awake. We were worried you were gonna sleep through to next week!"

"What's happening?" I said—or I tried to say; what came out was something closer to, "Whaspnin?"

"We're lettin' you rest up, of course!"

"Where are you?"

"I'm around, don't you worry about that. I'm just making sure you're comfortable. Now that you're awake, why don't you go on down the hall? They're waiting for you."

I sat up, surprised by how little my body ached after so long in the cell. I was in a plush bedroom as big as the whole square footage of the house I'd shared with Ma, beige mixed with soft highlights, draped in silk finery, and carpeted by a rug that looked like it could swallow my legs whole.

I was naked. A brown robe lay draped over a nearby lounger. Birdsong floated in through an open sash window, but beside that all was quiet; not the dead vacuum of the cell, but instead a peaceful pseudo-silence complete with the trickle of the breeze, the static of sifting sand and tumbling leaves.

Sleep beckoned me, if only to provide an escape to unfeeling oblivion.

But what good would that do? I sensed I was being given a choice: walk to the gallows with dignity, or be dragged kicking and screaming.

I wondered whether they would really kill me. Surely after putting so many others through pain and interrogation in whatever hole I'd been kept in the last few days, it wasn't beyond them. What further use could I be to them?

Instead of fear, I didn't feel much of anything beside a distant relief that it might soon be over. No, I wasn't going to hide. This was the home stretch. What was done was done, and no amount of cowering was going to change a damn thing.

"Screw it, Peters," I said. "I hope it's nice wherever you are, because I'll be joining you shortly." I pulled the robe over my bare shoulders and stepped into a pair of white loafers. "Put some beer on ice, my man. I'm coming." I laughed at the images my imagination conjured. "There better be a pool."

I took a deep breath and padded over to the door, pulling it open and stepping out onto a hallway I knew only too well, the very same one that led to the library— only I was much farther along its length.

Somewhere a grandfather clock was ticking and tocking, and somewhere else a little light jazz was playing, but otherwise it was the same. I headed along toward the very end, from where genteel elegant mansion folk had once filled the house with their fine chatter. Now there was only a delicate tinkling, drawing me closer. By the time I came to the door, I had identified it as the rattle of silverware on bone china.

"Ah, Deshun, there you are!" Mother Eden sat at the head of a wide parabola of ladies, all dressed in frocks and taking dainty sips from floral teacups. She beckoned me enthusiastically. "You're just in time. We were just fixing to head out!"

"Where?" I croaked.

"A little gathering. Should be exciting."

"For what?"

"It's a surprise. Don't you like surprises, Desh?"

The others watched me carefully with identical smiles. Among them were the twins and Mother Eden's mouthpiece, Tight Lips, along with a few more I recognized—though they were different from her usual flock. Her inner circle had undergone something of a reshuffle. That elephant in the room went unaddressed.

"Come on now, ladies, drink up! We've gotta make a good impression. Won't do to be late."

A dozen necks arced and gulped tea, and then the room was filled with the sound of rustling fabric as the ladies got to their feet. I stepped among them, embracing incredulity, and a few curtseyed to me when I passed. It seemed I was just another lady in a frock.

I came to stand by Mother Eden's side and shrugged. After a few moments watching her straighten the teapot before it was whisked away by brown-clad servants, I said, "Why am I here?"

"Well, Desh, seeing as you had such a hand in our new

way of doing things, I thought you deserved to see the results firsthand. Come on, ladies, let's hop to it!"

She took hold of my arm and steered me toward the door. I yielded to her touch. Before, I had wondered if I was up for a trip to the gallows. Now I yearned for it.

The procession of ladies descended the marble staircase and walked to a waiting convoy of motorcars. They were fine, freshly waxed things of beauty, of no make I recognized, and must have been manufactured in the Project workshops—most likely at quite some expense. The ladies stepped into them without a glance at their shining chrome-gilded curves, the luxury meaning nothing to them, and I climbed into the last with Mother Eden.

Looking out over the lawn, the memory of a great staring crowd beyond the gates flashed before my eyes. How long ago had that been? I had no way of knowing, but it seemed like a hundred years.

Today the lawn was peopled by its usual smattering of gardeners and groundsmen. But there was something markedly different about them, something that gave me a peek into what I'd missed; the changes Mother Eden had talked of were evidenced before my eyes.

They were all dressed in brown. Not a single face among them was from the White-Picket District or the mansions. They all fixated on the ground as the cars rattled by, as though looking up would bring instant death.

"Living out in the open," I muttered. I was squashed along one supple leather bench facing the rear of the cab, beside the twins and Tight Lips, and they giggled at my words.

Mother Eden, sitting alone on the opposite bench, smiled and took a deep satisfied breath. "Clear and true, Mr. Golding. I gotta hand it to you, things have never been so good. We owe you everything."

I shook my head, cursing under my breath as we headed through the gates and cruised along the main street toward the Project's outskirts. Soon we passed the White-Picket District, which looked much the same yet had altogether changed; the pretense of make-do mediocrity had been stripped away, revealing the neighborhood of demi-mansions they had been all along.

When the bunkhouses flashed past on the horizon, I noticed two major additions: first, a whole new building where the kids' play area used to be, the new corrugated roof glinting in the sun; second, an encircling tangle of razor wire running around the whole compound, presiding over an excavated moat.

It hit me with physical force: I'd seen it all before, in history class vid-docs. Dachau, Japan's Death Railway Camps, the USSR's Gulags, North Korea's Labor Colonies. It had been blossoming right in front of me. All it had taken were these final finishing touches to complete the picture.

I knew the ladies were watching for my reaction. I made sure I gave none.

The houses thinned out, and the protective screenings of palms disappeared to be replaced by rolling dunes.

Unforgiving sunlight crashed down on the cars, and I sensed the raging war between radiation and air-con upon the Alacantra-lined roof.

"Here we are," Mother Eden sighed. The town hall had come within sight, and we were making a beeline for it. People from all over were pouring in through the open doors, the guards standing sentinel around its edge. It didn't look like anybody was guarding the fences today; everyone's attention was directed inside.

The cars pulled up, and ebullient cries of "Mother Eden!" and "Welcome!" and "Ma'am, you look bea-*utiful* this evening!" came darting in through the window. Mother Eden held up a humble hand in recognition. To those finely dressed in white robes, she smiled and thanked individually, addressing each by name. To the rest—by far the majority—clad in blue and brown, she merely swept a hand at the center of the collective and moved on.

The mass weren't in the slightest put out by the snub, clamoring to get closer to the car, begging for a moment's attention, their hands held out to the windows. The cars pulled up and the ladies slipped out with refined elegance, parting the brown sea with no more than bows and curtseys. I was left staring after them with my lip curling until people started looking at me, turning their noses up in disappointment when I turned out to be an Undesirable.

I climbed out and followed the meat of the crowd pouring inside. The building was packed wall to wall. For a moment I considered watching from the doorway, but then a guard I recognized all too well materialized from nowhere and took my shoulder, pushing bunkhouse peasants aside and hauling me in his wake.

"Hello, John" I said.

"Mr. Golding."

We left the brown robes behind and passed haphazardly-seated White-Picket folk. "How's things?"

"Never better. Lots of change." He didn't look convinced. Those were Mother Eden's regurgitated words, not his. His face was dark and brooding, like a disgruntled teen.

"You don't look thrilled about it."

He didn't answer, kicking aside an errant brown robe with a steel-toed boot.

"You don't like change, huh? I bet none of you do." I watched his face carefully. "You've never known anything else."

Still he didn't answer. Now we were passing finely dressed mansion folk, seated with plenty of space, and the best view of the stage. Most had glasses of ice water or sparkling champagne in their hands. All of them were attended by a brown robe.

Some of these servants were fanning their masters, some were feeding them strawberries, and one was giving a foot massage.

I followed John around the side of the stage and behind the curtain. Mother Eden and her fine ladies were there waiting, their voices high pitched with anticipation. The guard remained by the flap and gave me a shove forward.

I tried to discern the babble, but it was too energetic and fragmented, passing between pairs and triplets in a dozen different conversations. One thing I managed to pick up was the tone; what I had at first taken to be excitement now seemed closer to concern and discontent. Their volume sparked a lick of dread dripping in my gut.

They milled and squawked like a flock of spooked gulls until Mother Eden thrust her wrinkled hands into the air.

The chatter died mid-gabble. Quiet as a whisper—a volume ill-fitting her usually stentorian contralto—Mother Eden said, "Friends, I appreciate everything you're saying, but my mind's made up."

I started despite myself when Tight Lips stepped forward and addressed her directly. "You can't! You can't do this!" Seeing such open effrontery set my jaw gaping. I pricked up my ears, poised to absorb every word, but then sharp pain erupted in my arm and I was being dragged aside. My old peeping neighbor had her claws dug fast into my flesh.

"What—" I started.

"Shh!" she hissed, mashing her finger against my lips. "Listen close, pig. You're on in two minutes, and I won't have you embarrass my mistress."

"On? What—"

"She struck me across the side of the head, cursing. "Quiet! See the color of your robe? What is it? You tell me!"

"Brown," I muttered.

"Right." She was still hissing, throwing furtive apologetic looks over at the ladies. "You're to be seen, not heard, unless called upon. Now, listen close!"

"Why am I—?" I caught the hand whistling up to strike my face and grunted, dropping my voice to a whisper. "All right, all right! *What* am I doing here?"

She tutted, as though I was a child being deliberately obtuse. "You're first hand to the lady, of course. You'll be attending to her from here on. Now, for the last time, *listen close!*"

I looked down at my robe as she started listing off my myriad duties, relating to the care and upkeep of Mother Eden and her dignified company. Then I glanced over to the ladies, all of them having now joined the fussing protest, Mother Eden at their head, unperturbed even under such bombardment.

So this was her plan? My ultimate defeat? Keeping me alive was no act of charity, I knew that, but this was no worse than before. In fact, it would be a marked improvement.

Perhaps it was to keep me where she could have an eye on me. But if she was worried about further insurrection, then why not just kill me?

It didn't add up.

The housemaid was still talking, those piggy suspicious eyes reveling in schooling me like a two-year-old. She prodded me in the small of the back to make me stand straighter, slapping my arms until I clasped my hands. "... you stand behind here, but to the side so as not to draw the eye; within earshot, but not so close as to impose; hold yourself in a manner befitting the dignity of your charge, but remain deferential. Make no eye contact, keep your chin aimed at your toes when a lady or gentleman passes, and address them by their rightful title. Be seen, not heard!"

I just nodded, and she started rattling off some pre-prepared responses should interaction with another person be required.

So a few things had changed.

The woman had expounded a pamphlet's worth of information in the last minute alone, and she didn't look set to slow up. But my eye was drawn to the ladies, still fussing, now in a tight circle of harsh whispers. I only caught a few words, but each snagged my attention.

"Really, Mother, I must protest!"

"You can't! You can't!"

"It ain't right. And so sudden. We're all behind you and no mistake, but if we could only understand *why*—"

The housemaid snapped her fingers in front of my eyes. "Pay attention, pig! Thirty seconds, and look at you. Chin to the skies, eyes roaming all over everything like you was Lord of the Manor!" She scowled. "I'll have you fixed right and proper, just you wait. I don't know what Mother Eden has in mind, keeping you around." She eyed me sulkily. "You don't deserve such a privilege."

I almost laughed, then looked at her afresh, standing there with that sourpuss expression. I understood then. I had taken the job she'd been working toward from the start.

A moment's sympathy for her was quickly checked by yet another slap to the face. "You got twenty seconds, now make yourself presentable and be ready."

"For what?"

"For anything!"

"Ladies!" Mother Eden's voice had a new tightness. The ladies blushed. Mother Eden composed herself, adjusting her dress and clearing her throat. The volume of the crowd had been steadily rising to a considerable racket, but her voice was clear above the noise. "I've made up my mind, that's that. Now, can I rely on the lot of you to be accommodating and uphold all we've built here?"

Tense silence and a few hiccuping weeps followed, then they each stiffly bowed in turn.

Mother Eden smiled around at them all. "Thank you all, ladies. Make me proud. Now, go on, take your seats."

They shuffled out, leaving Mother Eden with me and the housemaid.

She looked ruffled for a moment, then straightened her frock, and positioned herself in front of the curtain.

The housemaid dug her thumb painfully into my ribs, propelling me to her side. Mother Eden's gaze lingered on me, and her eyes twinkled momentarily before hardening to beady tiles of slate. She cleared her throat, nodding to the curtain.

I heard the housemaid hiss with fury, and despite myself I gripped the curtain and pulled it aside. Mother Eden didn't acknowledge I had moved at all. Instead, she held her head high and sauntered through the gap.

Sorry, Peters, I thought. *I'm so goddamn sorry.*

Then I followed her through the curtain, took my place some distance behind her, and faced the crowd. They quieted at once, gentry and peasant alike, all eyes upon us. Simultaneously I felt the aura of their affection for their savior and their loathing ire for me.

Mother Eden took her place by her podium and swept her arms wide, as though to embrace them all. "Friends, it's mighty fine of you to turn out on such a beautiful day to listen to an old coot like me." A ripple of laughter ran through the room, precipitated by the gentry in front and carried dutifully by the brown-clad folk by the doors. "You're all beat from our recent alterations, especially those who decided they preferred some privacy in the quieter parts of town, God bless 'em! Digging those moats and putting up all those fences takes it outta you."

Suddenly the clamoring praise the bunkhouse folk had shown for her when we'd arrived made a lot more sense. Not only had they been consigned to the true status of slaves and peasants, but they had been forced to dig the very moats that had finally segregated them physically, not just socially, from the rest of the Project. Their mindless groupie craze hadn't been that at all; they had been begging—*no more, please, no more, you win!* She had won their affection totally through brutality.

"I want to say once again, I regret y'all's decisions, but a choice is a choice. I just hope what we offer in exchange for helping out around the place are reparations enough to keep you fed and kicking!"

What went unsaid was what caused the rear section of the room to stiffen: *You had your chance, you dug your graves, so rot in 'em.* There would be no room in the mansion district for those with a change of heart. From now on, if you weren't a killer by heart, you served one.

"But I have something important to announce. One final change." She smiled sweetly. "Being a leader was never in the cards for me when I got here. I had to claw my way through the heathens who were flying Eden right into the ground. I am what I am today because I made it so. And I'd like to say, with the help of many fine men and women over the years"—she tipped her head to certain lords and ladies, who nodded back as her equals—"that we made this place fine as can be." She flapped her hands gently to quell the hubbub of ascent and adulation. "But all things come to an end, my darlings. There's no easy way to say it, so I'm just gonna say it: my time is over. I'm stepping down."

I had never known silence like that which followed, and I'm betting I never will again. You could have set a bomb off right in the heart of that crowd and the survivors wouldn't have paid the slightest notice. So many gaping mouths, so many bug-eyed stares. I was probably gawping along with the rest of them, but the world had gone hazy; some kind of milky foam seemed to lay over everything.

What was she doing? And why had I been put out here now if all she was going to do was leave?

I don't understand, I thought helplessly.

Yet Mother Eden always had a plan, and that scared the shit out of me.

She waited patiently, hands clasped, until the shock had had time to sink in and the beginnings of panic were spreading. Then, skillful as ever, she started up again at just the right moment and brought everyone to orderly attention. "I'm sure y'all got a heap of questions, and you'll get your answers in time. But right now we gotta take care of the important business: I gotta name a successor."

This time the reaction fractured the crowd. Those at the rear recoiled as though burned, most having come from democratic nations where the idea of monarchic inheritance was absurd; those in front leaned forward, knocking their personal aides aside, their eyes narrowed to predatory slits—I could have sworn some of them sported lolling tongues hanging from salivating jaws.

Mother Eden carried on as though oblivious. "The decision's made. No need to worry about anything. I chose wisely. My replacement is gonna take good care of the lot of you. Hell, maybe better than I ever could. That's an important part of being a leader: knowing when to step aside and let somebody better take up the slack."

There wasn't enough laughter in the world for the irony in that, but I couldn't muster a single titter. My diaphragm had turned to cold stone. She seemed to take up my whole field of vision, blotting out the whole room and all those hundreds of people. When her lips moved, every detail was burned into my memory, every slough of the wrinkles around her lips, every sticky squish of her lips: "Ladies and gentlemen, I present your new Mother: Lady Golding, formerly of Fremont, California."

It was funny. When Ma stepped out, I expected the bottom to fall out of everything. I thought I would faint, or scream, or just plain run for the door. The world would swirl and sweat would pop out on my forehead.

But instead I just shut down. All the pain, worry, and shock drained away like somebody had unplugged me. A full frontal lobotomy in two seconds flat.

She appeared from the far side of the stage, flanked by the ladies who had been in the car with me, and embraced Mother Eden. Then Mother Eden stepped aside, and Ma—Lady Golding—took her place at the podium and addressed her new flock.

Her introductory speech lasted a full ten minutes. By the end of it she had everyone on their feet in a full standing ovation. Even the bunkhouse folks at the back looked enamored. But I didn't hear a word of it. I just stared at her, unfeeling, hollowed out and blank, and when it was over I lifted the curtain aside for her and her disciples and bowed.

She ignored me. I wasn't there. Just a seamless background machine.

I caught Mother Eden's eye as she followed last in line. There was no smile on her face anymore, but those eyes told the whole story. At last, I knew just how far she would go to win.

A week later the Skyrail arrived and spat out a new crop of draftees, fresh faced and blinking under the desert sun. The whole Project turned out to welcome them. As First Hand to Lady Golding, I was among the few to attend with the fine folk from the mansions, all decked out in gleaming white robes.

The rest of the Brown Robes looked on from across the moats in the middle-distance, lined up solemnly against the chain link fences. Most had made some effort to clean themselves up, their faces scrubbed raw and their robes rung out in the well, but there was no hiding the accrued dirt packed forever into every pore and wrinkle.

Some might have genuinely hoped at a shot of getting a blue robe someday, maybe even a white one, by making a good impression. I wouldn't have known. I wasn't welcome in the bunkhouses anymore. They saw me as a traitor because of the perks mansion help got—most notably a real bed to sleep in on the East Wing, my own quarters, and indulgent meals made out of the fine folks' leftovers. I didn't blame them.

That was how complete Mother Eden's victory was. Even weeks later, I was still discovering ways she'd found to make my existence a little more miserable. Nothing too big that would make me snap, you understand. Just a hell of a lot of small things that added up. The tattered robes, the looks of derision, not getting to read the log to the kids, having garbage dumped on me by the guys I used to sweat with on the Beetle, the ugly conversation of the ladies and gentlemen at the dinner table, the way Lady Golding snapped her fingers when she wanted the table cleared.

A thousand tiny screws all tightening together. I was nothing.

The draftees off the Skyrail took in the sight of us silently waiting and tramped over with trepidation written on their faces—though, on a few, I noticed, was something just a little coy and curious. They were received with open arms by Lady Golding and introduced to her foremost disciples. At some point she waved their attention over to the Brown Robes, who stiffened as one, and that was that.

It got the message across. Fear was etched onto each of the arrivals' faces—though desperation and feral aggression piqued on a few. It was subtle, but it was there. I was an expert at spotting future mansion folks by now.

Later, they were all processed, which included an interview and full psych profile in isolation rooms beneath the surveillance bunker. That was how things were done now. I supervised the process and made sure everyone ended up where they belonged.

There was no lottery anymore. Placements were final, bar exceptional circumstances. Once judgment had passed, the draftees would be wearing the same colored robe for a very long time. I kept a close eye out for any sign of a potential troublemaker—someone like myself. I thanked God when I found no trace of one. I turned in my report and headed for home with my head down, taking my daily punishment from the bunkhouse folk, hoping Lady Golding was in a good mood when I got back. I might have been First Hand, but that didn't make me immune to reprimand. As it turned out, Lady Golding was fond of the lash.

Life took on a new rhythm. The dust settled. Many at the Project were far worse off, and for that very reason my lot was the worst of all. I was a spectator with no home, no family, and no identity; a slave to my own mother; traitor to my father, the kids in the bunkhouses, Peters, even myself.

Mother Eden retired to a small manor on the outskirts of the mansion district. Nobody saw her much, but she entertained her old inner circle often enough.

And she was always present when the Skyrail delivered fresh draftees, of course, front and center in Lady Golding's blossoming group of disciples. I always sensed her watching me when those poor bastards came tramping in from the desert. Because someday there would be another who would fight the system, hoping for something better. And when they showed up, it would be me who broke them.

Extract #18

Letter received by airdrop

Son,

I'll be honest, I thought you'd forget about me once you got over there. They must be putting a mind like yours to work like all hell, and it touches my heart to know you're still thinking of your old man.

Shame they had to blank out so much of your letter—at first I thought somebody had spilled a bottle of ink on the page. Funny, reading a real solid letter on paper like this. Makes me think of when I was a boy. Sorry, son, it looks like you put a lot of work into that letter, but they painted over almost all of it. But they left in enough for me to know the important things; what I got was real swell. It sounds like you're both having a blast over there.

Still don't understand why we can't vid-chat, or even have a damn telephone call! I'm sure it's a good reason, probably real technical. Stuff like that is always going to be beyond a blockhead like me. But I know it's just a matter of time. Once things settle down and all this political pushing and shoving blows over, they'll loosen up the rules a little.

For now it's enough to know you're out there making a difference and taking care of your Ma. I always knew you'd make me proud.

I appreciate the letter, I really do. But I know your time must be precious, and I want you to put every scrap of your smarts to use. We're all counting on people like you.

I want you to know I'm okay. Everything's fine here, just like always. Rent's behind and what they're saying on the TV scares the bejesus out of me, but how's that different from any other day? It sure gets quiet at the dinner table, then I put your mother's show tunes on and it's like you're both here with me. I know we'll be together again real soon. Nothing lasts forever.

I love you, son.

- Father

P.S. They left a couple of words in your letter that got me wondering. Something about your Ma enjoying the company of some pretty high-up people. Sounds great, she always was a people person.

Maybe she'll even swing a few perks for the both of you!

But do me a favor and keep an eye on her. She means well, your Ma, but sometimes she forgets about other people. She's not selfish, she's had to fight hard to make sure we were fed and watered. You get a thick skin doing the kind of things she's had to do. But I

trust you to step in if she gets a little
out of sorts.

You're the man of the house, now, Desh.
Take care of my angel.

Thanks for reading, folks.

With luck, you enjoyed the read. I certainly enjoyed writing this. If you have a spare moment, I'd dance at your wedding if you could drop by your retailer's website and leave an honest review.

Afterword

Our Fair Eden is the result of my thoughts on the forthcoming effects of climate change, and the cultural fixation of Western civilisation upon a snowballing catastrophe. We sense the coming storm, yet we can do little to stop it—some even revel in the fact that they'll be dead when the consequences hit. Treaties promise what governments have no intention of delivering, and research that could avert disaster goes unfunded.

Granted, the picture I have illustrated here is grim. But I fear it is not too far beyond reality.

Today we face myriad challenges that will affect us globally, something the human race hasn't evolved to cope with. Our actions will echo across the face of the Earth and through the pages of history. It's a lot of responsibility to shoulder in only a few generations. We're still learning.

But, eventually, things *will* reach a turning point, and we need to be ready.

With luck, things will go better than they go for Desh on his travels to Eden.

Harry Manners
Coventry, England
28th November 2014

Acknowledgments

My thanks to my wonderful editors, Amy Maddox and Claire Rushbrook. Their contributions to the pacing and authenticity of the book, especially regarding Mother Eden, were invaluable.

Anne Victory, my proofreader, proved once again that she is second to none, and my readers have been spared many a blunder thanks to her work.

My cover designer, Levente Szabo, has outdone himself in producing a true piece of art. As always, he was a delight.

My formatters over at Polgarus Studio have put together the eye-candy you're currently reading. It goes without saying that their patience and all-round loveliness made all the difference.

To my first reader, Emma, to whom this book is dedicated: the book wouldn't be what it is without you. Thanks for stomaching a first draft that could have very well ended up in the bin.

And to all my readers and booksellers out there: thank you for picking up this book and lending me your eyes for a while. I hope I did it justice.

Subscribe to the Mailing List

Want to keep up to date on all my books? Sign up to my newsletter for updates on discounts and new releases.

I never spam my readers, but I will send you sneak peaks and exclusives and freebies every now and then to let you know that I love you.

If you're interested in being an advance reader, get in touch!

Join the list: http://www.eepurl.com/V4niL

Other Books by Harry Manners

Ruin (The Ruin Saga #1)

The End cost humanity six billion lives. Almost every person on Earth vanished when the lights went out, computers turned to dust, and planes fell from the sky. Only scattered survivors remained, surrounded by a world empty and quiet.

Now, forty years on, civilisation is failing. The ways of the Old World have been forgotten, and those who knew its wonders are ageing. All that stands between the British Isles and a new Dark Age is the mission of New Canterbury, desperate to save books, art, and the knowledge needed to begin again.

Famine has devastated the land and refugees wander in their thousands. Anger is growing against the city and the demands of its sacred mission. In the wild lands surrounding New Canterbury, dark secrets fester, supernatural forces have awoken, and somewhere an army is on the move, hell-bent on ending the Old World forever.

The End was just the beginning.

Other Books by Harry Manners

Brink (Ruin Saga #2)

Earth has been almost silent for forty years. The apocalypse left behind only fragments of civilisation, surrounded by a sea of barbarism.

But now the true End is in sight: the horizon is alight with burning villages, two cities lie in the shadow of an army gathering in the north, intent on ending the old world forever. And somewhere, a supernatural force is on the move, pushing its servants into place: a young girl with special powers, and a man whose destiny might decide the fate of all.

While ominous swarms of pigeons plague the sky, the world becomes slowly quieter, and dark forgotten secrets are revealed – secrets of betrayal, love, and obsession – the army in the north prepares to leave.

The epic Ruin Saga continues in summer 2015…

Other Books by Harry Manners

No Way Home

Stories From Which There is No Escape.

Nothing terrifies us more than being stranded. Helpless, forsaken, cut-off. Locked in a place from which there is no escape, no way to get home.

A soldier trapped in an endless war dies over and over, only to be awakened each time to fight again – one of the last remaining few seeking to save mankind from extinction.

In rural 70s England, an RAF radio engineer returns to an abandoned military installation, but begins to suffer hallucinations, shifts in time and memories that are not his own.

A widower, one of ten thousand civilian space explorers, is sent alone to determine his assigned planet's suitability for human colonisation, but stumbles across a woman who is part of the same programme and shouldn't be there at all.

A suicidal woman in a poverty-stricken near-future America, where political apathy has allowed special interests to gain control of the country, takes part in a particularly unpleasant crowd-funding platform, established by the nation's moneyed elite to engage the masses.

An assassin from the future, sent back in time to murder an insurgent, is left stranded when he fails in his mission and knows he will soon cease to exist.

These sometimes dark, sometimes heart-warming, but always insightful stories and more are to be found in *No Way Home*, where eight of the most exciting new voices in speculative fiction explore the mental, physical and even meta-physical boundaries that imprison us when we are lost.

About the Author

Harry Manners lives in Bedfordshire, England. When he's not writing, he studies Physics, reads a ton-load of books, and generally nerds out—for which he is staunchly unapologetic. Our Fair Eden is his second novel.

Website

www.harrymanners.net

Facebook

www.facebook.com/OfficialHarryManners

Twitter

@harry_a_manners

Blog

www.harrymanners.wordpress.com

www.ingramcontent.com/pod-product-compliance
Lightning Source LLC
Chambersburg PA
CBHW020924120726
47905CB00008B/2374